Praise for the Novels of Jamil Nasir

QUASAR

"Fresh and innovative . . . a promising debut." *The Washington Post*

THE HIGHER SPACE

"A charming blend of mysticism and chaos theory." *Locus*

TOWER OF DREAMS

"Unusual setting and poetic language . . . fresh and intriguing." *The Denver Post*

DISTANCE HAZE

"Captivating." *Publishers Weekly*

THE HOUSES OF TIME

"Mind-bending . . . a wildly imaginative romp." *Philadelphia Literary Examiner*

Short Trips

JAMIL NASIR

iUniverse, Inc.
New York   Bloomington

iUniverse books may be ordered through booksellers or by contacting:

iUniverse
1663 Liberty Drive
Bloomington, IN 47403
www.iuniverse.com
1-800-Authors (1-800-288-4677)

ISBN: 978-1-4502-1369-1 (sc)
ISBN: 978-1-4502-1370-7 (ebook)

Printed in the United States of America

iUniverse rev. date: 03/31/2010

Contents

The Heaven Tree

Garbage cans banging woke me up after midnight.

I lay still, hoping they wouldn't do it again. But they did, louder, with a lot of muffled giggling. I sat up and looked into shadows cast by streetlight through backyard trees and bushes. In the shadows pale figures moved.

"Shhh!" I hissed, loud enough to be heard in the next block. But *they* didn't hear—a garbage can lid rattled to the ground, and a giggle became a laugh.

"Stupid—" I hissed.

A window shot up next door and a ringing screech drowned out my feeble warning. "Get out of there! Get out of there this minute or I'll call the police!"

Startled silence followed by attempted quietness exploded into more giggling.

"Just you wait, you devils," screeched Mrs. Nicholson, and slammed her window shut.

I sighed and went downstairs. By the time the rotating blue and white lights pulled silently up to Mrs. Nicholson's curb, I had smoothed the long side-hairs over my bald spot and tied a robe over my belly. I stepped out onto damp front lawn grass. The leaves on my maple tree were perfectly still, and the street was quiet, dark except where a large moth fluttered around Mrs. Nicholson's porch light.

A policeman was climbing Mrs. Nicholson's porch with heavy steps and a jingling of handcuffs. The screen door opened, there was a low-voiced argument, and then the policeman stumped back down and across to my lawn.

I met him there. "Hello, Alan," I said.

"Hello, John," he said quietly, not slowing his long steps toward the walk that runs past my electric meter and forsythia bushes. I fell in behind him. A lone cricket creaked under the bushes.

"What are you going to do to them?" I asked.

"Arrest some or all of them for vagrancy and disturbing the peace. This is the third night this month."

The uncut grass of the backyard tickled my ankles. Streetlight speckled Alan's broad back.

"They didn't make much noise, Alan. And it was my garbage cans, not hers."

"Disturbing the peace is disturbing the peace, no matter whose garbage cans they are," said Alan, holding a tree branch so it wouldn't whip back on me. "Look at this place."

Beyond the sagging link fence separating my back yard from the Langley place, tall weeds cast spiny shadows on crab grass; skunk cabbage and wild rhubarb mingled shadowy leaves under untrimmed tree branches; ivy twined around the columns of a leaning back porch and poked into the darkness of broken windows.

"Place ought to be condemned," said Alan, stepping over a trampled down part of the fence. "Someone ought to call the Health Department."

I followed him, trying to keep my slippered feet off thorns. The weathered boards of the back porch creaked under us. Frightened whispers came from the darkness inside the open back door.

Alan switched on a flashlight and a streak of white and silver fled into the darkness of the house. I followed his heavy, steady tread along a mildewed hall, into what had once been Louise Ann Langley's clean, fussy front room.

It wasn't clean and fussy anymore. A collection of old mattresses and cushions were spread on the floor, tattered blankets and even some hay strewn over them. A brown stain down one wall showed where the roof leaked. The furniture Louise Ann had been so proud of was broken up and piled against one wall, and cowering among the pieces were the current residents of the house, blinking their silver eyes in Alan's light.

"They all here?' he asked, shining the light over their gleaming silver hair and pale skin.

"Yes. Three females and two males."

"Which ones do you figure did the banging?"

I thought fast, for an insurance agent.

"That one over in the corner. Ananka. Ananka, come here."

There was a muffled cry, and one of the silver-haired creatures tried to burrow deeper behind a broken sofa.

I made my voice stern. "Ananka, come here. The policeman wants you to come out right now."

Ananka sobbed, slowly untangled herself from behind the sofa, and stepped into the light, trembling violently.

"Come here," I said again, pointing to a spot right in front of Alan.

She edged forward, sobbing, looking up into his face with her beautiful wide eyes.

Alan muttered a curse. When Ananka stopped in front of him, he said: "This can't be the one, John. She's not—she can't be sixteen years old."

"She's the one I saw. Ananka, this policeman is going to take you away to jail."

One of the males crouching in the pile of furniture started to blubber.

Ananka made a little helpless gesture then, spreading her hands and closing her eyes as if expecting to be seized on the spot and put in chains. It gave me chills; Ananka had had Crane's Syndrome almost four years now, and was heartbreakingly beautiful and young.

"I've read they don't do too well in jail," I said. "She'll probably be dead in a few weeks if you take her."

He stood looking at her.

I pushed my luck a little further. "They won't cause any more disturbances. I'll be responsible."

"That's what you said the last time."

He took a threatening step toward Ananka.

"Do you want me to take you away in my police car?" he demanded fiercely.

She shook her head, eyes still closed, tears running down her face.

"How about the rest of you?" he snarled.

They scrambled deeper into the pile of furniture.

"If you make *any more noise,*" bellowed Alan, "I'm going to take all of you away in my police car and put you in jail. Understand?"

I had a hard time keeping up with him on the way back to his car. When we were almost there, I said: "I'll see to them, Alan, I promise."

He turned and jabbed a large finger at me. "I'm not kidding, John. I can't keep coming out here every week. The Department has new guidelines on the Craners: we have to arrest them and send them to relocation centers if we get complaints. The City is under a lot of pressure to get them off the streets."

"That's not fair. They aren't hurting anybody."

"You better tell that to your neighbor. If she calls me again, I'm going to take them in. I don't care how young they are. That's just all there is to it."

He got in the car, blue and white lights still rotating on top, and rushed away from the curb with the slightest squeal of tires on the cool pavement.

On my way up to bed, I wondered if it would make any difference to him that Ananka was almost seventy years old.

✳ ✳ ✳ ✳

The next morning there was banging on my kitchen door. I stumbled downstairs, opening my eyes enough to see that it was eight-thirty and beams of yellow light someone else might have called cheerful were slanting through the windows.

Two Craners, Benjamin and Caroline, were at the door. Benjamin wore a dirty sleeveless sweatshirt and ancient dress pants torn off at the knee; Caroline had on a ragged dress three sizes too big for her.

"Do you have any more of those—anything to eat?" asked

Benjamin politely, wrinkling his brow to make his face serious and grown up. I remembered when he had been Ben Wachter, the fat, imperious lawyer at the end of the block; now he was a tall, muscular boy with dirt smudges on his face. His eyes hadn't yet turned completely—there were still little flecks of brown in them.

"No more food for you," I said angrily. "You promised you wouldn't make any more noise at night."

"We won't," said Caroline. She had had the Syndrome almost as long as Ananka: her eyes were silver-grey, her tangled hair deep silver, her voice sweet as a bell.

"That's what you said last time."

"Well—we—we had—it fell down, by accident," struggled Benjamin, as if vaguely aware he had once been a great advocate. "We won't—anymore."

"The Mopsers knocked it down," put in Caroline.

"The who?"

"They're mean. They have big hairy wings, and big noses."

"And claws," said Benjamin.

"And eyeglasses," said Caroline.

"You can't see them—in the day," blurted Benjamin. "They hang—upside down—on the—" he waved his hands agitatedly.

I stared at them.

"We're hungry," said Caroline earnestly.

My defenses caved. "Well, you tell the others not to make any more noise, or there'll be no more food for you, Mopsers or no Mopsers," I said sternly. I rummaged in the refrigerator and found some stale bread, two peaches, and half a can of baked beans. "And don't go into Mrs. Nicholson's yard. *Ever.* Have you been remembering not to go into Mrs. Nicholson's yard?"

"Yes," said Benjamin, accepting the food.

"Oh, yes," said Caroline, wide-eyed.

"Thank you," said Benjamin gravely, and headed back down the garden, Caroline skipping behind tugging at this sweatshirt.

After breakfast I showered, shaved even though it was Saturday, oiled my hair carefully over my bald spot, and put on the blue suit I wear to interview prospective accounts. Then I went across to Mrs. Nicholson's front porch and rang the doorbell.

The door opened wide enough to show a pale eye and wrinkled cheek.

"Yes?"

"Mrs. Nicholson? I'm John Roberts, your next-door neighbor."

"Yes?'

"I'd like to talk to you about the Crane's Syndrome people that live behind us."

"What about them?"

"Well—"

"Just a minute." A chain rattled off, the door opened, and I stepped into Mrs. Nicholson's front hall. It was spotlessly clean, with a grey rug and a dark, elderly knick-knack cabinet, but dimness hung in the corners like accumulated stale air or gloomy thoughts. Mrs. Nicholson herself was tall and bony, with white hair and frosty blue eyes.

"You're the man who keeps persuading the police not to arrest them," she told me. "I intend to put in a complaint about you."

"Ma'am, they can't help what they do. They can't think straight. It's a disease."

"Which they caught by fornication and adultery, every one of them. I'm a simple woman, Mr. Roberts, but I believe it's a judgment of God."

I followed her into a sitting room with ruffled curtains pulled close, crowded with faded furniture and more stale air.

"It's a virus, Mrs. Nicholson," I said, sitting on a sofa with a dry, musty smell. "Haven't you seen the TV specials? Crane's virus reverses the biological process in the cells responsible for aging. It's wonderful, in a way. The scientists are trying to find a way to use it as a kind of elixir of youth without the hallucinations and loss of thinking ability—"

"God meant for man to grow old and die, Mr. Roberts," said Mrs. Nicholson, and I shifted my eyes under her cold gaze.

"You've got a house full of beautiful antique furniture here," I ventured finally. "Are you insured? I can get you a fire policy that—"

"This furniture is not *antique*, Mr. Roberts. We bought it the year after we were married, me and my late husband, God rest his

6

soul. He died a year ago, and my relations persuaded me I would be more comfortable in the city than on our farm. A great mistake. Sodom and Gommorah, and the police not even willing to protect decent people."

"Mrs. Nicholson," I coaxed, "will you come out back with me? I want to introduce you to one of them."

"I will not! I'm going to have them taken away! Every one of them!"

But she followed me down her narrow back hallway. She hadn't had visitors in a long time, I guessed, and she wasn't going to give me up so easily. I unbolted, unchained, and unlocked the kitchen door, and we stepped onto patio bricks crumbling and mossy from tree dampness. An aluminum lawn table and two aluminum chairs were sticky with tree resin and scattered with winged seed ponds. The air was cool, and birds twittered in green shade. Farther off was the sound of leisurely weekend traffic on Thayer Avenue. Through the shrubs that lined Mrs. Nicholson's fence, I saw a silvery figure poking around in one of my garbage cans.

"Ananka," I called gently.

The figure jumped, ready to run.

"Ananka," I called again. "Come here, honey. I want you to meet someone."

She stayed warily still, watching with large, alert eyes as I led Mrs. Nicholson to the bottom of the garden.

"I'll give you an orange."

She hopped lightly over the fence. Mrs. Nicholson shrank back. I grabbed Ananka's hand, pulled her closer.

It was rare to see a four-year Craner—they all seemed to wander off somewhere after awhile—her silver gazelle eyes, thick silver hair, ivory skin, delicate pouting lips were astonishingly beautiful. A small, exquisite breast peeped through a tear in her scavenged shirt, and her legs were slender and strong below tattered shorts.

"Can you say 'Hello, Mrs. Nicholson'?" I coaxed her.

"Hello, Mrs. Nubberson," she muttered shyly.

"Cover yourself, girl, aren't you ashamed?" scolded Mrs. Nicholson, but her eyes were not unkind. I pulled Ananka's shirt so that the breast was hidden.

"Isn't she something?" I said, smoothing tangles out of her hair. "Four years ago she was a crotchety old lady who watched Bible TV all day and yelled at kids that walked on her lawn. Her husband Ralph got the Syndrome from one of the first Craners to wander into the neighborhood, before the epidemic really took off. They called her Alisa, and she slept under a picnic table in Montgomery Park for a few months, and I think most of the men in the neighborhood took a whirl with her. No one had ever seen anybody that beautiful before. I know Les Mansfield caught it from her. And Ralph Langley was pretty frisky for an old guy. Anyway, pretty soon his hair was turning from white to silver, and his old thin body getting tall and straight. Louise Ann--Ananka—had a fit and threw him out. He slept in the park for awhile, getting younger and stronger every day. He used to come around and ask for food, his clothes all dirty and his eyes turning silver.

"'Johnny-boy, you got to try this,' he told me once. 'I feel like—I don't know, but I ain't felt this way in a long time.' Then after awhile he didn't recognize me anymore.

"Louise Ann took him back in after he reached that stage. I guess she loved him. And also, by that time he was big and handsome in a way the old Ralph never was. You wouldn't think it of an old lady like that, but pretty soon the fat seemed to be melting off her, and her hair turning silver.

"That was four years ago. About two years ago Ralph wandered off somewhere, the way they do, and Louise Ann started calling herself Ananka, and the other Craners from the neighborhood have been with her since. Right, honey?"

She nodded obediently, without understanding. Then she put her arms around me and buried her head in my shoulder.

"Dubby, can I have my orange now?" she asked. Dubby was the name the Craners had for me.

Mrs. Nicholson's head jerked, and she looked at me in sudden horror.

"You!" she gasped, and backed away, reached her kitchen door with long strides, and slammed and locked it behind her.

Late that night there was a tremendous noise in the Langley yard, a confusion of shouts, screams, and animal snarls. I had reached my back fence, slipperless and sleep-blind, side-hairs hanging down my face, when I collided with a sobbing Roberta. I held her.

"Ananka," was all she could sob. "Ananka."

I ran, thorns cutting my feet.

Three Craners knelt in the tall weeds, metallic hair and pale skin lit by moon and streetlight. I pushed a blubbering Les aside and saw Ananka lying on the ground, glistening dark liquid smeared on her shirt.

"What happened?" I hissed, and when they only went on moaning, grabbed Les fiercely by the collar and shook him, yelling: "What happened?"

He sobbed: "A bad doggie--'Nanka gave him some bread—he—he—"

I knelt over her. She was breathing.

"Pick her up," I yelled over their noise. "Pick her up and carry her up to my house. Come on, she's not dead, you idiots! Les, you hear me?"

I finally got Les and Benjamin to lift her. Then, as if suddenly struck by the importance of their mission, they ran headlong into my yard. I followed as fast as I could, cursing.

"Don't drop her! Slow down!" I puffed, caught up with them at the kitchen door, and switched on the light. They laid her on the yellow formica table, knocking down the salt and pepper shakers.

Her right hand and forearm were mangled, blood spattered on her shirt and shorts. She was chalk-white, eyes slitted, breath shallow. I was dialing 911 with trembling hands when there was a heavy knock at the front door. I dropped the phone and ran to open it.

It was Alan, and behind him Mrs. Nicholson in a robe with yellowed lace at the cuffs. Alan opened his mouth sternly, but I started yelling. I don't remember what I said. He strode into the kitchen. When he saw Ananka, his jaw got square.

"Help me carry her," he said.

She was surprisingly heavy. Mrs. Nicholson held the screen

door. When the Craners saw us carrying Ananka toward the squad car, they set up a howling.

"Be still this minute! They're not going to hurt her!" Mrs Nicholson snapped, shooing them with one hand and the hem of her robe. We laid Ananka in the back seat, I squatting by her head. As we squealed away, I thought I saw Mrs. Nicholson with her arm around one of the male Craners, smoothing his hair like a little boy's.

※ ※ ※ ※

Dawn was pale in the sky, quiet and grey along the street when Ananka and I got back from the hospital in a cab. I got her under one arm and the cabbie got her under the other and we walked her wobbly legs upstairs to the tiny guest bedroom with the floral bedspread and wallpaper. I gave the cabbie a beer and a big tip, and when I went back upstairs she was asleep, her face pale and serene.

I went to bed too, woke up around noon, took a shower, then tapped at the guest bedroom door. There was no answer. I turned the knob quietly and peeked in. Ananka was crouching on the windowsill in a little wedge of sunlight, wearing her clean hospital nightgown, bandaged arm hanging at her side. She seemed to be staring out at the Langley yard.

I put my arms around her, eased her down off the sill. She felt hot and her cheeks were flushed.

"You have to stay in bed, honey," I told her. "The doctor said so."

She put her well hand out toward the window. "Ralph," she said.

"You remember Ralph?" I asked, walking her to the bed. "I thought you'd forgotten about old Ralph."

I got her to lie down, tucked the covers over her, smoothed her hair. Her eyes were still fixed on the window.

"You want me to move you over there so you can look out?"

She nodded.

I got her out of bed again, sat her in the faded pink armchair, got the mattress off, pushed the frame over by the window, and was sweating and grunting when the doorbell rang. It was a grey, tired-looking man in white with a black medical bag.

"I'm the paramedic," he said. "They should have told you I'd be coming."

"Oh yeah. Her rabies shots." I led him up to the bedroom.

Ananka was crouching on the windowsill again. I gathered her down, sat her in the armchair. The paramedic stared at her open-mouthed, then he busied himself with his black bag. I thought his hands shook a little.

"Want a beer?" I asked him on the way downstairs, after he had given her the shot.

He frowned. "Yeah."

We sat at the kitchen table with cans in front of us.

"You a doctor?" I asked him.

"No." He watched me steadily from protruding, muddy eyes. He had longish sandy hair, not too clean, combed back from his forehead, face wrinkles he didn't seem old enough for. "Couldn't get in."

"I've heard it's tough. I'm an insurance salesman myself."

He nodded and took a long drink.

"Now, Crane's Syndrome." I said. "I've seen a lot of programs on it, but—"

"It's a virus," he said. "Sexually transmitted. Corrects information loss in cell DNA."

"I've heard that," I said. "But why does it make them, you know, feeble-minded?"

"Not feeble-minded. Synaptically retrograded."

"What?"

"Retrograded." He looked at his watch. "You now how Crane's Syndrome works?"

"Well—"

"There's a class of viruses—called retroviruses—that punch holes in cells and attack their DNA. DNA is the information-bearing molecule in the cell that tells it how to grow and what functions to perform, right? Most retroviruses reprogram the DNA so the cell becomes a little factory manufacturing more viruses. That's how viruses reproduce. That's how they make you sick.

"Except for Crane's virus. Its program is different. Nobody knows why or how. Somewhere, somehow, it picked up a perfect template of human DNA, and when it penetrates a cell it actually corrects defects, imperfections or mistakes in the DNA, using the same DNA-programming mechanism normal viruses use, but in this case reversing the effects of aging. Aging happens when cells divide a number of times and DNA information is damaged or lost. Happens all the time. The Crane's Syndrome virus goes in and fixes that. Right?"

I nodded.

"Well, Crane's Syndrome attacks the nerve cells of the brain too. But brain tissue ages differently than other tissue. What happens is, as you age, synaptogenesis occurs—connections form between brain cells, reflecting your experiences and the growth of reasoning ability. Well, Crane's virus' action on cell DNA causes the brain cells to revert to their original, youthful form—they gradually withdraw their connections from each other. That's the retrograde part. As the cells get less and less interconnected the patient forgets things, loses built-up cognitive structures, until finally, in theory, he ends up with the brain of a newborn infant, completely unformed, unstructured, and without preconceptions."

"So they see the world like little children."

He shrugged, idly tapping his empty can on the table. "Cognitive tests show their senses are sharp like children's."

I got him another beer from the refrigerator. "So how do they die? Do they die, ever?"

"I've seen dead ones. Accidents, falls, poison."

"But I mean *natural* death. They don't ever grow old and die? The TV says there have been mysterious—"

"The TV is a bunch of morons. Some nut says he's seen Craners fly into the air or vanish and the TV reports it as fact, but when the government does controlled longitudinal studies, they call that a cover-up. The Syndrome has only been observed for nine years, not long enough to find out much about it."

"But there've been so many reports—"

He shrugged irritably, looked at his watch.

"I've got to go," he said, and finished the rest of his beer in one long drink. "I'm late for my next appointment." He stood up, suddenly anxious.

"I'm not supposed to drink on duty," he mumbled resentfully as I let him out.

I took Ananka oranges and jelly toast—her favorite foods—for dinner, but she hardly noticed. She chewed absently, staring out the window. I watched her curiously. She seemed to stare not at her old homestead, but at the oak tree that branched stories above it.

"What do you see up in that big old tree?" I asked, trying to coax a piece of jelly toast into her mouth.

"Ralph."

"Ralph? Honey, Ralph isn't up there."

She was silent, chewing meditatively.

The next couple of days her fever went down and she started paying more attention to things around her. I rescheduled appointments, called in sick at the office, fed her oranges, jelly toast, peanut butter, mashed potatoes, and ice cream until you would have thought she would get fat; but she didn't. She stayed amazingly beautiful, and her sweet voice filled my house with a kind of silver light. The paramedic (whose name was Payden) didn't stay to talk anymore; he gave her her shots with hands that I thought trembled, answered my questions and pleasantries in monosyllables. His eyes avoided Ananka: instead he attended to the devices that measured her— thermometer, stethoscope, blood-pressure cuff. Benjamin and the girls came up every day for food. I didn't see Les. I didn't see or hear Mrs. Nicholson.

Tuesday night I put Ananka in bed and fixed her a bowl of mashed potatoes with milk and butter. I sat in the pink armchair next to the bed, working on a TV dinner.

"Ananka, what happened to Ralph?" I asked after we had chewed for awhile.

"Went to heaven," she said matter-of-factly through a mouthful of mashed potatoes.

"You mean he died?"

"No. Climbed."

"Climbed what?"

She pointed out the window with her spoon.

"He climbed that tree to heaven?"

She nodded. "Can I have some ice cream?"

I went downstairs and got her a bowl, with chocolate sauce.

"Well—where is heaven?" I asked, watching her maul the ice cream clumsily.

She waved her spoon at the ceiling, scattering creamy drops.

I wiped them up with my napkin. "What's it like?"

"Pretty." Her eyes were suddenly excited. "Blue. Blue like high grass. The wind ruffles it. Clouds blow like big cows." She laughed. "The sun is an old man looking down. Pretty."

I tried to read her eyes. They turned back to the ice cream. "That's where people go when they die?"

"No. You climb."

"Why don't *you* climb up there?"

"Not ready yet. Almost ready."

She gave me a wining smile and her bowl flipped over and smeared ice cream down her front like black and vanilla blood.

"Ooooh!" she gasped, and laughed.

I peeled off the ruined sheets, scooped as much half-melted gook as I could back into the bowl, led her to the bathroom. I ran water in the tub, taped a plastic trash bag over her bandaged arm.

"You remember how to take a bath?" I asked her.

She shook her head shyly.

I wielded a bar of soap. "When I go out, take off all your clothes and get in the water and rub yourself all over with this. Don't get it in your eyes—"

She took off all her clothes—her hospital gown—in one quick motion, struck a lewd pose, and laughed delightedly at the shock on my face. I handed her the soap, staring dizzily at silver tresses falling past carved ivory shoulders, the slender, laughing belly, delighted silver eyes.

14

She held the soap out to me. "You."

"Oh no."

I backed out and went downstairs, shaking my head. I was on my second beer before I realized that the running and splashing of water upstairs was louder than it should be. I ran back up. Water streamed down the hall from under the bathroom door, and when I yanked it open a three-inch wave drowned my slippers. Ananka sat in the overflowing tub splashing and singing, the soap floating unheeded in a corner. I waded in and turned off the faucets.

She grabbed my arm and tipped me into the bathtub. I went under in a cloud of floating silver hair, like a man drowned by a mermaid. I came up coughing, Ananka was laughing, and more water than ever was pouring onto the floor.

"Be serious, honey," I pleaded, too waterlogged to be angry. I stood up in the bathtub in my soaking clothes and she pulled me down again with a splash. Then she was on top of me, straddling me with her strong legs, looking into my eyes with her hypnotic ones, and kissing me.

"Love 'Nanka?" she murmured, caressing my wet hair, her breath sweet and musky. "Want to climb up to heaven with 'Nanka and Ralph? Want to?"

I heaved out of the water with my last strength, spilling her backwards with a splash and a flash of long legs, ran out of there, trailing gallons of water.

Many beers later I was sitting on the dark patio, smelling cool humid leaves and thinking to the best of my ability, when a pale movement caught my eye. I squinted into Mrs. Nicholson's back yard. Someone crept through its shadows.

I stood up. "Hey!"

The figure froze, becoming part of a tree shadow. I walked unsteadily to the fence.

"Les," I said as sternly as my condition allowed. "Les, if that's you, I want you to come here right this minute."

The pale figure edged forward and Les looked down at me with frightened eyes.

"Didn't I tell you *never* to go into Mrs. Nicholson's yard?" I snarled. "You'll get everybody in trouble, you stupid lout. What have you got in your hand there?"

His huge left hand uncurled slowly and he looked down into it, seeming as shocked as I was. Two fresh oranges lay in his palm.

"You—you broke into her house?" I gasped. "To steal food?"

He shook his head desperately. "She asked me," he moaned.

"Don't you lie to me! Why would she ask you, you—?"

"To help her."

"Help her do what?"

"Climb."

I was still swaying with my mouth open when he shrank away into the darkness at the bottom of the garden.

As soon as I had my breath back I marched over to Mrs. Nicholson's front porch. Four days of newspapers lay ungathered on the steps. I rang the doorbell and waited, then rang and waited twice more, then started to hammer. I was about to go back and call the police when bolts clicked and the door opened an inch. An eye looked out.

"Mrs. Nicholson?"

"Yes?"

"Are you all right?"

"Yes."

"I—I haven't seen you for a few days—I just thought I'd come over and check if—"

"I'm quite all right, thank you," she said. "Thank you for asking." And she shut the door.

I walked back across my lawn, thinking. That was Mrs. Nicholson, all right—there was no mistaking her voice. But the voice was a little different too; a shade deeper, a taste slower. Younger.

I had a hard time sleeping that night.

#

The next day I got into my blue suit and went to work, making Ananka promise to be good and leaving the door unlocked for Payden. When I got home in the evening, she was sitting cross-legged on the kitchen table, eating peanut butter out of a jar with her finger. She smiled brilliantly at me.

"Did the man come?" I asked, putting groceries away in the refrigerator.

She nodded, and laughed excitedly.

"What are you so happy about?" I asked, suddenly suspicious.

"Nothing." She looked demure, waggled a peanut butter-covered finger at me, and blushed.

I cooked dinner in a bad mood. I was dishing up the mashed potatoes before I realized what was wrong: I was jealous. Stupid, I told myself as I carried the dinner tray up the stairs. Ananka was close to seventy, well past the age of consent. And if Payden wanted to violate the laws against sexual contact with persons known to be infected with Crane's Syndrome and turn into a pea-brain, that was his business.

Ananka seemed to feel the weight of my thoughts. We ate in silence. The next afternoon when I came home from work she was gone.

I climbed over the fence and picked my way through the Langley yard in the long yellow light, burrs sticking to my pants, grasshoppers jumping around my feet. Ananka was squatting on the broken-down front porch, gazing out at Thayer Avenue. She smiled at me, stretched her arms up for a hug. Her bandage had gotten smudged with dirt, but she seemed altogether well, just like the old Ananka. Craners heal fast, they say. I stooped and held her, drinking in the young, sweet feeling of her. She looked into my eyes, then looked past me and laughed, as if at something joyful in the distance. All I could see was afternoon traffic on Thayer.

"Come up later—if you want some oranges," I told her.

She gave another happy laugh.

I straightened and walked away heavily. Just before I rounded the corner of the house she called out: "Dubby?"

I looked back.

"Everybody has to climb."

I nodded, went on.

My house seemed elderly and shabby, aged yellow sunlight lighting dusty silence. I moved the guest room furniture back the way it had been before, ate dinner alone in the kitchen, stacking the dishes in the sink. Nobody came up begging for food, which was unusual. After dinner I tried to watch TV. A storm was brewing, thunder muttering above the perky game-show host's voice, and a copper-colored dusk was falling early. I finally turned the TV off and stood outside my front door smelling the wet electrical air, watching the high distances mist faintly. When the wind gusted and the first big drops spattered through the maple tree, I went back inside. On my way to shut the upstairs windows I caught sight of someone in the hall mirror: a fat little man with stubby, careful hands slung self-consciously at this sides. There were deep creases between the edges of his nose and lips, and above his creased forehead a stiff unnatural surface of hair thinly covered his scalp from ear to ear. Rain was drumming on the roof now, and I could hear the bedroom curtains flapping. I found some scissors and went into the bathroom, cut off the long side hairs that covered my head and threw them into the wastebasket, where they lay exhausted and oily. When I was done, the face in the mirror was egg-like and fleshy, vulnerable, the eyes hot. I fell asleep with rain pounding on the roof, and had uneasy dreams.

Much later I woke in a crash of thunder and ran from the room, blundered downstairs and through the kitchen, fumbled with locks until the door flew open, ran down waterlogged grass to where a half-foot pool had formed at the bottom of the garden. Rain flayed through bowed branches, and my pajamas were as soaked as if I had been swimming. The streetlight flickered off in a burst of lightning, and thunder crackled almost instantly. I slogged through tall weeds, climbed the porch and plunged through the black doorway of the Langley house.

I blundered into a wall, stood dripping in the darkness.

"Ananka?" I called. "Ananka, I'm ready. I want to go with you."

There was silence except for rain drumming on the side of the house, pattering through a broken window. I felt my way along the wall. The air was wet, mildewed; in one place water spattered down from a leak. A faint light flickered ahead of me. I went through a doorway. Four fair-skinned, silver-haired figures sat very still around a guttering candle in Louise Ann Langley's old living room.

"Ananka?" I said timidly.

"She's not here," said Benjamin, rousing himself from his stillness. "She's gone."

"Gone? Where?" I demanded, advancing into the room with what I could muster of my old sternness. "Where?"

"She cli-," started Roberta, but cut off at a sharp look from the others.

I stared for a few seconds, then ran wildly out into the rain where the old oak tree stood. Up among swaying, shaking branches way at the top, I thought I saw a pale figure. I jumped and grabbed a low branch, pulled with all my might.

"Ananka!" I screamed, but it was drowned in lightning and thunder.

I clawed and scrambled, holding tight to the slippery branches, blinded by rain, breath tearing at my lungs, lightning crashing, leaves hissing, the lights of the town dim and watery far below, and finally I reached a place where the branches were thin and the trunk bent dangerously under me. I hung there in rain and wind.

A yard above the reach of my hands, hanging from the last branches that melted off into the air, Ananka's half-unraveled arm-bandage swayed and shook.

And then a bolt of lightning forked down, lighting bright white a country I had never known: clouds like towers, cliffs, and plains shifting and rushing to a dark horizon, the tops of trees a rippling and dashing sea, and between, a vault where shimmered a billion gleaming drops in which I could almost hear the sweet voices of the dead.

The Nomalers

On a bright October morning Ralph Jennings and I, wearing gray suits, rattled over the brown fields of Southeastern Iowa in an airport rental car.

Ralph was driving and giving me instructions: "Remember not to stare. The clients are self-conscious about being different, and they don't like strangers. Let me do the talking. No matter what strange things you see, *don't stare*." He added as an afterthought: "And don't let the Old Nomaler fool you. He's a smart old bird."

I tried to look grave. Meeting The Client is the first tiny step they let you take toward being a real lawyer.

A town posted "Priopolis Speed Limit 25" came and went in a flash of hamburger joint, gas station, and trailer-sized white houses. A few miles later we turned on a bumpy road with a sign that said "Private-Keep Out" and stopped at a shack with a wire fence stretching into the distance in both directions. A man came out of the shack.

He was of medium height, thin, with lank brown hair. His nose dropped in a thin, straight line from forehead to lip, and his eyes were so close together he looked cross-eyed. Big teeth stuck out crookedly between thin lips. He was like something you would see in an aquarium, on the other side of the glass.

"Ralph Jennings and Blaine Ramsey to see Mr. Nomaler," Ralph said, and gave the man his driver's license. The man looked at me. I dug out my driver's license. He took them both into the shack.

"Security," Ralph explained.

A few minutes later the man brought our licenses back.

"OK," was all he said.

A couple of miles on through the bare, rolling farmland we came over a rise and saw an enormous, three-storey farmhouse. It was a jumble of additions, wings, annexes, enlargements, connecting buildings, barns, outbuildings, garages, even a shingled tower, all weathered into a gray fortress that looked like it would hold a hundred people. Smoke drifted from several chimneys. Ralph pulled up to a leaning porch stacked with boxes and junk. Two young men came out onto the porch. They looked like twins of the man at the security shack.

"Lawyer Jennings?" one asked, and they led us into a big front hall without shaking hands.

Comfortable domestic things were going on in the hall. A middle-aged man smoked a pipe in a greasy armchair. Three ten-year-olds made a terrific noise playing cards on a threadbare carpet. An aproned woman chased a baby who was running away with someone's shoe. There was a smell of lunch cooking.

Everyone, from the man to the baby, had the same thin, flat nose, squeezed together eyes, buck teeth, lank hair.

I tried not to stare. Everyone was staring at us. The baby started to cry and dropped the shoe, and the aproned woman swept him away to another room.

"The Old Nomaler's busy," said one of the young men. "He wants you to wait."

"We'll be glad to," said Ralph, who hates waiting for anything.

They led us up some stairs and down a narrow passage to a small, dim room. Ralph set his briefcase on a swaying coffee table with a strip of formica missing, and asked: "Can you show me to the bathroom?" They led him off like a prisoner. I sat on a bloated vinyl sofa and tried not to breathe a sour smell. After a minute, I opened a window and leaned out of it. Fir trees growing almost against the house gave me a breath of cool, aromatic air.

Down in the yard, a boy was yelling, "Train coming! Train coming!"

Train tracks ran a hundred yards behind the house. Seven or eight little boys, some almost babies, quickly gathered by a rusted tractor below my window. An older boy, about twelve, balanced on the tractor's seat. As the train rumbled past, he called out numbers. It took me a minute to figure out that they were the four- and five-digit identification numbers on the boxcars. The little boys sat on the ground, rigid with concentration.

When the fifty-odd cars had passed, the older boy yelled: "Total!"

"Five hundred and twenty thousand , two hundred and twenty-three," hollered back the little boys almost in unison.

Steps in the passage announced the two Nomalers marching Ralph back from the bathroom. Both of them stared at the open window, then at me. One brushed past me and shut it severely. Then they stalked off without a word.

"You shouldn't touch anything," Ralph murmured, sitting on the sofa with a creak. "They don't like it." He pulled his briefcase near to his feet like a protective talisman.

Half an hour later the two Nomalers led us through a maze of halls, rooms, stairways, foyers, ramps, basements, balconies, and passages. When we finally reached the Old Nomaler's room there was no way to tell what part of the house we were in, or how to get back.

The room opened off a landing at the top of a dark, creaking staircase. A confused babble came from a half-dozen TVs ranged around an old man propped in a shabby king-size bed. When he saw us he nodded to another man, who started turning the TVs off. The old man looked like all the other Nomalers except that he was wrinkled and bald, with wing-like fringes of white hair. He wore dirty pajamas, and a quilt was pulled up to his middle. Around his bed were cardboard boxes full of papers, broken lamps, old bicycle parts, moth-eaten stuffed animals, and other things. Piles of papers lay on ancient desks pushed against the walls. Three worn black rotary telephones sat on one desk next to an obsolete desk-top calculator. A dozen folding chairs were set around.

"Lawyer Jennings," the old man honked, ducking his head and waving. "Brought somebody along with you, I see." He held a pair of bifocals against his vertical nose.

"This is Blaine Ramsey," said Ralph, patting my shoulder

warmly, "one of our most competent and trusted associates." I had been the only associate free when the Nomaler matter came in.

"How do you do, sir," I said.

"How de do, how de do. Well, sit down, sit down. You remember Derek Dan, there, Lawyer Jennings." He nodded at the middle-aged Nomaler who had turned off the TVs.

"Of course. Hello, Derek," said Ralph.

"Lawyer Jennings," said the man.

We took two folding chairs. I got out a note pad and tried to look competent and trustworthy. Derek Dan Nomaler sat where he could read what I wrote down.

"You've heard about this here new rulemaking up in St. Paul," said the old man. "The shipping insurance regulation for the Mississippi River?"

"I hadn't before you directed my attention to it," said Ralph. "I read it before we flew out of Washington last night."

"What do you make of it?"

Ralph gave him a couple of paragraphs of jargon that sounded good without meaning anything. When he was done, Old Nomaler said: "I want you to get rid of that regulation, put things back to the way they were before."

Ralph appeared judicious. "Well, there may be grounds for doing that. Federal pre-emption, perhaps other jurisdictional problems. The difficulty, of course, is standing to appear before the Minnesota Commission. Since the rule by its terms affects shipping interests only, we would effectively have to own a Minnesota shipping company to be an aggrieved party under the appeals statue."

"We'll buy one," said the Old Nomaler.

Ralph took that like a man, even nodding as if he had thought of it first.

"Of course, we could handle such a purchase for you. However, may I point out that the Nomalers have no conceivable interest in overturning a Minnesota shipping rule. You don't own any concerns that could possibly be affected by it. What do you hope to gain?"

The Old Nomaler gave a honking laugh.

"You always ask the same question, Lawyer Jennings, and I

always give you the same answer: you just let me take care of that and you see to your own side of it."

The Nomalers' shipping company purchase went through a month later, Ralph hinting darkly that they had overpaid almost a million dollars to close the deal that fast, and in February our appeal came up for hearing before the Minnesota Public Service Commission, Docks Division. The sky in St. Paul was like dirty snow propped just out of reach, the sidewalks cordoned off below twenty-foot ice stalactites that loomed from the parapets of tall buildings. But the streets were mostly deserted: everybody with sense walked in their shirtsleeves through the glassed-in "skyways" that ran at second story height between most of the buildings. There was even a roundabout way to walk all the way from our hotel to the Public Service Commission, which Ralph took, I puffing behind with two bursting litigation bags. An hour later I sat next to him in a small, dingy hearing room as he spoke emotionally about the great water-ways of our nation, the free commerce that had always moved on those waterways, the humble men whose dreams created that commerce, the dangers of governmental strangulation of free enterprise...my attention wandered after awhile. The regulation we were seeking to overturn was about as far as you could get from interesting: it simply required shipping using Minnesota docks to carry a particular kind of liability insurance. The only interesting thing about the whole case, as far as I was concerned, was why the Nomalers cared about it in the first place. I glanced idly around the hearing room.

From the last row of seats provided for interested members of the public, someone was staring at me. A woman.

Ralph got done with his argument and sat down, and an Associate Commission Counsel stood up and launched into an even more boring argument in favor of the rule. I studied the woman out of the corner of my eye. She seemed to watch me with a weird, hungry stare. She was an interesting specimen herself: in a perfect world she might have been beautiful, with a mane of black hair and large, burning eyes, but some stress or sorrow of this world had streaked her hair gray, hollowed out her cheeks, eaten away the flesh of her bone-thin body.

The Associate Commission Counsel's voice finally droned away to silence. There was a pause, during which the few retirees in the public seating dozed and the room's radiators could be heard faintly ticking out heat; then Administrative Law Judge Sneed roused himself to turn over a sheet of paper and clear his throat and say: "Finally, on behalf of the Council Against Domination, a consumer group certified under Commission Rule 846.C.ii.(j), we will hear from Mr. Timothy Nolan."

The hungry-looking woman pulled a sheaf of papers out of a black vinyl case and handed them to the man next to her. He came forward. He was fat, with jiggly cheeks, a bulbous nose, and hair worn in a kind of Afro. His face had an injured, anxious look, like a boy spanked for things he didn't do. Something about him seemed oddly familiar.

He stood awkwardly in front of Judge Sneed's table, shuffled through his papers for an uncomfortable time, then started in a high, quavering voice: "Yes, Your Honor. I'm coming before this Commission, because it is my painful duty to...to correct the gross, distorted view of this case offered by the appellants." He glanced at Ralph and me with a mixture of wrath and apprehension.

"This issue is nothing like what they say it is. They have mischaracterized it. They are wrong on every single point they have brought out. This rule ought to stand just the way it is. It's an abomination—it's shameful—But *why* do you think these appellants have come before this Commission to try to strike down this rule? Mr. *Jennings*," he spat the word out with much quivering of the cheeks, "has made a lot of fancy arguments which—which— But let me tell you the *real* reason, your Honor, the *real* reason."

He shuffled through his papers with trembling hands and started out in a dramatic voice: "Your Honor, the shipping insurance rates are going up. Yes, the only two companies offering the exact kind of insurance required by this rule have taken big losses in a harbor accident in the mosquito-infested region of Malaysia. Only a few people know that. Mr. Jennings' clients know it, but they aren't telling. No, you Honor. They haven't presented it to this honorable Commission. The insurance rates will go up by a factor of ten in the next months."

I was uncomfortably aware of the thin woman's eyes on me.

"If their insurance rates go up that much, the barge companies using the Mississippi River will have to raise their freight tariffs. To avoid the higher tariffs, farmers will start moving their produce by rail instead of barge, as a result of which the Minnesota and Southern Railroad Company will start making a profit for the first time in 24 years, prompting a consortium of Australian investors who are looking for railroads to buy to try to acquire a controlling share in it, causing the Federal Government, which has to approve sales of railroads to foreign interested, to require Australia to lift trade barriers on U.S. farm produce in return; when Australia does that, the selling price of U.S. corn will rise 2½ cents a bushel, making it profitable for Southeastern Iowa farmers to switch from wheat to corn as their preferred crop, slowing the chromium phosphate depletion of their soil and thus making their crops less vulnerable to a grain blight that *is spreading now from Mexico.*" He looked up to shake his fist. Judge Sneed watched him, wide-eyed. "If the Southeastern Iowa farmers keep growing wheat, the blight will wipe them out in five years, and they'll have to sell their land at bankruptcy prices. To Mr. Jennings' clients—the *Nomalers!*"

He stalked back to his seat, quivering.

Judge Sneed let go of the edge of his table and took a breath.

"Thank you, Mr. Nolan," he said. "Any rebuttal?"

"No, Your Honor," Ralph said sweetly.

After the hearing adjourned, Ralph made important noises into his cell phone in the lobby, then said to me: "We've located a potential Minneapolis buyer for the Nomalers' shipping company. I have a hearing in Florida tomorrow on the *Hess* matter; I want you to stay here for a day or two so you can ferry the papers down to the Nomalers if this Minneapolis company makes us an offer."

He was already reading the *Hess* pleadings when a cab took his gray profile off in the direction of the airport.

I got lost in the skyway maze on the way back to the hotel. After I had gone through the second-floor lobby of the First Bank Building for the third time, I put my litigation bags down in front of a fast food place to wipe my brow and get my bearings. That's when I saw Timothy Nolan of the Council Against Domination.

He didn't see me. He was sitting by the window of the fast food place, gorging himself and crying. As I watched, he stuffed a hamburger, fruit yogurt, fried chicken, chocolate cake, French fries, coleslaw, a pickle, and a grilled cheese sandwich into his mouth until his cheeks ballooned, tears streaming from eyes that stared into a fearful distance.

※　※　※　※

Later I slouched on my hotel bed and tried to read a science fiction magazine. The gray light outside my window was getting grayer when someone knocked at the door.

It was the Council Against Domination woman, dark eyes burning in her gaunt face, long, bony hands twitching on the same black vinyl case she had brought to the Docks Division hearing.

After I had stared at her for a good long time, she murmured: "Can I come in? I have something to discuss with you."

I got out of the way, closed the door and my mouth behind her.

"Sure," I said stupidly. "Come in."

She gave me what was probably supposed to be a smile, threw her coat on the bed, and walked stiffly to look out at where snow was starting to filter out of a gray sky onto the gray city of St. Paul.

I cleared my throat. She whirled in alarm, then gave me another emotionless smile, tossed a lock of graying hair out of her eyes.

"I'm hungry," she said. "Can you buy me dinner?"

She looked hungry. I fumbled with room service menus, the telephone, ordered dinner for two. When I finished, she was leaning against the wall, hugging her vinyl case against her skinny chest.

"I can tell you about the Nomalers," she said. "I know you're curious about them."

"What about them?" I ask stiffly, aware of the rules against Discussing Client Confidences.

"Everything. How they're planning to drive all the other farmers out of business, dominate the whole country. Everything."

"You don't really believe that fairy tale Nolan told at the hearing?"

"It's the truth."

"Come on—everyone in the room was trying not to laugh. Not the biggest MIT genius with the fastest computer is going to tell you things like that an insurance rule in Minnesota will cause a grain blight in Iowa."

"Computers can only think about numbers. Nomalers can think about *things*."

The telephone on the bed stand rang. She took two quick steps and answered it before I could move.

"Hello?" she murmured in a languid, steamy voice. "I'm sorry, he's—busy. Can he call you back?" Then: "Oh." She held the phone out to me.

It was Ralph, in Florida. He sounded a little funny, but he only said: "I just heard from our Minneapolis buyers. They're going to make us an offer. You can pick up the papers tonight. The Kristensen Transport Company." He gave me the address. "I'll call the Nomalers to set up a time when you can take the papers down."

When I hung up, the woman went on talking as if nothing had happened: "We know the grain blight is what the Nomalers are counting on in challenging the rule. Tim figured it out, replicated their analysis."

"Uh-huh."

"Yes. You see, he used to be one of them."

That stopped me. I suddenly realized why Nolan had looked so familiar: the narrow forehead, close fish-eyes, bobbing Adam's-apple—but force-fed fat, with a cheap nose job and a perm.

"They sent him to college as an experiment. Their young don't go to school—they bribed some state education officials to certify a home program. Tim was one of their best—trainees. But in college he found out how evil they are, turned against them. He's been fighting them ever since."

The pride in her voice made me wonder: "He met you in college?"

She shrugged.

"I think you're both a couple of nuts," I said. "How—"

"Tim calculated that you would be wondering about the Nomalers," she broke in. "How do you explain that I knew that?"

There was a knock at the door and a muffled voice said: "Room service."

The woman had a sudden urge to use the bathroom.

I opened the door and a cheerful kid wearing pink and gold with epaulets wheeled in a hot cart and set the little table by the window. He was taking the covers off the plates when he stopped in the middle of asking me had I seen the basketball game, and his face got red. The Council Against Domination woman had come out of the bathroom wearing nothing but a towel. A small towel.

"Darling, is dinner—oh, excuse me," she said, and smiled winningly at the kid. When he had left, still red, I closed my mouth far enough to ask: "What are you—?"

The phone rang. We both dived for it. I got it, but not before she had delivered a very sexy giggle into the mouthpiece.

"Hello, Blaine Ramsey? This is Derek Dan Nomaler," came a staticky, faraway voice.

"Hello, Mr. Nomaler!" I said, trying to sound cordial and businesslike. The woman was crawling on me, breathing like a locomotive. Her towel had gotten lost. She put her mouth near the telephone and panted: "Come on, baby, let's do it some more—"

I got my hand on her face and pushed. She bit me.

"Ramsey," came the distant, crackly voice. "Are you there?"

"Yes, sir!"

"The Old Nomaler'll be ready to see you at eight o'clock tomorrow night to sign them papers. You hear me, Ramsey?"

The woman was doing her best to kick a hole in my ribcage, laughing wildly.

"I'll be there! Thank you, sir!"

I hung up and let go of her. She backed away, rubbing her neck, which realized I had been squeezing. Her naked body wasn't bad looking, if you liked them gray and gaunt. Her eyes were shining.

"I have to dress," she said, and ran into the bathroom, slamming the door.

In thirty seconds I went through a range of emotions, settling finally on wild curiosity. The woman's black vinyl case was lying on the bed. I unzipped it.

An inner ID tag said: "If Lost, Please Return To: Ms. Jessica Ann Leighton, 301 Elm Street, Minneapolis, Minn. 52217," written small and neat. Nolan's notes from the hearing were in a different hand, wavering and scribbly. The only other thing in the case was a big diagram made of pieces of notepaper scotch-taped together. I unfolded it and laid it on the bed.

It was some kind of flow chart, drawn in ball-point pen, with hundreds of square, round, triangular, and diamond-shaped boxes connected by lines, arrows, and symbols. I read the writing in some of the boxes. One said: "Piedmont 351, vel. 345 mph, alt. 18500 ft., acc. .05 g, vect. 87/108/??" and a lot of other even less comprehensible stuff. Another said: "Precip. 82%, vix(alt)=" and ended in something like the General Theory of Relativity. In the very center, with many lines and arrows leading to it, was a big red magic marker star.

The bathroom door opened, there was a sharp drawn breath, and then the woman was between me and diagram, pushing me away with one hand and folding it up with the other. When she had it and Nolan's notes back in the case, she tossed back her hair and looked me in the face. She was breathing hard, and in her eyes was exultation and hatred.

"Goodbye, Mr. *Ramsey*," she spat, and ran out of there.

I paced the room a little, watching dinner for two congeal on the table by the window and trying to make any sense at all of Ms. Jessica Ann Leighton. Finally, I figured I needed professional help. I called the firm's Washington number. It was pretty late, but one of the paralegals, Edward Bolingbroke III, was still in the office. He wasn't happy about the assignment I gave him, but an hour later he called back.

"There's a lot in the Nomaler files," he told me. "I haven't been able to review all of it, but I can give you a start. First thing we handled for them was a tort case, wrongful death. About twenty years back. One of the Nomaler boys had a car accident with a gasoline truck that made weekly deliveries to a gas station down there. Freak impact flipped the truck into somebody's wheat field. Both drivers got out, nobody got hurt, but some gas spilled and caught fire, started a pretty bad brush fire. It was late summer—dry. The wind was blowing in such a way that the fire burned up to a big chemical storage tank owned by a local company, full of methy—methyl-iso—no, methyliso—anyway, something poisonous they use for making pesticides. The tank caught fire and blew up, and a cloud of poison smoke blew almost a mile and settled smack onto a local farmer's house. Killed the farmer and most of his family. It just happened that he was a big wheel around there, had organized local opposition to the Nomalers, boycotting their wholesale outlets, refusing to sell them land and so forth. Survivors brought suit in the county court. Your friend Jennings got the venue changed, and the jury denied liability for lack of proximate cause: unforeseeable freak chain of events. The case of *Leighton v. Nomaler*, affirmed by the Iowa Court of Appeals at—."

"Leighton?"

"Samuel Arthur Leighton was the farmer's name."

I was silent until Eddie said, "You still there? Want to hear the next one?"

"Yeah."

"This might have been luck, but...It was an acquisition we handled for them—a series of acquisitions. In the spring of 1973 the Nomalers mortgaged everything they had, took out business loans, sold off land, and invested ten million dollars in guess what? Unprofitable Texas oil wells. A few months later the OPEC oil embargo hit and Texas oil wells got obscenely profitable. They sold out their holdings a few years later, just before prices dipped again. Jennings handled the sales. Overall, they made more then eighty million on the deal. I'll tell you, Blaine, either these folks are damn lucky, or..."

"Or, what?"

"Or nothing. They're just damn lucky. That's as far as I've gotten so far."

The next afternoon I flew to Iowa City with the Kristensen purchase contract papers and rented a car. I took Interstate 80 west, turned south on highway 149, and west again on a country route. Between country songs and ads for hog wormer and feed corn, the radio weatherman was predicting light snow and twenty degrees below zero.

The twenty degrees below zero I could believe, but by the time I reached Priopolis it was pitch dark and the light snow had turned heavy. I could barely see the "Private—Keep Out" sign marking the Nomalers' road. I crawled along at 10 mph through foot-deep snow, past the dark guardhouse. By the time I saw the lights of the main farmhouse, it was almost nine-thirty. A hundred yards away from the house my car stuck in a snowdrift and I couldn't get it unstuck. I trudged up to the porch Ralph and I had used before. The wind through my overcoat was numbing. I pounded on the door with a hand that felt like a piece of wood.

The door cracked wide enough for yellow light to show swirling snowflakes and a narrow, cross-eyed woman's face that shrilled: "Go away! You're at the wrong place!" She tried to close it, but I stuck my foot in the crack.

I worked my frozen lips. "I'm the lawyer—."

She was screeching at someone inside. A second later the door jerked open and a shotgun barrel hovered in front of my nose.

"What do you want?" rasped the skinny, fish-like man holding it.

"I'm the lawyer—from Minneapolis—I brought the papers—."

"Where's your car"

"Got stuck—up the road."

"Let's see your I.D."

I pulled out my license with foot-thick fingers and gave it to him. Another man took it away somewhere.

"Can I come in?"

"Not yet."

Heat flowing out of the door brought some feeling back into me. By the time the other man came back with my license, I was warm enough to be mad as hell.

But since these folks were Ralph's clients, I limited my remarks to, "I appreciate your hospitality," as they let me in. They ignored me. The one with the shotgun locked it in a closet, bolted and chained the porch door. Then they all went off without a word. The hall was still, empty, warm, and smelled of dust and firewood. Now and then a floorboard creaked somewhere. I stood on the doormat, snow melting off my coat and hair. I noticed the mat didn't say "Welcome" on it.

Finally two Nomalers came down the hall. One said: "The Old Nomaler's ready to see you." We took the scenic route to his room, and soon I was again basking in his beneficent gaze, Derek Dan hanging around behind my chair close enough to pick my pockets.

"No offense," honked the Old Nomaler, waving a hand at me. "Folks got to be careful who they let in these days."

I got the Kristensen papers in order and handed him a set, explained the details of the purchase offer. I could feel Derek Dan's eyes over my shoulder, could hear the moaning wind banging something loose against the side of the house. I felt suddenly alone and vulnerable, like a diver in the kingdom of the fish people. I missed Ralph, with his gray head, opaque eyes, careful hands, his steadfast refusal to believe in anything but winning cases.

After I explained the deal, the Old Nomaler signed each paper in exactly the right place.

"Mr. Nomaler," I said as I put them away, "I'd like to ask a favor. The weather's pretty bad out. My car's stuck in the snow, and I don't think I could possibly get back to Iowa City tonight anyway. Could you put me up for the night?"

He thought about it for a long time, eyes rolling up to look at the ceiling. Finally he said: "Well, I suppose so, I suppose so. Be murder to turn a feller out on a night like this." He honked with laughter. "Derek Dan, see to it."

I followed Derek Dan onto the dark landing, where my two

escorts stood against the wall. He took one of them into a small side room and closed the door. The other watched me like he might miss something important if he blinked.

A low-voiced argument started in the side room. As it got heated, I caught a few words: "responsibility," "never," "Nomaler," and "murder."

But they came out deadpan as ever. Derek Dan went back into the Old Nomaler's room. The other two walked me through the house to a small, dim room.

"Woman's coming to make the bed," one of them said, and shut the door. A key turned in the lock.

I took off my coat and sat in a deep, smelly armchair. A wobbly night-table and a metal bed frame with a lumpy mattress made up the rest of the furniture. Wind gusted strongly outside a small window.

There was a knock, the key turned, and a young Nomaler woman poked her head in.

"I come to make the bed," she said, and flushed deeply, as if that might give me ideas.

"I won't watch," I said.

But I did, while she worked rapidly and expertly with the sheets and blankets. A homemade dress—purple with little white flowers—hung on her as on a clothes rack. Her thin hair was parted in the middle and tied behind with a drooping ribbon. Her close-together eyes had a look of timid sincerity.

"I'll get you your dinner," she said when she had turned back the cover and smoothed it.

"It's very kind of you."

"Well—the Old Nomaler said to do it. I wouldn't dare on my own account."

She flushed again and went out, and a little while later came back with a tray. She set it on the night-table, which rocked drunkenly.

"My name's Emily Del," she said, "I'll be back to clear away when you're done."

"Blaine," I said, and held out my hand. She shook it inexpertly, went out quickly.

The food was odd: thin, lukewarm broth, unfamiliar vegetables, and home-baked bread, all spiced heavily with something strange. After I ate it, I felt peculiar. I was trying to pin down the feeling when Emily Del came in again. She closed the door and leaned her back against it.

"Where are you from?" she asked.

"Washington D.C."

"Is that far away?"

"About a thousand miles away."

"Still in Iowa, though, isn't it?"

"No, but it's still in America."

She nodded thoughtfully, as if weighing that. Then she came over to where I was sitting on the bed.

"If I asked you to do something," she said, "would you promise not to tell anyone?"

"I guess so."

She undid the top button of her dress and pulled out a tattered, years-old *People* magazine, sat down beside me, too excited now to be shy, and opened it to a well-worn page with a color photo of a movie star.

"Can you read her name?" she breathed, her finger on the caption.

"Natassia Kinsky."

It took her a few tries to get it right. "I think she's *so* pretty," she sighed, gazing at the picture. "I wish I looked just like her."

I studied her narrow face, snaggled teeth.

She got up and moved away timidly. "Thank you for reading her name to me."

"Can't you read?"

"'*Course* I can read. But not hard words like that. And I couldn't show it to any of the boys—they'd take it away." She slipped the magazine back inside her dress.

"The boys read better?"

"Well, yes. They have to because they're the Calculators. We're the Breeders. There's plenty of things we do better than them. That's called Division of Labor. The famous Henry Ford Nomaler invented it."

"But what's the point of it?"

"To spread the Nomaler way of life all around the world, of course. Don't you think the Nomaler way of life is superior to any other you've seen?" It sounded like a quotation.

"Sure."

"There you are, then." She came close again, looking anxiously into my face. "You won't tell anybody, will you? We aren't supposed to talk to strangers."

I said of course I wouldn't.

It was almost midnight when I got undressed and got between the covers that Emily Del's deft, skinny hands had made up; but I couldn't sleep. I lay there and listened to the wind shake the house. The strange feeling from the Nomaler food had crept into my brain, making it strangely clear, thoughts ranged neatly in rows like pieces on a chessboard. After awhile I nudged one of them tentatively: my wondering about Jessica Ann Leighton and Timothy Nolan. Thought patterns built effortlessly around it.

Unless Jessica Ann was just crazy, she had been trying to advertise yesterday that she was in my hotel room naked. She had given her pitch to anyone who would listen, but had stopped pitching it right after Derek Dan Nomaler's phone call. That made it look like her public relations effort was aimed at the Nomalers. But why? Thoughts whirled like jigsaw puzzle pieces, settling finally into an odd pattern. Jessica Ann had told me that Nolan had "calculated" that I was curious about the Nomalers. If you believed that, silly as it sounded, and believed that Nolan used the same methods the Nomalers did, then the Nomalers might also be able to "calculate" that I was curious, perhaps could also "calculate" that Nolan had "calculated" it and had sent Jessica Ann to take advantage of it. Derek Dan Nomaler had heard a woman in the throes of passion in my room yesterday, and could confirm who it was if he checked with the hotel and ran across a certain bell-boy. And if they found out all that, the Nomalers would surely wonder whether I was still their zealous legal advocate, or whether Jessica Ann Leighton – whose father they had killed – had turned my head with her emaciated charms. If that was part of Nolan's plan, had he known somehow that I would be staying overnight in the Nomaler house? Could he have "calculated" the snowstorm? One of the boxes on the diagram in Jessica Ann's vinyl case had said "Precip. 82%"; did that symbolize light snow turned unexpectedly heavy? The same diagram had a big red star in the middle; what—or who—was that? Some calamity the Council Against Domination had prepared and sent into the Nomaler household along with me? Was I messenger of doom to my own clients? I leapt up, ran from the room and down narrow, twisting corridors. I had to see the Old Nomaler, warn him about the Red Star, tell him—

I woke with a start, wind howling faintly outside the window. I lay in the dark awhile, trying to get the dream out of my head, cursing the Nomalers' strange food. Gradually I became aware of an uncomfortable pressure in my bladder. I got out of bed and dressed without turning on the light.

Emily Del had forgotten to lock the door. I stepped into the hall and tried to remember whether I had passed a bathroom on my trip down from the Old Nomaler's room.

"Hello?" I said to no one.

There was a dim light at one end of the hall. I went that way, floorboards squeaking faintly. There was no other sound but the distant gusting of wind. I went down some stairs, along another hall, looking through open doorways for a bathroom. One doorway showed a small, plain chapel with pews and an alter below a crucifix flanked by candles. For no particular reason, I went in.

The crucifix was carved wood, and there was something strange about it; as I got closer I saw that the figure of the Messiah was dressed in farm boots, overalls, and a hat. Its face was thin, with a long, perpendicular nose, eyes so close together they looked crossed, buck teeth jutting out at different angles. Underneath the crucifix was a plaque: "Jacob John Nomaler, Murdered January 9, 1919." That gave me a funny feeling. I backed away, backed into the first row of pews so hard I sat down. A hymnal lay open on the pew, a rough, hand-sewn book crudely printed. It was open to a hymn called "Rivers of Their Blood." The first verse went:

> We will swim in
> Rivers of their blood,
> We will soar in
> Regions of the sun,
> We will show them
> What is meant to be.
> We will drown them
> In righteousness' sweet sea.

I go up and walked as fast and quietly as I could in the direction of my room. It took me three or four minutes to realize I was lost. When I stopped to get my bearings, I heard voices coming faintly down a flight of stairs.

I started to hurry in the other direction, but stopped myself. I was these folks' *lawyer*, for God's sake. If they wanted to practice bizarre religions, I should be glad. I would just go up and ask whoever was there to show me the bathroom. I started up the stairs.

I stopped again almost at once. I recognized one of the voices. It was the Old Nomaler's, and I was on the staircase below his room.

His voice was doing strange things. It droned with a stream of words, like an auctioneer singing a Gregorian chant. It was punctuated by mechanical clicking, rustling of paper, and monosyllables in other voices.

I poked my head cautiously above the top stair. In dim yellow lamplight the Old Nomaler sat in his bed, an I.V. in one arm, face flushed and eyes flashing. On each side of him sat a middle-aged Nomaler holding him by the hand. One of them was Derek Dan. A dozen others sat in a crowded circle around the bed, rifling through cardboard boxes of papers. A younger Nomaler sat a little way off talking into a telephone; another was writing furiously on a thick tablet; a third was tacking pages from the tablet onto a corked wall. An old-fashioned desk-top calculator rested on Derek Dan's lap, and his free hand flew over the keys.

"...Ramseyum cognation Leightonee Nolanor in homology, apposition, cause, proportion, context," the Old Nomaler's voice droned, "opportunity, confidence factor, relation Jenningsum Jenningsee— "

"Innocence pathway," rapped Derek Dan.

"Guilt pathway," rapped the middle-aged Nomaler on the Old Nomaler's other side.

"—rapport, intersection, eliminate below-ten, above-ten, ignore Leightonum, Leightonor—"

The Nomalers with the cardboard boxes shuffled papers rapidly and began weaving words into the Old Nomaler's canticle: "libidinous," "financial," "eighty-three," "adverse," "input need hotelus," "inhibitor guilt pathway."

"Maximum destructive," said Derek Dan.

"Projection," said the other middle-aged Nomaler.

The one at the telephone was dialing.

A few inches behind me, a voice screamed: "Emergency stop!"

Wiry hands grabbed me, hustled me up the stairs and into the room. Two dozen fish-faces stared without expression.

"Is there a bathroom around here?" I quavered, pulling my collar straight.

The Old Nomaler laughed feverishly.

"Listening?" he demanded.

The three Nomalers who had grabbed me nodded.

"What else?"

"I was just looking for the bathroom," I said weakly. "I got lost, and—"

The Old Nomaler laughed again, loud and long and crazy. "Take him to the bathroom!" he screamed savagely, veins in his neck and forehead distended. Then he started his crazy laughing again, his eyes on my face staring and murderous, jagged, rotten teeth bared.

The three Nomalers marched me to a windowless bathroom with an old-fashioned toilet you pulled a chain to flush, a bathtub standing on enameled claws, and a mirror with the silver flaking off the back. I stood over the toilet for five minutes, but nothing would come out. My face in the mirror looked wild. When I opened the door, the three Nomalers were standing in a row. They marched me through the house in dizzying spirals, and my room appeared when I least expected it. I went in meekly, the door was closed and locked, and their footsteps went away.

It was 3:00 a.m. I sat in the smelly armchair without turning on the light, thinking about the Old Nomaler's crazy, murderous face. I sat there an hour before I heard rapid footsteps in the hall. I did a silent back-flip and crouched behind the armchair.

The key turned and a dark streak hit the bed with a maddened keening.

I dived on the streak.

It was like fighting a bale of wire and sharp elbows.

It whimpered "Help!" in a woman's voice. I pulled the face close to mine. Emily Del was sobbing with fear.

"They're going to kill us," she sobbed. "They're coming! We have to get away!"

"Who?" I hissed.

"The Calculators! They were whispering outside my door. I talked to you, and you saw the Central Processor, and they're coming! They'll fry us and eat us like they did to—!"

I put my hand over her mouth, didn't breathe. I thought a floorboard had creaked in the hall. Thinking fast, I jumped to the door, reversed the key, and locked it from the inside.

The knob turned silently.

I grabbed my coat off the chair, opened the room's window and storm window as quietly as I could. A gust of snowflakes swirled in. The tops of young fir trees were within diving distance of the window.

"Come on!" I hissed at Emily Del, and dived into one. It bent almost double, and I slid feet-first into snow above my knees. Emily Del came down the same way, her dress over her head. Bitter wind cut deep into me. My hands had already gone numb. Emily Del was wearing only her purple housedress.

"Come on!" I yelled above the storm. I grabbed her hand and dragged her in the direction I thought my rental car must be. Fifty yards from the house she fell in the snow. When I picked her up, she was stiff with cold. I unbuttoned my coat, wrapped half around her, and we stumbled on. The snow cleared for a second between gusts, and I saw the car, snow drifted to the roof.

My keys weren't in the coat pocket where I had left them. The car doors were locked. I hadn't locked them. Suddenly I knew what had happened.

Emily Del was slipping to the ground. I held her. "We have to get back to the house," I yelled in her ear.

Her face was still, preoccupied, eyes almost closed.

"I can't," she murmured.

"We have to! They tricked us, to get us outside. They wouldn't have killed us—that would mean trouble. They don't do things that way. They analyze, calculate, manipulate—they can't get into trouble for this—we snuck out, forgot the car keys. How do they do it? And without computers!"

A smile of pride came into her sleeping face. "Computers can only think about numbers," she slurred, "Nomalers can thinks about *things*. Nomalers—."

And she was gone.

I held her cold body in my arms. I could faintly see the dark hulk of the house in the snow. "You bastards!" I screamed against the wind.

That seemed to get results. A metal shriek drowned the roar of the storm. A fiery mass plummeted from the clouds straight onto the house, and the walls burst outward in blinding flames, hurling streamers of fire and debris like a Fourth of July rocket, throwing weird shadows in the snow.

I dived behind the car just in time to escape a shower of hot metal and burning wood that broke the windows and thudded into the snow, hissing and steaming. When I poked my head out to look, only splinters of the house were standing, and the whole area was burning fiercely, hissing and sparking.

I picked up Emily Del and slogged nearer the fire. There was no need to get in the car now. There was plenty of heat.

I woke the next afternoon in an Iowa City hospital—in a private room, bought with the firm's group health insurance. There was nothing much wrong with me. Emily Del was recovering from acute hypothermia in another room.

An orderly brought me some stuff that was supposed to be food, and a newspaper. Banner headlines on the front page said: AIR CRASH KILLS HUNDREDS IN IOWA.

"A commercial airliner collided with a private plane over Southeastern Iowa early this morning, crashing into a crowded farmhouse in what aviation officials are calling a freak accident. Blizzard conditions kept the rescue teams from reaching the crash site for nearly two hours. Of the estimated two hundred people aboard National flight 351 and in the farmhouse, only two are known to have survived." There were gruesome details of the carnage, and descriptions of disaster workers' heroic battle with the elements, then: "The tragedy began when Timothy A. Nolan, a Minneapolis resident, flew a rented aircraft out of a small airfield near Minneapolis. While flying conditions were marginal, according to Elstein Wiggs, flight controller at the airport, Nolan, a licensed pilot, was determined to reach Priopolis, Iowa that evening. An unexpectedly heavy snowstorm interfered with transponders carried by Nolan's plane and the airliner, devices normally enabling air traffic controllers to track planes and warn them of danger."

The telephone by my bed rang. It was Ralph Jennings, full of questions.

"I hope you managed to save the Kristensen purchase papers?" was the first one.

I admitted that I hadn't.

"Damn it, Ramsey—Does Ms. Nomaler still want to sell the company?"

"I don't know."

"Damn it, Ramsey, what have you been *doing* up there?"

I got him off the phone with promises to straighten everything out. Directory assistance gave me Jessica Ann Leighton's Minneapolis number.

"Hello, this is Blaine Ramsey," I said when she answered.

There was silence on the other end of the line.

"I just wanted to tell you that I'm now inclined to believe you about the Nomalers," I went on. "And I wanted to ask whether you and Nolan set up that whole charade with me at the hotel to divert their attention, so they would be too busy to calculate what someone like Nolan might do with an airplane and a freak snowstorm –"

Her voice was icy. "I have no idea what you're talking about," she said. "Please don't bother me again." And she hung up.

I stared at the telephone. Its expression revealed nothing.

Anyway, we won our appeal. You can use Minnesota docks as much as you want without state liability insurance.

The Book Of St. Farrin

I woke up on the concrete floor of a subbasement utility tunnel with the first syllables of the scum warning in my ears, and before I was awake, I was running. I had worn armor once, chased scums through the dark dirty places where they lived: I knew the surrender period after the bullhorn warning; I knew the dead silence when the hunt began; I knew that the ninth subbasement of the Utopia Luxury Apartment Complex was a place where you wouldn't risk taking scums alive.

I had slept in the utility tunnel because it opened on two unused stairwells. I dived down the urine-smelling blackness of the first—but too late. As I ran, a blinding pulse of violet light seared the concrete next to me.

I jumped the handrail, hit the flight below with my shoulder, jumped another rail, another. Bright light blossomed above me in the stairwell. I could hear the faint rush of a Black Angel's wings.

And then there were no more stairs, just a gray concrete wall at the extreme depth of the building with a foot-wide crack where the foundation of the Utopia Luxury Apartments had shifted. Concrete teeth tore at me as I rammed myself into it. Inside it widened. I hugged the ground as violet light flamed above me, breathed dust the Angels hands made smashing the wall open. It was no good to him just to kill me—he had to take back one of my thumbs to get his bounty money.

I wormed blindly into the crack. Suddenly there was empty

space under me. I pitched into blackness, tumbling in an avalanche of stones and dust. When I stopped I was half buried in rubble.

I dragged myself up. The Angel's light moved somewhere far above me, showing a steep slope that a few pebbles rattled down. I stumbled and slid the rest of the way down it. At the bottom a black tunnel opened. I plunged into it, turning on my own small light. Broken rock crunched under my feet. Cement dust stung my throat. I passed what might once have been a window, choked with concrete now, and facing downward.

After a while, cracked paving stones showed under the rubble of the floor. The ceiling receded into darkness. I turned a sharp corner, and my light showed windows, doorways, walls.

Everyone knew the City was built over an older city that had been destroyed in the Fire. The Ur, they called it, but no one ever went there—its radioactive ruin was hidden under a thick blanket of entombment concrete. I guessed that was the crumbling ceiling that arched out of reach of my light, held by reinforced concrete pillars like huge stalagmites. The massive buildings that stood partly crushed under it were made of brown stone, worn and pocked with age, with arched windows and doors. There were the remains of columns and fountains, carvings worn smooth in the stone. Pitch dark surrounded the beam of my light as I wandered, an aimless sightseer, chasing startled shadows. Silence lay everywhere like thick layers of dust.

My light was fading. I turned it off to save the battery, sat against a broken stone column. The darkness was dead, dry, still—but after a while I saw a flickering light, almost faint enough to be imaginary. I had never heard of Angels tracking scums through the Ur, but I moved silently behind the column, holding my breath.

Silence hissed in my ears. The light didn't get any closer. I crept along cracked paving stones toward it, until I could see that it came from a place in the middle of the street, like a window set in the ground. It flickered, changing colors, making the dead stone of the buildings seem to move, summoning ghostly faces to their windows.

It was a video screen, half buried in hard dirt, flashing silent static. I dug it out with my fingernails. It didn't come easily—there was nothing to show it hadn't been there for the hundreds of years since the Fire. Its casing was corroded metal thirty centimeters square by five thick, of strange design. There were buttons below the screen, with strange markings. I touched one of them.

The screen stopped flashing and a picture appeared. It was a picture of the building facing me on that street, a massive ruin with huge doors of rusted metal, and hollow, high windows. In the picture the building was dark, but not pitch-dark—maybe moonlight-behind-clouds dark—the metal doors were polished silver, the walls smooth and uncracked. The windows were dark, but there was an air of life about the place, as if everybody was sleeping or had just gone away. Mist floated in the street. For a long time the picture stayed like that, and I watched it, wondering what it meant.

Then one of the polished metal doors swung open and somebody came out.

I dropped the screen, shone my light at the building. It was lifeless, doors rusted shut, windows blank, walls leaning.

I picked up the screen. The figure was coming toward me.

It was some ancient video recording, I told myself, maybe an archaeological find. Maybe I could sell it in the City. The thought helped me stand my ground.

The figure on the screen came close and looked into my eyes.

It was a beautiful dark-haired girl.

I knew she wasn't real, but I stared. Her eyes were large and luminous, somehow sad. She wore a long black gown. She put the palms of her hands together and raised them to her lips, as if in greeting.

"Toori protect me," I muttered, and passed my hand through the space in front of me where the girl would be if there was a girl. There was only dry, still air.

She smiled sadly and passed her hand through the air the same way I had.

"Toori protect me," I said. This had to be worth money in the City. Maybe enough to buy me a job authorization, a room in the apartment blocks, a wife –

"Who are you?" I asked her. "An interactive simulation? Can you hear me?"

She touched her lips with two fingers and shook her head, as if telling me she didn't understand.

"Out," I said, gesturing furiously upward. "How do you get out?"

She shook her head.

"I live up there," I said, pounding myself on the chest. "Want to get out."

She studied me closely, then walked away from the screen.

"Wait! Come back!" I shouted in the dead air, banging on the screen. In a while she did, waving me to follow her.

I got the idea, though it was strange. I walked the same way in the real buried city as she was walking in the virtual intact one.

She went quickly, glancing back now and then, as if I was really walking behind her instead of following a 3-D animated map. On the screen, the buildings we passed were stately, well tended. Where I was, they were crumbling or tumbled into shattered heaps, plunged in blackness except where my light shone. On the screen, there were no people except the woman. Where I was, there was no one but me.

After a few hundred meters she stopped and pointed at a low doorway. I tilted the screen up to look at a tower, rising toward a dark sky heavy with clouds. In the beam of my light, the tower had a few stones missing, but was solid as far up as I could see. The door was metal and took all my strength to open, with a loud squawking of hinges. A stone stairway spiraled into darkness.

I climbed them a long way. At the top, my light showed rough foundation concrete—but there was a crack between concrete and stone. I slipped the ancient TV-thing into my dirty jumpsuit, hoisted myself up, and after some hard scrambling came out in a cave that water had hollowed under a City street drain. I curled up in a dry corner and slept.

In dreams I carried the ancient TV-thing through the City, running from thieves, holding it high above the grasping hands of beggars, hiding from the police bribe-takers, resisting the electronically enhanced blandishments of prostitutes, running to the higher levels of the City, where the rich corporations lived--

I woke pawing blindly for it.

The cave was dark. Dim red light came through the drain grating from curfew warning holos that floated above the streets outside. I drank from a trickle of drain water and lay back down. Darkness and silence drove thoughts through my head; how I had lost my job as a police bounty hunter to a younger, more aggressive recruit, become a scum—Socially Controlled Unproductive Member—how I had escaped from the indentured labor factory that made food for a world still poisoned and blackened, had hidden in basements and condemned buildings, running now myself from the hunters. After a while I didn't want to think anymore. I propped the TV-thing on my chest and pushed the strange buttons until the screen glowed, lighting the cave walls dim gray.

I wondered if it would pick up a City channel, but it showed the underground building with the metal doors exactly as before— night-dark, misty, deserted. One of the doors swung open. The beautiful girl came out, came toward the screen. Her eyes were searching and grave. Looking into them I fell asleep again.

Slowly the night wore away.

But not before, groping painfully in dreams and looking into her eyes on waking, I had recognized her.

I knew who she was. And I knew the TV-thing was going to make me rich.

When day came, I pushed the drain grating up and crawled out. The dim, crowded street smelled like smoke, garbage, and sweat. Vendors called their wares from pushcarts. Between the tops of the hundred-story buildings floated advertising holos, sweet dreams you could buy if you had enough money. At the corner two police Angels stood, black helmets swiveling.

A few blocks away I waited in line for a phone booth, and when the plastic doors jammed shut behind me, took the TV-thing from my jumpsuit and turned it on. I punched the City's only free phone number. A simulated face appeared: "Thank you for dialing the RAD Cola Corporation Neurological Volunteers Line. We at RAD Cola – "

"Cut that." I held up the screen. By now the beautiful girl was gazing out of it. "Take a look at this—have somebody important look at it. I'll be back in touch. My name is Farrin."

I broke the connection, slipped the screen back into my suit, left the booth. Cold, acrid rain was starting to fall. A few blocks away, a warm, perfumed breeze caressed my face.

High between the buildings a RAD Cola ad-holo was forming, familiar logo shimmering. The faithful on the street were kneeling. I leaned against a wall and let the psionic images flow through me. A wide field appeared, filled with crystal sunlight that could only have existed before the Fire. Tall grass waved in a breeze. Birds sang and insects hummed. Across the field, through a patch of tiny flowers, a figure ran, long dress fluttering, dark eyes laughing, carrying two can of RAD Cola. The fragrance and electricity of her body enfolded me as she handed me one of the icy cans and we drank, the bubbly brown liquid impossibly tempting—even more, in that second, than the curve of her shoulders, her short, lustrous hair, her breasts pressing at the thin material of the dress, her eyes. Then it was over. The scene receded high into the air, collapsed into the red-and-white logo. People moaned, stumbled to their feet. RAD Cola was the richest corporation in the City—because of the psi advertising technology only it had, and because of the Holy Beloved, Toori Sith, the model who had starred in the ads since the beginning.

And whose face gazed from the screen of the ancient TV-thing I had found in the Ur.

Across the street, people were crowding eagerly through the massive doors of a twenty-story concrete dome. Above the doors, red neon letters said CHURCH OF BEAUTY. In the entrance, a prostitute caressed me with implanted electrodes that sent shudders through my body.

Services were starting, the acres of concrete crowded with people facing a two-story dais. The Burning was in progress. Half a dozen figures hung above the dais, and a white-surpliced priest, brightly haloed with light from his electroneural enhancers, was setting fire to them. The figures were ultraflammable plastic, and burst into flames that quickly consumed them. The first was a man nailed to a T-shaped piece of wood. Next a man in an orange robe, with a faint, inward smile. Then a bearded man with a sad, compassionate face. Then another robed man with only flames where his head and hands should be. As each of the figures was engulfed, the priest's voice boomed through the dome: "Death has overtaken you."

And ten thousand voices murmured the response: "Death has overtaken all."

Near me, a group of factory workers wore heavy plastic clothes and helmets covered with gray dust. An old man, probably almost fifty, leaned on a cane, face twitching with some sickness. Two ragged, empty-faced children, holding hands. A man sleeping under a heap of rags on the floor. A half-naked girl with bruises on her face and arms. Faces gaunt and haunted, bodies thin.

The Burning over, the priest turned to the people with hands raised, enhancement auras crackling.

"Death has overtaken the world," he intoned.

"There is nothing left," the murmur welled up.

"The Fire has come."

"There is nothing left."

"Beauty has died."

A ritual sigh from ten thousand throats.

The priest effortlessly held a huge book open before him.

"I read from the Book of Saint Debbie, Chapter One.

"'After the Great Fire the world was burned, and into it was born a baby, called Debbie. All around was the fire-sickness, and

51

the buildings lay upon each other like slain creatures, but one man was wealthy: Alan, the father of Debbie. His Corporation had as much knowledge and riches as were then to be had.

"'Alan said: 'I will not let my daughter see this world, for such a world is not fit to be born into.' So saying, he built a palace around her, filled with all the things that were Before, spending upon it as much as would sustain a million men. There were spacious halls and soft beds, greenhouses holographed like fields and woods. No people were let in except they were fed and washed, and skillful at telling beautiful stories of outside. Debbie ate only fresh milk and fruit and baked bread, bought for fortunes. She played in fields and forests, and had pet dogs, and at night lay in her bed watching the moon rise over the woods. Her father guarded her well; twenty thousand men labored to keep Debbie.

"'Debbie grew to six years old knowing nothing of the Fire.

"'So was Debbie saved.

"'But outside, the Death Mother stalked the earth, embracing all that lived, and when she heard of Debbie she was jealous with wrath. So she called to Debbie in her dreams.

"'In her dreams, all around were broken buildings, and people thin and gray, all the trees burned to ashes, the rivers black, and the sky dark. Her father and the others told her not to heed such foolish dreams, but one night she woke and crept to a door her father had told her never to open. She opened it and there were all the things she had dreamed, and the Death Mother stalking over the earth. When she saw Debbie, she said: 'Come here, pretty child.' But Debbie ran from her through the broken buildings, and hid.

"'The Death Mother seeks her still, walking over the earth, and so will she walk until she finds her. Only then, at the time of the End, will the world be healed.'"

There was rapt silence, and then the priest started to chant, his enhanced voice rich and melodious. The people answered in the same music, full of sorrow and ecstasy. As the chanting rose, the Images appeared above us: gigantic holographs of the earth ravaged and blackened, forests in cinders, cities turned to dust, rivers running with debris, the sky black and roiling, people blank-eyed, ragged, and skeletal, bodies in mass graves, the vacant upturned faces of starving children, then sprouting from all this the Fire itself, mushrooming sky-tall flame boiling into poison smoke. And finally, as the chanting reached its height, emerging from the flames along fashion-show catwalks or through the idealized landscapes of ad-holos, the Holy Ones themselves, sleek, stylish, and beautiful, and greatest of all, crew-cut and wearing a revealing leather dress, dark eyes smiling while the full lips sipped a can of RAD Cola, was Toori Sith.

The flames and smoke subsided around Her. The people raised their hands to Her, suddenly silent. Then the Image faded, and they began silently crowding toward the doors. The girl with the bruises was crying uncontrollably.

On the street, half a dozen big men in gray waterproofs were watching the people pour out of the church. As I passed, two started pushing through the crowd.

I tried to run. I heard the explosion, felt the pain. I cradled the TV-thing inside my jumpsuit as I fell. People's legs blurred around me, and then I could see only dirty water running over the concrete where I lay, and then even that blurred and went away.

✳ ✳ ✳ ✳

I woke in a cubicle of glaring white, strapped to a table. Above me, a dozen robot arms held surgical instruments. My reflection in a blank video screen was unfamiliar: my ragged beard and hair had been shaved, my skin scrubbed clean.

The screen lit up, showing three men. Two were fleshy angels from before the Fire, tall and strong; one was old enough to have white hair, but his skin was pinkish, his eyes clear blue, teeth even and white. The third man looked more like a City dweller—small and thin, with gray skin and muddy eyes—but clean, and wearing an impossibly expensive suit.

The white-haired man turned on a speaker above my head. He smiled kindly.

"Welcome to the RAD Cola Corporation Central Compound, Mr. Farrin," he said. "I apologize for any inconvenience. I regret also that we can't talk face to face. We have the cleanest closed loop on the planet here, and we have to be very careful about outside contacts to maintain it.

"We want to talk to you about the simulation device our Field Operations people found on you this afternoon. We'd like to know who made it, and who hired you to approach us with it."

The three of them waited.

My voice cracked as I said, "I'll sell it to you."

"We're confident you'll sell it to us, Mr. Farrin," said the white-haired man. "We're not nearly as confident that our purchase will not be followed by further blackmail demands, either by your organization, using similar devices, or by others. I think you'll understand that we can't allow that to happen."

"No one hired me," I said. "I found it."

The white-haired man was replaced on the screen by a man with a shaved head lying in a cubicle like mine. Robot arms approached him. A surgical saw cut into his head with a high pitched whine. I shut my eyes.

"No blackmail," I rasped. "I found it in the Ur – "

"Toori Sith is unfortunately already part of the so-called Church of Beauty's liturgy," said the white-haired man. "An ancient-looking video screen showing her in the Ur could drive half the City wild in the belief that she is Debbie, the child who must die before the world can be healed."

I opened my eyes. The three men were back, watching me calmly.

"Whoever made the device knows that an uproar over Toori Sith could cost RAD Cola revenue. We can't allow that. So, again, Mr. Farrin: who hired you to sell us the device?"

"I found it. In the Ur. She showed me the way out – "

Liquid started to move through a transparent tube attached to my arm. Suddenly I was dizzy.

"Good night, Mr. Farrin," said the white-haired man.

I didn't wake up again until someone pulled the tube out of my arm. I felt sick for a minute. Then my eyes focused.

A Black Angel stood over me, filling the cubicle.

I screamed. The Angel's hands broke the straps holding me like rubber bands. Then it pulled off its helmet.

There was no one inside.

Someone had programmed it to come in and break me loose. And now a recorded message was coming from it's hollow neck: "The Holy One has learned that you used to operate a suit like this. The Holy One sends this as a gift and bids you attend her on the 392nd floor. Go secretly and quickly. I am one willing to risk his life in the service of the Holy One."

I sat on the table and stared at the hollow Angel. When I was done staring I began to disassemble it. I worked as fast as I could.

Forty-five minutes later the suit and I were spliced as well as I could manage alone. It helped that my head was shaved and washed, baring the electrode hookups and injector nozzles the Department had planted in my skull years ago. I hoped that not too many were rusted out. I hit a keypad inside the wrist: the suit hummed to life like a small nuclear plant. A sound-like buzz in an unobtrusive temporal synapse told me that its batteries were fully charged. I checked through other sensory and parasensory inputs. There was static in some of the channels —probably bad sockets on my side—but I could work with it.

Medium-range sensors swam up out of the babble of suit inputs. The building rippled away in all directions as a parasensory multi-D diagram. I was in a cell block on the 101st floor. The cells around me were empty. Three quickly pulsing and two slowly pulsing green/hard/hot ciphers – three waking and two sleeping men – were in a room down a hall, collocated with military hardware. An elevator shaft near them rose 291 more floors.

I lasered a circuit in my cubicle door, jumped down the hall, nerve-gassed the guards before they could move.

No alarms were signaling anywhere that I could see/hear/smell.

The elevator car was on the 59th floor. I pried open the elevator doors, grabbed one of the metal guides in the shaft, and activated my thruster. I went up the shaft fast.

Halfway to 392, emergency logic was firing all around me. I

didn't try to read it, went faster. Heavy grates were closing above, sealing off 392. I shot through in time, yanked open the elevator doors, and stepped out.

Into incinerating, white-hot pain.

Then it was gone: I was lying on a floor, still alive. An overload like that would take a military-grade neural scrambler. Which apparently RAD Cola had. But somebody had turned it off.

I got up, got a visual. The wall opposite the elevator was three-meter-thick mirrored steel, coated ten centimeters deep with laser-refracting plastic. As I watched, it seamed and split apart. Security logic boiled and fumed nearby, suggesting a manual override. As I went through the opening in the wall a simulated polite voice told my audial sensors: "You are cleared for entry. Please be aware that any activation of weapons will precipitate an instantaneous preemptive strike by automated systems."

The wall clicked shut behind me. I was in a big space filled with unfamiliar inputs. A gemlike blue female cipher was static sixty meters away. I ate the distance with enhanced strides, stood in front of it.

I got a visual.

It was deep blue dusk. A few stars twinkled in the sky; I knew they were stars because I had seen pictures. There were plants too; not in environment tanks like at the Public Museum, but growing right out of the ground, crowding each other, some taller than a man. The Holy Beloved Toori Sith stood holding the thorny stem of a deep red flower, her eyes vague and dreamy. Wires were plugged in to her head.

"Beautiful rose," she murmured. "She bloomed last night, in the dark. I smelled her while I was sleeping . . . " Her voice was soft as the breeze that stirred the plants.

"I'm here," I said. "But I have only about three minutes before I'll be gone again." My sensors were picking up world-class firepower massing outside the metal walls of the garden.

The Angel's harsh voice seemed to hurt her, and she shivered, looked up at its helmet. "Take me to the place with the silver doors."

I ogled her with my locals.

"The place with the silver doors," she said again. "On the screen."

"I can't take you there. That place is poisoned, radioactive."

She looked back at the rose. "You prayed to me when you were in trouble . . . "

"Yes."

" . . . did I help you?" She looked up again, her eyes more beautiful than anything in the world.

"Yes."

A massive disturbance in the garden's security circuitry activated sonic alarms.

"Help me," she whispered.

"I can't."

She closed her eyes and rubbed the flower against her face so that a thorn cut a deep gash at the corner of her mouth.

"Please," she whispered.

I hesitated, but then the Angel gently unplugged the leads in her head, picked her up effortlessly.

"Which way?" I transmitted.

She pointed.

I carried her to a wall. She put her hand on it, and three meters of metal slid aside. Beyond was a hall with windows, and beyond the windows, nothing—open air, night.

I shattered a pane of shatterproof glass. War machines were screaming down the hall, bellowing all-frequency warnings. I jumped out the window.

We fell fifty stories.

I keyed my wrist pad and the Angel's wings came out. We sliced through night above lights, smoke, and giant holos. The City was an illuminated map under me. I wheeled around to head for the Utopia Luxury Apartment Complex tenement two sectors away, felt/watched it come closer on my display, one of its eight spokes collapsed into rubble.

Soon we were sailing between buildings. I brought the Angel down, then pulled the suit off as fast as I could, hiding the pieces under garbage piled up on the street. The glowing, abstract spaces of the Angel collapsed into a smelly, murky alley that Toori Sith's short silver holo-dress faintly illuminated.

I took her hand and we ran, through empty alleys under towering red curfew holos. Rain fell on a cold wind. At the edge of the Utopia's wrecked wing we crawled into a crack between tumbled slabs of concrete.

Toori Sith was shivering. She sat huddled against the concrete, hugging her beautiful legs against her chest. I watched her for a while.

Finally, I said: "Let me call them. Tell them where you are. They'll take you back."

She shook her head, rested it on her knees. A little bloodstained water ran down her chin.

Fearfully, I put my arms around her. She leaned against me, shivering. I felt the way you would expect to feel holding a goddess.

Then all that was gone.

I was standing on what, in antiquity, had been called a beach. It was wide and blinding white, ran up to thick green vegetation, down into water. The water stretched to the horizon, shades of transparent blue. A wave washed around my feet. The sun was hot, and graceful things with sweet, mewling voices wheeled high in the air.

It was deserted, except for Toori Sith. She wore a pair of shorts, her body slender, young, and brown, the breeze ruffling her short hair. She took my hand and we walked together.

"Is this an advertisement?" I asked after a while.

"This is my talent," she said. "I can bring people to these places."

"Not RAD Cola. You."

"The Corporation only records and amplifies. I bring."

"You have psi powers, then. You're a mutant."

She didn't say anything.

"Who are you really?"

"I don't know."

I waited for her to explain that.

"Eight days ago I had an anti-aging treatment. I don't remember much before that —disconnected images, dreams. The treatments do something to your brain."

She took my hands and put my fingers on the metal sockets under her hair. She lifted her arms, and there were sockets in her armpits. There were sockets in the soles of her feet.

"I heard about the video screen you brought from my informants in the Corporation, made them show it to me. When I turned it on, a girl came out of a building. She was exactly like me, except that she didn't have these." She showed tiny sockets in the fold of skin between thumb and forefinger. "She smiled at me and put her hands together, like this, then went back into the building and closed the door. The screen went off, and they couldn't get it to go back on."

She knelt, drawing patterns in the sand until a wave washed them away, then drawing more patterns.

"I think I remember standing in front of that building a long, long time ago, dressed the way she was dressed. A long time ago, before RAD Cola and the anti-aging and the advertising . . . "

She was silent, gazing at the water.

"I have to see it," she said finally.

"But the City," I said, "is full of poison, radiation. Especially the Ur. Look at me." I held out gray, wrinkled hands that looked dead in the bright sunlight. Then, for a second, we were back in the City, huddled together in the concrete crevice, poison rain pouring down on a cold wind. When the beach returned, I went on: "It'll kill you, like the rest of us."

She didn't answer. She stood up and stretched, waded out and slipped into the waves. For a while I seemed to hear the sighing breath of the ocean, to see Toori Sith floating in its green depths, asleep. Then I was back in the City, she sleeping quietly against my chest.

I woke her a few hours later. The rain had stopped, but the red holos still hung angrily a hundred meters above the streets. She didn't seem to remember me, or where she was, but she wasn't scared.

"We better move now," I told her. "Dead time."

She nodded, wiping sleep from her eyes. I helped her up and we crept through rubble into the sagging hulk of the Utopia Luxury Apartments' wrecked wing, along a dark, mildewed hallway with peeling walls and holes in the ceiling that night sky showed through.

The bolt on a metal door was broken; it creaked open to show descending stairs. I used a small detachable light I had taken from the Angel. We went down nine levels, along a concrete passage dripping with water, then down a utility tunnel where dull yellow illumination tiles gave light. Then down another stairwell, until were facing the crack that led to the Ur, torn wide open by the Angel's smashing hands. There was a way to climb down if you were careful. We stumbled down the slope at the bottom, raising dust like ghosts around us, and faced the crumbling mouth of the Ur tunnel.

"Down there," I said.

She followed me, our feet crunching on shattered rock, our breath echoing like whispered voices, until the passage opened onto the ancient street. I couldn't remember which way to go, so we wandered, holding hands, shining the light at the buildings, she silent and intent.

Then, suddenly, we were there, the massive, leaning building with the metal doors looming before us.

"Here," I murmured, pointing at a square indentation in the hard dirt of the street.

But she wasn't listening. She was staring at the doors.

One of them was opening. It swung heavily, silently, just as on the TV-thing; but on the TV-thing the doors shone like silver—here they were dull gray, eaten by green oxides.

Out of the blackness beyond the door hobbled a hunched figure in ragged robes, a hood hiding its face. A pair of trembling, skeletal hands reached up to put the hood back.

It was an old, old woman, so old she had no hair, no eyes, so old that her blind stone-gray face was stretched over the skull like dry paper, pocked with the purple blotches of radiation sickness. A smell came from her like the smell of refrigerated dead things.

Toori Sith's hand was trembling. I couldn't move.

The ancient woman slowly reached out her hand.

Toori Sith's hand unlocked itself from mine. My feet were planted to the ground. I couldn't move even to look at her. I hissed: "Run!"

Then my mouth was stopped.

Toori Sith walked forward. She climbed the steps to the door, raised her slender white hand, and took the ancient woman's claw.

"Mother," she breathed, her voice soft and sweet in that dead place.

The ancient woman backed up, drawing her into darkness. The door swung slowly and heavily closed, shutting finally with a dull clang.

I stood for a long time, unable to move.

Hours later, when I stumbled from the Utopia Luxury Apartments' wrecked wing, squinting in the gray daylight, a flash of color caught my eye, a tiny jot of green against the gray. Through a crack in the sidewalk paving, a single leaf, tender and thin, thrust itself against the whole gray mass of the City. I knelt wonderingly to look at it.

The Allah Stairs

When my brother and I were little boys, we had for a neighbor a littler boy named Laziz Tarash. Laziz lived in a second-floor apartment next to ours with his large, loud mother and small, quiet father. Uncle Nabil lived downstairs, and Grandfather lived down the street. Outside our front windows was an empty lot where a stonecutter sat all day under a corrugated iron shade and chipped blocks of stone, and beyond that, over the roofs of the stone houses, the land fell away in rocky hills grown with camel-thorns and dusty-green scrub.

Laziz was a pale, puffy boy whose cherubic face turned pink in the winter cold. His mother was pale and puffy too, but his father was dark and thin, silent, serious and bald. We used to see him hurrying out in the mornings while we waited for the car that took us to school, wearing a baggy suit and clutching a scuffed leather satchel. I have the impression that he worked at the bank. I don't think I ever heard him say a word. But Mrs. Tarash said many: all day you could hear her piercing nasal voice through the apartment walls, raised in command or complaint against the maid, her husband, the tradesmen, or Laziz.

Laziz went to our school, St. George's, where my father and grandfather had gone. He was too young to be studious, but he wasn't loud and unruly like the other little boys. In winter, during recess, he would huddle in a sheltered corner against the wind and rain, hands in the pockets of his blue sailor coat, standing first on one foot and then on the other. He didn't have any friends. If you

63

asked him to play he would just give you a shy, faraway smile, and not answer. But there was a tree in a courtyard at the very end of the playground, and sometimes when it rained, or when it got very windy, Laeth and I would find Laziz standing under the tree, his nose running and his cheeks fiery pink, and he would tell us stories.

The stories were about his father, about how Allah had punished him for doing bad things to Laziz.

There was one that he told over and over in his lisping baby's voice: "Last night my father spanked me for not doing my schoolwork. And then I knocked on Allah's door and climbed up the Allah stairs, up, up, up, up, up. And I talked to Allah and told him. And I went and got the monkeys. They took my father and tied him to a tree and hit him!" Here there were sound effects and the waving of a fat little fist. "And they kept hitting him and hitting him until blood came out and he died!" Then he would laugh happily.

Of course, when we teased him he shut up and got his faraway look again.

Time went slowly for awhile; nothing ever changed in our little town. Then we moved to a different country, where we lived in the city and had city friends. We went away to college, Grandfather died, and I got married. It was almost 20 years later before Laeth and I stood again in the dusty playground of St. George's Boy's School. I was a lawyer, getting a stoop from leaning over my desk all day. Laeth, who had been almost as small and cherubic as Laziz, was now broad-shouldered and bearded, and losing his hair. The town had changed too. There were big buildings and smooth roads, washing machines and color TVs, and hardly anyone rode donkeys anymore. Someone had introduced a machine that could chip stone smoother and more quickly than any stonecutter.

We walked around the playground gingerly, hands in our pockets, as if we might break something. It was morning class period, and a kindergarten song came faintly through the sunlight from the far end of the school building. Everything was smaller than I remembered – olive trees that had seemed towering were scarcely over your head; the long, long playground was a walk of fifty paces.

"Here's where we used to play marbles," said Laeth.

"And cars," I said.

"Remember the *moulokhia* they used to serve in the cafeteria? That was like mucus?"

At the end of the playground was a tiny courtyard. In the courtyard stood a tree.

"Laziz Tarash!" we both said when we saw it.

"The Allah stairs," said Laeth, and we laughed. At that moment there was a rustling in the tree. A pair of beady eyes peered at us; and a small brown shape scampered up a branch and out of sight.

"A monkey!" said Laeth.

"Can't be," I said. "There are no monkeys around here."

We went into the school building and collared a boy on his way to the bathroom, made him tell us where Mr. 'Odeh's class was, and when the noon bell rang we met Mr. 'Odeh in the hall. We shook hands and told him who we were. He had diminished in size along with the rest of the school; he was now just a round-shouldered, potbellied man whose bald head barely reached my chin.

"Have lunch with me," he said, and led us across the playground, which was now filling up with boys, dust, and noise, out the tall iron gate, and down the block to a little apartment with an arched ceiling and thick stone walls.

"Of course I remember you," he told us as he took plates and cups from a cupboard. "I remember all my students. I remember how many times I had to slap their hands to make them learn their multiplication tables."

"Then perhaps you remember what became of Ramsey Abu-Nouwar, sir," I said.

"Ah, that one . . . " said Mr. 'Odeh, and we were off on the life histories of ancient school friends, forgotten long ago and not remembered until we set foot back in St. George's. Laeth wanted to know about Kais Najjar and Gaby Khano. I was interested in Haseeb Al-Rahman. We were sipping tiny cups of coffee before we came to Laziz Tarash.

"Ah, that one," said Mr. 'Odeh, shaking his head. "A sad story. He works in the Gulf Bank here." He tipped his head in the direction of the market.

"What is sad about that, sir?"

"His father. Didn't you hear? It happened many years ago, soon after the war. Your uncle didn't tell you? Died, yes – a strange case. Ran into the street at two o'clock one morning in his nightshirt, screaming. Yes, they were still in the same building where you lived. He fell in the middle of the street and died. A man who got to him said he was raving on and on. About monkeys. Monkeys chasing him or beating him, I don't know. Yes, monkeys.

"Laziz was still a small boy then. He and his mother moved in with the mother's family in Abu Ghair, up the hill. Poor boy. Many years ago."

We had walked Mr. 'Odeh back to his afternoon geometry class and were outside the school gate before Laeth said to me: "Monkeys."

"Strange," I said.

The next day we visited our old apartment building. It looked small and shabby next to the modern edifices that now lined the street, and the little shop on the corner had become a supermarket and gas station. We knocked at the downstairs apartment (Uncle Nabil had long since emigrated to Australia); the old man who answered told us that the two upstairs apartments were vacant, and gave us the keys. Climbing to the second floor, it struck me that the building stairwell was the only part of the whole town that hadn't changed in 20 years – the echoes of our footsteps, the dusty smell, the afternoon sunlight through dusty glass – I half expected to open our apartment door on the faded woven rug and dark, elderly china cabinets, see my mother in the kitchen as she used to be when we came home from school, humming obsolete songs as she swept or washed dishes.

But the apartment was empty, sunlight lying silent on the dusty floor tiles, whitewashed walls echoing our footsteps. I went onto the tiny veranda behind the kitchen.

"For years and years," I told Laeth, "there was a big tin back here with a label that said 'Vegetable Ghee.' That's my most vivid memory of this place."

"Don't you remember mom and dad screaming at each other, and dad bringing flowers later?" asked Laeth.

We had the keys to the Tarash's apartment, so out of curiosity we took a look.

"Watch out for monkeys," Laeth said as the lock clicked open. We had debated the monkey question the night before, sitting under the pine trees in Grandfather's garden, breathing still night air perfumed with jasmine. Laeth had read that delusional episodes or images could be passed subliminally within families, especially from parents to children.

"Probably Laziz picked up a delusional paranoid complex about monkeys from Mr. Tarash, and combined it with the father-hating phase of the Oedipal cycle, resulting in the stories he told," Laeth said. "Later, Mr. Tarash's complex must have blossomed into a full-fledged psychotic episode, causing him to have a coronary or stroke."

Laeth is a psychiatric intern; I never argue with him for fear of being psychoanalyzed. And anyway, the Tarash's apartment seemed to bear out his theory of perfectly normal mental illness. There were no signs of monkeys, Allah, or stairs that went up, up, up, up, up.

At least not until we came to Laziz's bedroom. It was a tiny room facing out over the dusty fig trees and clotheslines in the backyard.

"Where are the Allah stairs, do you suppose?" I joked. And suddenly they were there, rising from the center of the floor into a bright rectangle near the ceiling, rough stone steps that an intense radiance poured down, paling the sunlight.

As soon as Laeth and I let go of each other and I could think again, I waved my hands at them.

"Go away," I pleaded. They did, leaving the room empty and dusty, the afternoon sunlight quiet and bright.

"My God," said Laeth.

"What shall we do?"

"Make them come back."

"Are you crazy?"

"Laziz climbed them, and he's all right."

"You're not actually thinking of *climbing* them?"

"We have to."

He was right. Otherwise crawl to our graves a stooped lawyer and a bald psychiatrist, not even able to pretend we had tried to grasp at something magic when it was shown to us.

"Allah stairs," I said, and they were there, fading everything else with their brilliance.

We edged to the bottom of them, clutching each other like little boys, looking up into the bright rectangle. There was only blinding radiance up there, with a hint of movement, like the inside of a sunlit cloud. We climbed. At the top we stood in a place made of molten light, the stairs a dark tunnel behind. The light was so intense that it made Laeth's body and what I could see of mine translucent. It flowed and boiled like white hot lava. Then things started to take shape in it: divided, darkened, condensed into a jungle scene. A strange jungle scene. Everything was a little bit wrong, as though the trees, vines, bushes, and grasses had been shaped by someone who had heard about jungles but never seen one. The white, boiling light was visible at a distance, as if the jungle was an island floating in it.

In front of us stood a big tree full of monkeys, fierce monkeys with claws and fangs and snarling faces. They were tying something to one of the top branches. As I looked closer, I realized it was Mr. Tarash. He had on his baggy suit and his satchel was tied around his neck with a leather thong. He thrashed and howled in terror. As we watched, the monkey started to beat him with sticks and rocks. Blood started to patter through the leaves.

"My God!" said Laeth, too loudly. The monkeys stopped and looked down. Then, howling, snarling, hurling their sticks and stones, they swung and scampered and dove through the branches toward us.

We ran – down the Allah stairs, out of the Tarash's apartment, out of the building, didn't stop running until we reached the corner. The old men sitting on stools in the shade of the gas station stared. I straightened my shirt collar. Laeth brushed dust off his pants. No demonic monkeys from another dimension chased us. Everything seemed normal, except for the two strange young men racing down the street.

We caught a taxi. By the time we got to the Gulf Bank on

Salah-i-Din Street near the market, it was late afternoon. The bank manager was a fussy little man with a big moustache, who wanted to know if Laziz was in trouble. We told him no, we were just old school friends. Finally there was a barely audible knock and Laziz sidled nervously into the office.

He looked amazingly like his father: small, thin, bald, haunted. He even wore a baggy suit, and you could imagine that he carried a scuffed leather satchel. He licked his lips and tried to smile when we told him who we were, and shook hands.

"Welcome. Welcome," he kept murmuring breathlessly. "Welcome. Welcome." He seemed to sense some calamity.

"We thought perhaps, since we're in town only for a few days, we could have your company this evening," I said.

Laziz murmured polite things. The bank manager's face softened. He looked at his watch.

"You still have 25 minutes in your shift. I will let you go early today. It will come out of your annual leave, of course."

On the sidewalk, when he saw the taxi, Laziz put up a feeble resistance.

"But – but where are we going?" he asked.

"Sightseeing," I growled, and shoved him into the back seat.

As we neared the street where our old apartment building stood, Laziz started to sweat.

"I want to go home," he whined. "Where are you taking me?"

When we sent the taxi away and started walking toward the stairwell door, he tried to bolt. We caught him in half a dozen steps, each held him firmly by an arm, marched him into the building. The deep transparent blue of evening filled the street, and there was no one to see us. Inside, his legs went limp, and we had to drag him up the stairs whining and weeping. I still had the keys to the apartment. We dragged him into the little back bedroom and balanced him on his feet. He was mumbling incoherently.

"Remember the stories you used to tell us in school?" I asked. "Maybe you can explain something for us. Can you, Laziz?"

He seemed to be praying, making the gestures of blessing with trembling hands. I said, "Allah stairs," and when they appeared he screamed and ran into Laeth on his way to the door. We got him by the arms again and hustled him up the Allah stairs.

Again the molten light; again the malformed jungle with the tree of fierce monkeys. The monkeys had just finished tying Mr. Tarash to one of the top branches, leather satchel dangling from his neck, thrashing and howling in terror. They began beating him; blood pattered through the leaves. Laziz stared fixedly. Soon Laeth and I had to look away – Mr. Tarash was a bloody pulp, not thrashing anymore – but Laziz still stared, as if he had lost the power to move.

After awhile the sound of beating stopped and something fell to the ground with a sickening thud. Laeth touched my arm and pointed into the distance, where the outlines of the jungle faded into molten light. Two figures, one large and one small, walked along a jungle path toward us, holding hands. As they got nearer, I recognized them.

One was a large shapeless woman, puffy and pale. She wore a shabby housedress I remembered from twenty years before. In fact, everything about her was the same except her voice: apparently her complaints had been stilled, because she beamed silently around at everything with astonished satisfaction, especially at the little boy she held by the hand.

He was a pale and puffy little boy about six years old, with a fat cherubic face. He strutted proudly next to his mother, gazing imperiously around. He wore a long purple robe with planets and stars on it, and a matching purple pointed hat. He had on cowboy boots with jingling spurs, and over the robe a set of silver cowboy six-guns. There was a moustache painted on his face.

The two of them stopped a few feet away from us. Mrs. Tarash didn't seem to notice us; she just kept staring around with a look of complete admiration. The young Laziz studied us.

Finally he gestured at the older Laziz.

"I thought I took care of you," he said, nodding toward the tree. Then he cried shrilly: "Monkeys!" They came swarming down, howling and snarling.

The older Laziz screamed, pushing Laeth into me, and by the

time we got back on our feet he had just disappeared down the Allah stairs, the monkeys racing after him. We followed.

Moonlight filled the apartment through blank windows. The rooms were full of scuffling and hissing that could have been a hundred demon monkeys, or could have been something else. No monkeys were visible. The front door stood open. We ran down the stairs and into the street. Halfway across, two men crouched over someone who seemed to be lying down. As we got nearer, I could see it was Laziz, sprawled on his face.

One of the men looked at us in shock. "Dead," he said.

"Monkeys," said the other. "He was screaming something about monkeys."

Pine Needle Whiskey

He was a skinny, stoop-shouldered long-hair, balding and melancholy, like a Frank Zappa Rip Van Winkle who had fallen asleep in these north woods back in the 1960s and couldn't believe what he'd seen since waking up. He watched me from 20 yards up the shoulder as the old man who had picked me up in North Hole rattled off in his ancient pickup. A knapsack faded the same color as the summer grass lay near him.

I lugged my own knapsack toward him. "Hi."

He nodded.

"Al." I shook his bony hand. "Where you headed?"

"Willis," he mumbled in a hollow voice. "Coast."

"Same here. How long you been waiting?" He was dusty and creased, the way people get sleeping in fields and under trees.

"Week." I stared at him. He nodded mournfully. "No through traffic. Folks go up to work at the stone quarry and come back." He licked his lips. "Can I bum a dollar?"

I got one out for him and watch him trudge down to where the road disappeared into the pine-choked landscape of low hills and marshes, dust floating behind his tattered hightops. At a bend in the road an unpainted frame building with two gas pumps was posted "General Store." Behind it a dirt track ran between half a dozen tiny clapboard houses, one with an old lady dressed from head to foot in black sitting on a tiny porch. A cloud of gnats hung in the air; a couple of crows flapped and cawed in a pine across the two lanes of patched asphalt. A sign that said "Thunder Bay

238" faced me in the late afternoon light. After Thunder Bay it was 1500 more miles to Vancouver, where restless youths like me were drifting that year.

A couple of cars rattled by at 70 miles an hour, ignoring my thumb and raising clouds of dust that settled lazily in the lengthening yellow light. A figure was laboring up the shoulder. It was the old lady in black. As she got close I saw that she wore big boots, and her face sagged with wrinkles that threatened to cover her eyes.

She shot a stream of tobacco from the corner of her mouth. She had the heavy, powerful nose of an Indian. "You want to buy liquor?" she rasped, looking at me narrowly.

An engine roared and an old undercoat-gray Firebird swooped across the road. The old lady and I leaped up the sloping grass shoulder. The car slowed down and delicately ran over my knapsack, suspension bouncing, then came to a stop.

A big Indian sat behind the wheel. The sallow man in the passenger seat held a naked pint bottle half-full of amber liquid. Their rough clothes were dusty as with stone quarry work, their faces flushed, veins distended, the way drunks get when they're ready to make noise and fight. But they didn't make any noise or any move to get out of the car. They sat perfectly still, their red, swollen eyes staring fixedly at me.

For 30 seconds, a minute, they stared.

Then the Indian gunned the car and it pelted us with dirt and stones squealing down the road. It screeched into the General Store's dirt parking lot. The two riders slammed out and into the store, whooping.

"Drunks," croaked the old lady disgustedly. "Don't do like them. I get you stuff don't make you crazy. I make it myself." She winked at me. "Trust grandma."

"Don't buy nothing from her!" somebody yelled.

The hitchhiker Willis was jogging painfully up the shoulder, narrow shoulders raised with exertion, weak eyes staring.

"You don't need nothing from her," he gasped as he got near. "I should have told you."

"This boy your friend?" The old lady asked me scornfully. "*This*

74

boy? He's gonna make you crazy." She watched me narrowly for another minute. Then she started hobbling back down the shoulder toward the store and the dirt street.

The afternoon light was getting shaded with blue around the edges, especially in the hollows of distant mountains. The air was cool and still, a few birds singing. My legs were shaking as if they were having a hard time holding me up.

"We better spend the night in the woods," said Willis, picking up his knapsack. I picked mine up; it had a dusty tire track across it. "They're starting to drink that stuff. It makes them crazy."

A while later I scrambled up a steep slope behind him in chilly purple dusk, pushing through the branches of shoulder-tall baby pines like spiny sleeping creatures, their cool smell filling the air. The shack town was out of sight through the forest behind us.

A long, inhuman scream swooped over the hills, raising my hair.

Willis reared straight up as if burned. He started to run.

"Hey!" My feet tore at the slope to keep up with him

At the top we plunged among full-grown trees. Pine needle walls and carpet muffled our steps and wild breathing. Dusk flashed between black branches that whipped and scratched me. There was a rustling overhead. Willis was climbing a tree. I struggled up after him.

It was a huge pine with thick branches, and soon we were above the darkness of the forest, with a vast view of the jeweled void darkly illuminating blacked tree-muffled hollows and hills of a landscape that hid –

"What? What is it?" I hissed, hands shaking so I could barely hold the branch we were crouching on. "Are they coming? What are they trying – trying to do us?"

He was staring away into the air.

Finally he murmured to himself with deep thoughtfulness: "*These bodies are known to have an end: but the dweller in the body is eternal, imperishable, infinite.*"

Pause.

"As a man casting off worn-out garments takes others that are new, so the dweller in the body casting off – "

He lunged off the branch.

In that instant his face showed horror; with wild clawing and my hand rammed under his arm he managed to scramble back on. He was gasping. I could see his heart pounding in his face.

He started to cry.

"I only been here a week," he blubbered. "I can still get away. I can – "

"What do you mean?"

"I – I drank some of her stuff when I first got here. Pine needle whiskey. I didn't know! Only a dollar a pint -- but it makes you crazy!

"They're from *out there*," he hissed, cringing and waving a bony hand at the cold, moonless sky. His teeth chattered. "*She* says they're prisoners. *Giant thoughts* – come screaming out of the sky at you – her whiskey makes – a hole in your head to let them in – but I can still get away – I only drank a little, I can – " the words snuffled into feeble crying.

I stared at him open-mouthed. But relief crept over me. I had heard how wood alcohol can make you crazy. I thought for a minute; then I said: "Look, Willis. Let's get down out of this tree, and I'll tell you what we'll do. Neither of us wants to stick around here, right? Let's find our knapsacks and find someplace to sleep, and in the morning we'll hike for it. We'll cut through the woods and meet up with the road a few miles away, and just keep walking. I've got a jar of peanut butter in my knapsack for food."

"I got a canteen of water," he chimed in anxiously.

"Okay, then, we're set. Let's get down out of here."

"I only been here a week," he sniffled as we climbed down. My arms and legs felt weak with shaking. "They got no hold over me. I'll just walk away. Nobody can stop me."

At the bottom of the tree it was dark and stuffy and still. We groped through cool pine branches toward crickets singing, and came out at the top of the slope with the baby pines under a blue-black sky, black outlines of the forest all around.

"I guess we came up this way," I said, taking a direction. "Look, here's one." I picked up the knapsack and held it close to my face in the dark. "It's yours." I handed it to him. "Could I have a drink of your water? I'm dry as a bone."

"Let's not drink too much tonight," he said anxiously, unbuckling the knapsack and pulling out a big canteen. "We're going to need it tomorrow. We're going to do a lot of walking, I can tell you. I bet we'll walk twenty miles."

The notion seemed to comfort him. He handed me the canteen.

I swigged a big mouthful.

It burned.

I sprayed most of it on the ground. I stared at him goggle eyed.

"This is – alcohol, man," I spluttered. It tasted strongly of pine.

"It is not." The whites of his eyes were big in the dark.

"It is."

He grabbed the canteen and sniffed it, took a sip and puckered his mouth, then spit it out. He spit several more times, face convulsed.

"Hey, man," he said shakily, his voice on the verge of breaking. "Hey, man, I been drinking out of this."

I stared at him a minute more. "You're crazy," I finally said in disgust. I turned around and started feeling my way down the slope between the baby pines. "You're nuts."

"Hey, wait a minute. Wait for me." His voice fluted and trembled. I could hear him fumbling with the knapsack.

I ignored him, pushing branches aside and straining my eyes at the ground. I was almost among the crickets in the dark trees at the bottom when a terrible drunken shriek came through the night air. I froze. It was like the yell that had set us running before.

"Willis?" I hissed up the slope after a minute. I remembered now that we were pals and were going to stick together until we got out of here. "Willis?"

No answer. No sound but the crickets.

I started back up the slope as silently as I could, ears straining. "Willis, man," I hissed. "Are you there? Did you hear that?"

My foot kicked something, giving me a start. My knapsack. I picked it up and walked to where Willis had been a minute ago. There was nothing there now but baby trees and chilly darkness against the backdrop of deeper darkness.

"Willis?" I tried lamely again.

I hoisted my knapsack and started along parallel to the big trees at the top of the slope. I guessed the old lady had been right about Willis: he was crazy, whether from drinking her pine needle liquor or some other cause. The other people around here seemed to be uncontrollable screaming drunks and maybe dangerous. The only thing that made sense was to take my own advice and find someplace to sleep, then sneak away in the morning. If twenty or thirty miles of walking would get me to another town, I wouldn't complain.

I came to a place where dim starlight showed a thinning in the trees like a crooked path into the woods with big rocks jutting out of the ground along the middle of it. I picked my way into it, tree-darkness soft and deep on both sides, the rocks adding a damp, mossy smell to the pine-scented night.

Branches rustled to my left.

I froze, staring into the blackness, straining to hear over the pounding of my heart. There were black bear in these woods, I knew, and badgers, fox, and deer. And –

"Willis?" I said weakly.

Crickets answered.

I started moving again.

A twig snapped.

There was more rustling, then the pounding of feet and harsh breathing as I ran in terror and a pale face swerved out of the darkness, attached to a wiry body that knocked me down, crushing my face into the ground and twisting my arm up behind me.

Breath gusted on my neck.

"Where is she?" it hissed through gritted teeth. "Tell me, or I'll pith you right here."

It was Willis's voice, but with a strange intonation, precise and compressed, as if somebody else was doing the talking.

I sobbed about being sorry I had left him.

"You're awfully clever," he sneered in my ear. "But I can smell it on you. Now *tell me* – where is she? How many others have escaped with her?"

"Willis," I sobbed. "Is that you? I'm sorry, but I – I don't know what you're saying."

My arm got let go and I got rolled over onto a big slab slab of rock, Willis kneeling on my chest and looking down into my face with intense, focused eyes I felt I had never seen before. He was that different than he had been half an hour ago.

He stared, stared into my eyes.

Then it was strange. The tablespoon of liquor I had swallowed seemed to suddenly hit me with hallucinogenic force: I felt groggy and sensate, my back to the strong quiet rock, wood and air around me, stars above, and in the aromatic darkness I seemed to feel suddenly the vast motion of the cosmos, all the galaxies circling, whirling, like water down a drain to –

Where? A strange feeling came over me in a rush, that I knew the answer but had forgotten it.

And in that second Willis's alien eyes seemed to drill into me, and I felt that he saw into me, saw everything about me; and for a second I thought I saw into him – into a deep strangeness that made me shiver, a freedom so vast it was like being lost, and a vast knowledge.

Then he was standing up, and pulling me up by the arm.

"Okay," he muttered. "You're not one of them. But you know where she is. Take me to her."

"Who? The old lady?"

He nodded, eyes distant.

"But -- you know where she is as well as I do. Back at the town. Isn't she?"

He gave me a thin-lipped, humorless smile. "Please pretend I don't know. Pretend I don't know anything about anyone around here, or where they are. And that I need to gather this information. Now, take me to her."

✳ ✳ ✳ ✳

From behind pine bushes across the road, the greenish halogen light on the side of the General Store was like a single spot of consciousness in a profoundly sleeping land, moths and bugs dancing crazily around it over the dirt parking lot.

"Let's get out of here," I whispered to Willis, my teeth chattering in the damp cold before dawn. My fear had increased as we had gotten closer to the shack town.

"You talk to them," Willis said. "Find out where the old woman is."

The glint in his eyes in the dark brought the enormous whirling feeling again, and the certainty that I had forgotten the answer to a vast, important riddle –

A smell of damp dust came up from the parking lot as we crossed it. The wooden door at the top of two warped steps was open a crack, letting out a sliver of light. I pushed it open all the way.

It was a general store all right, with everything from clothes to motor oil to faded boxes of cookies, stacked on unpainted wooden shelves reaching the ceiling behind over-painted wooden counters. A single dim bulb behind the back counter filled the shelves of shadows. The back counter had three soda fountain stools in front of it, a grill and coffee machine behind it, and a big, fat man on top of it, snoring softly.

The plywood floor squeaked slightly as we tiptoed over to him. His face had a brick-red flush, and he gave off the sweetish pine-needle smell of liquor. Little bubbles formed at the edge of his lips when he exhaled.

"Willis, let's get out of here," I whispered urgently. "They're probably all hopped up on --"

A sound came from the open door. Willis and I turned fast.

Huge arms wrapped around us, squashing us against each other.

"Haw haw haw!" bellowed the man who had been snoring. He was a giant, tremendously strong. His rough, rancid jacket scraped my face. I bucked, kicked. My half open eyes saw Willis's teeth bring a red stain from his bicep.

"Haw haw haw!" He crushed us until the blood pounding in my head covered the boom of feet on the plywood floor. In a throbbing tunnel of black I saw them: the two drunks who had run over my knapsack, and the old lady in black.

She hobbled close, peering at Willis and me with granite eyes under folds of skin.

"One of these?" she croaked, pinching me with a hard calloused hand.

"Must be, eh," said the Indian. "The transmission sounded like it came in real close. They're the only ones around here besides us."

"G-got to be the long-hair one, eh," started the other, sallow man, pointing at Willis with a hand trembling with drink. "'E w-was awake the other day, but then he stopped drinking the j-juice. Must've left a hole in 'im where *they* could get in."

The old lady looked at Willis gloatingly.

"Then wake him," she crowed. "Wake him up again."

The giant let me go so suddenly I almost fell, had to lean on the side counter to catch my breath. The Indian and the giant wrestled Willis on to the back counter with a bang.

"Pull me out. Hurry. Pull me out," Willis whined breathlessly in the strange, precise voice.

The old lady rushed to stand over him, glaring down at him with frightening hatred.

"Yah, you go back, you son of a bitch," she spat at Willis. "Go back and tell them. *We got free.* And we gonna set all the other ones free. *All the other ones you send here,* you – " she poured out a stream of filthy curses.

The sallow man had unscrewed the cap of a pint bottle, and now his narrow back came between me and Willis, so I heard rather than saw the keening through gritted teeth, the spluttering and gagging, Willis's legs twisting in the Indian's stone-hard hands, then a choked gurgling and coughing, and finally desperate gulping, until the sallow man threw the empty bottle away into a corner.

The old lady's eyes were burning at me.

When I shrank back she creased her wrinkles into what I guessed was a supposed to be a reassuring smile.

"Your friend gonna be all right," she crooned. "He drank it voluntary, the first time. Just like you got to do. You gonna drink, hah? You wanna go free, hah?"

I watched her fearfully, her shaking hands, blazing eyes.

"You don't wanna go free?" She demanded. "You like this world, all this death, torturing, hunger, people killing each other? Whatever crimes we did *out there*, we shouldn't deserve this. Nobody should deserve this."

"L-long-hairs coming awake, eh," stuttered the sallow man behind her.

"Get him up," she said without taking her eyes off me. "Let him talk to his friend. Your friend gonna talk to you," she said to me. "Listen to your friend."

The three men pulled Willis into a sitting position, then up onto his feet, where he stood swaying dangerously. His face was changed again, congested with drink, hollow chest heaving, eyes stupefied.

The sallow man put another uncapped pint bottle into his hand.

"Give it to 'im, Willy," the sallow man said to him loudly. "T-tell 'im it ain't so bad."

Willis got his balance and shuffled forward, held the bottle up to my face. The wild, alcoholic smell of pine burned my nose.

"It ain't so bad," he mumbled. "Try it."

"Willis – ?"

"Do I look drunk, man?" He mumbled earnestly. His face was close to mine, eyes cocked off in two different directions. "'Cause I ain't. *This stuff makes me remember who I am, man.* I can't never die." A big tear rolled down his cheek. *"I'm free."*

At that moment the sallow man blurted fearfully: "Hey, it's the OPP, eh."

Out the door I could see rotating red and white lights like the sweeping wings of angels.

Heavy feet thumped on the two wooden steps.

A big man came in the door, wearing the clean beige uniform

and wide-brimmed hat of the Ontario Provincial Police. His pink neck bulged from a stiff collar and he had a big black holster on his hip. The plywood floor creaked and bent under his solid weight.

The Indian and the sallow man stood perfectly still, hands hanging awkwardly. Willis had a stupid, polite look, as if concentrating on the bottle in his hands. The old lady and the giant shuffled nervously behind me.

It seemed to take forever for my breath to squeeze out of my lungs, swirl up my windpipe, and burst from lips in a sob of accusation. I skittered around the Indian to the policeman, forced my sobbing into words, leveling my finger –

He cut me off after two broken sentences.

"Haven't I told you time and time again *you're to leave passers-by alone?*" He glared fiercely around the room, but especially at the old lady. He had a big, hard voice that somehow reminded you of the gun on his hip. "Do I have to put the whole lot of you in jail to get my point across that *I mean business?*" He smacked one meaty hand into the other in time with the words. "And who's this?" He looked at Willis. "A new one?"

"He – he sneaked into the store at night," the old lady said, meaning me. "I heared them fighting. He's probably gonna steal the store. I come running."

The others murmured agreement.

The policeman shook his head in disgust. "How many times do you think I'm going to believe that story?" He sighed. "All right, you come with me," he said. I stuck close to his meaty back as he strode out the door.

There was the faintest transparency in the darkness over the black tree horizon, and the air was like chill water.

"They're harmless," the policeman said wearily as I trotted behind him toward his big white car. "Drunks. Their parents were drunks. I always check if I see the lights on at night. I can take you about 50 miles toward Thunder Bay, if you're going that way. Even though hitchhiking is illegal in this Province." He gave me a stern look.

I was sitting numbly in the front seat with the metal grating behind my head, shotgun and police radio fastened to the dashboard in front of me, the policeman putting the car in gear, when he looked at me and said: "Don't you have a backpack or anything?"

It was back in the store, with my sleeping bag, maps, and peanut butter in it.

"Go ahead and get it. Don't worry, they won't bother you."

When I pushed open the door, trembling violently, the General Store was empty, its heavy, breath-stained air silent. My knapsack was slumped against the wall. I got hold of it and turned – and almost fell over the old lady.

"You," she muttered.

I banged my head on the wall in terror. She crowded me eagerly, slate-gray eyes fixed greedily on me.

"*You're* a prisoner, just like us," she hissed. "Don't you know who you are? You can't never die, never be hurt. Only way to punish you is make you forget, forget who you are, put you crawling on this world like a maggot, shaking with fear. Don't you wanna go free?

"You ever wanna go free, come see grandma." She winked at me. "Trust grandma."

And flying down the road an hour later next to the quiet policeman, dawn tinting the road and sky pink ahead of us, I reached into my knapsack for a map and felt the cool, sticky shape of a full pint bottle.

Not Even Ashes

If I hadn't liked garbage dumps, I would never have seen her.

I had a cabin on a Titan III transport that took 87 days to carry 1000 people and 50,000 tons of aluminum from Callisto to Earth. I spent most of my time in the ship bars, but down the passage from my cabin was a maintenance hatch, and below that a garbage port that dumped every 48 hours. The hatch was kept locked, but in my job lock-decoding implants are standard equipment. Drinking helps ship claustrophobia, but there's nothing like watching a big gravity wheel drop garbage into infinite emptiness.

That's how it was that 85 days out from Callisto, two days before we docked at Rupert Sheldrake Station, I lay on the humming metal floor of a dark, empty passageway with my face against a tiny view-port. The inside of the garbage bay was lit dim red. That's when I saw her.

At first there was a white blur not far from the view-port. After a while it started to look like a face, a woman's face with the eyes closed, wedged into a jumble of plastic containers. I squinted at it, trying to see a scrap of garbage instead of a face. A smaller blur next to what looked like the face started to look like a hand.

A cold feeling went through me.

A green light marked the bay emergency hatch. My watch said four minutes until dump: it took one and a half of those to break the hatch lock. When the hatch slid open the green light turned red and started to blink.

A metal ladder went down into garbage. I half fell down it

and tried to stand on a jumble of jagged scrap metal, breathing sour fumes. I took a few steps, fell through a hole, climbed out with scratches all over me, took a few more steps, and was almost standing on the face. It *was* a face, asleep or dead, not moving. I grabbed the hand that was near it and pulled.

An alarm horn blared and the red light filling the bay flashed.

The woman's body was limp. I dragged it to the ladder, got it over my shoulders. A rusty screeching was the bay doors starting to move; garbage shifted under my feet. Twelve weeks of drinking hadn't done my physique any good, but I went up that ladder fast. The emergency hatch had closed automatically for pressure lock, but there was a manual release. Air whistled past me as I struggled through. I flipped the hatch shut, heard the rumble of the port opening, the roar of air exploding into vacuum. My heart was pounding. The woman slumped on the floor in front of me looked dead and wasn't wearing any clothes.

She wasn't breathing either. I carried her up metal stairs to the passenger level. There was no one around, just a long, metal corridor that sloped upward out of sight in both directions. It was geomagnetic night-time aboard ship, and everybody who wasn't sleeping was in the bars, restaurants, and stimudromes topside. There's nothing else to do in outer space, except go crazy.

With the woman on my bunk and me standing over her, there was barely room to close my cabin hatch. She lay with her head flopped back, chalk white and inert, a couple of spacesuit breathing jacks showing on the pale flesh near her armpits. I got the nozzle of my first-aid epinephrine inhaler into her mouth, pressed the button. The inhaler made noise and her chest arched. I took it away and she seemed to sigh, her chest relaxing again. I did the same thing again, then a third time. She lay still, refusing to be alive.

"God damn you," I told her.

She took a deep breath by herself.

I gave her another jolt and she almost jumped off the bunk.

"Easy," I said, holding her bare shoulders. She stared at me with wild eyes.

"What is it?" she gasped. "What's happening?"

"You're all right. Take it easy. I'm going to get you a doctor."

She started to cry. She looked scared.

I let go of her with one hand, typed an access code on the bunk console.

"Wait," she rasped. She seemed suddenly dizzily awake, wary. "What—how did I get here?"

"I brought you. As a matter of fact, I found you in a garbage bay."

"You're a ship employee?" she asked weakly, lying back on the pillow. Inhaled epinephrine wears off fast.

"No. Lady, it's time for the doctor."

"Please don't call anyone."

I stared at her. She looked back with pleading, fading eyes. She grabbed my hands clumsily. "Please don't tell them about me. I'll tell you why…" Her hands trembled. "Please. Please. Promise?" Her eyes crossed, closed, and she was asleep.

Don't ask me why I didn't call the doctor—or the ship police. Maybe I'm too used to breaking rules—after all, that's my job. I just sat on the edge of the bunk and looked over her muscular, moon-gravity-thin body, paper-white skin, dark blue hair. Other than the passive-breathing jacks and a small neural jack behind her ear she showed no signs of endogenous hardware. She was scraped and cut from lying in the garbage bay, and there was an injection mark on her left forearm. That made me think. Finally I rolled her under the covers, turned off the light and went out.

You had to shove to get through the crowds on the entertainment deck. There was the smell of psuedopium, sweat, spicy food, the babble of voices, music. Twelve weeks in a space transport makes people celebrate just to stay alive. The whores and hustlers on the deck would hardly listen to my questions about a thin, blue-haired girl. After awhile I got tired of being jostled. I shuffled back to my cabin, turned off the light, and lay on the floor with my wadded-up jacket for a pillow.

✳ ✳ ✳ ✳

When I woke up next day period the woman was still asleep, but she had a pulse and her skin had some color. I took a shower. When I was back in the cabin knotting a tie, a movement made me turn.

She had dragged herself upright in the bunk, trying to open her eyes, panic fighting drugged sleepiness in her face. When I came close she lifted her arm as if to ward off a blow, tears running down her cheeks.

I retreated to the vendor console and punched up coffee with double caffeine. It took some coaxing to get her to sip from the steaming plastic cup, but it did her good; soon she could hold the cup herself. Her large, black eyes slowly got awake and sane—but not happy.

"What time is it?" she asked, rubbing her face. "What day is it?" Her voice was hoarse. She didn't seem to notice she was naked.

"10:10 SGT, Tuesday. When did you go to sleep?"

"I don't remember exactly. I'm hungry."

"We'll eat. But we need to talk first."

I watched her wary eyes turn sleepy. She lay back in the bunk and stretched so that I could get a good look at her breasts and the strong, lean line of her stomach. She knew she was naked after all, it seemed.

"I'm feeling drowsy," she said. "Probably after-effects of the... couldn't we...?"

"Sure." I punched the vendor again, sat on the edge of the bunk with another cup of coffee. She made no move to take it.

"Sorry to interrupt you," I said. "You were about to tell me who tried to kill you and why, and why you don't want to see a doctor, and whether I'm going to go to jail for keeping you here. Lady, I'm counting the seconds before I get on the phone to the ship cops."

She sat up, panting with fear. "No—not now. You've got to trust me. As soon as we get to Earth and I'm safe, I'll tell you. I promise. There'll be reward money – "

I shook my head. "Those endo lie-detector rigs are out of my price-range. Suppose you're a gangster or a smuggler. Then the police ask me, 'Mr. Karmade, is it your normal procedure when you find people stripped and doped and tossed in garbage bays, to conceal them and fail to inform the authorities?' 'No sir, but she told me she would explain everything, and there was reward money, and she spread out on the bunk in such an appealing way – '"

She sat up and slapped me across the face, hard. When I had wiped the water out of my eyes, I sighed and started to type the server access code.

She said, "Wait."

She sat back again, pulling a blanket around her as if she was cold. After a while she started to talk. Her voice was low, controlled. "Maybe you heard about the disturbances on Callisto."

"Rumors. Power blackouts, a plant at Buri impact basin closing temporarily. Nothing on the video. I was at Ottar, and there was no trouble there."

"There wasn't anything on the video. We kept it off the video and out of the production reports, arrested survivors from the plants that were attacked to keep them from talking. The System Government doesn't want publicity, not yet. We don't know exactly what's happening, but it looks like a full-scale Zaghreb rebellion. All the plants in the Southern Hemisphere are closed—two were completely destroyed. Troop carriers are on their way from Earth. All transmissions are being monitored by jamming satellites. Production reports are being faked for the closed plants. Travel to the Southern Hemisphere is suspended. Unofficially, of course.

"I was part of an InterPol intelligence team that came out two transports ago, when the first disturbances were reported. Six of us took mining jobs at plants where there had been incidents. I was in Lodurr when it was overrun. I hid at the bottom of a mine-shaft for two days. I'm carrying information vital to the defense of the System."

"To the defense of the System?" I said, surprised. "What can a few devil-worshippers in old-fashioned spacesuits possibly – "

"I thought the same until I saw them at Lodurr. There are more than we thought, a lot more. They're getting modern equipment from somewhere. And they brought—things—with them. Strange machines. At least I think they're machines." She shuddered suddenly, and looked into my eyes.

I studied her. "If you're with InterPol," I said after a while, "the ship police aren't going to bother you. They'll fight each other to kiss your ass."

"The Zaghrebs have agents on this ship. We knew that when we boarded. We didn't think they'd try anything on a System vessel, but three of them grabbed me two nights ago, searched my cabin, interrogated me. The last thing I remember is getting some kind of shot. They must have dumped me in the garbage bay where you found me. If they think I'm dead it suits me fine. I don't want them to try me again. It's not likely they have informants on the ship police, but it's not impossible either. If you hide me for two more days, until we dock at Rupert Sheldrake, there'll be reward money when I reach Los Angeles headquarters." Suddenly her voice broke. "The things they did to me – "

I watched her while she trembled and cried. When she was quieter, I said, "It's a nice story. If it's true."

Her voice was shaky. "There are two men in Cabin 804—Gunnar Lee and Yusef Gradenko—from my InterPol team. Only the three of us are still alive. Tell them I sent you. Tell them what happened. But don't let the Zaghrebs follow you."

✳ ✳ ✳ ✳

Cabin 804 was halfway around the wheel from mine. I waited until the passage was empty, then knocked.

There was no answer, no sound but the deep endless hum of the transport. The inside of the cabin was blanketed with scrambler waves that jangled my surveillance earpiece—but I had a hunch. It took me thirty seconds to break the door lock. Inside, it was dark and silent. I switched on the light.

There were two men in the cabin. One of them had thinning brown hair and a hooked nose. He lay peacefully on the lower bunk, wearing pajamas, covers pulled up to his chest. It was hard to tell what the other man looked like: he lay crumpled by the shower door, naked, and there was a lot of dried blood on him.

I moved slowly to the man in the bunk. His right temple was a blackened crater, and there was blood on his pillow. I crouched over the man on the floor. His left eye was a deep, crisped hole.

I went through the cabin. In the breast pocket of a corfam jacket was an I.D. card that projected the image of the man on the bed. The image said: "My name is Yusef I. Gradenko, InterPol System Detail three – "

I wandered among the crowds on the entertainment deck until processors in my surveillance package signaled that there was no one shadowing me. Then I took a circuitous route back to my cabin.

The woman was crouched in the shower cubicle, and didn't come out until I had the door shut.

"What did they say?" she asked anxiously. "Why did it take you so long?"

"Your friends are dead," I said. She searched my eyes. Then she sat on the bunk.

"I'm sorry," I said.

"How?" Her voice was ashen.

"Spark-cut. Expert work."

She nodded slowly. After a while she looked at me.

"You'll let me stay here?"

"Yes."

She nodded again.

I argued with the cabin vendor, then finally got a bottle of liquor and a set of cheap unisex clothes. The woman took the clothes into the shower cubicle, slid the door shut. Atomized water hissed. I filled two glasses with medicinal-smelling green liquid. When she came out I was on my second glass.

The cheap jumpsuit made her look beautiful somehow. She picked up her glass, smelled it, drank it suddenly. I filled it again. She sat down. We looked at nothing and drank.

After a while I asked: "How did you happen into OPI? That's rough work."

"I was born on Callisto. It's my home. Earth is off-planet to me."

"That's a little unorthodox for an InterPol agent, isn't it? I thought Earth was supposed to be Home Planet."

She shrugged. "Everybody on Callisto is a little bit Zaghreb. The difference is that we know we need Earth to survive. The Zaghrebs think Callisto could be independent."

"And they worship something that's not from Earth. Something they found on Callisto."

"They worship the Void. The infinite nothingness. The emptiness that goes on forever. Something we on Callisto are born looking at."

Her voice sank. "Earth people are like hothouse plants. You can't see out and you don't want to see out. I spent a year on the Neptune Orbiter, a tiny lighted space in the infinite night. The sun there is a bright star, no more. Daylight there is darker than the darkest night on Earth. With the cabin lights out I could look through the port and see Neptune, huge and green and white, rolling through the night, secret, frozen, gigantic; and looking away from the planet, there was nothing—blackness, emptiness, silence—me floating in it—never ending – "

"People aren't made to see such things."

She looked at me as if surprised I was still there. "People are made to see all sights, all visions," she said.

After that we drank a lot. I tried to keep the conversation going. Her parents had been miners on Callisto. Her mother had died there. I told her about going into the New York Warrens as a rookie policeman. My head felt big and hot. She had been on low-orbital reconnaissance over Neptune. Her black eyes were huge, luminous, liquid. Around midnight I remember wondering why she didn't look drunk.

The next thing I remember is waking up on the floor with a headache and a mouthful of dust. It was dark. My watch said nine a.m. SGT. I sat up as slowly as I could, and stood up even more slowly. I kept one hand on the wall and tried to balance on my feet. My head was somewhere near the ceiling.

I groped for the door handle, opened the cabin door. My idea was to hobble up to the entertainment deck and get some real coffee. Hallway light showed that the cabin bunk was empty.

I thought about that for a second, then switched on the cabin light. The woman wasn't in the cabin. I slid the shower door open. She wasn't in the shower. Suddenly I was wide awake.

✳ ✳ ✳ ✳

The tether ride down from Rupert Sheldrake was uninteresting until we were below the clouds, gliding toward JFK in the rain, and then you could see the giant buildings, mile after mile of them, rising out of the smog.

We plunged into the smog and the ground came up and bumped us. I let most of the other passengers wrestle each other out before I followed them down the grey metal tunnel to the customs cubicles. After I had been decontaminated, x-rayed, searched, and interrogated on my political beliefs, I lugged my suitcase through a crowded terminal concourse echoing with flight announcements. At a bend in the concourse, someone had spray-painted on the concrete wall: "Fuck Earth."

Suddenly I was dizzy. My ears rang and a headache fireballed behind my eyes. My suitcase sagged from my hand, and the scuffed, litter-strewn floor oozed toward me.

"Let me help you there, buddy," a hoarse voice said, and a hard hand closed on my arm. On my other side a bald, wrinkle-faced man was putting a sonic tube away in a raincoat. He grabbed my other arm, picked up my suitcase, and grinned.

"Jeez, you don't look so good," he said. "You better come with us."

I had no choice. By the time the trembling weakness left me I was in the back seat of an unmarked rotor-car lifting off a police landing diamond outside the terminal. The big man with the hoarse voice sat next to me. He didn't answer my questions about what the fuck they thought they were doing.

InterPol New York Headquarters towered square and gigantic into a concrete-grey sky. On the 205th floor a quiet paneled hall led to a door that said R.E. Schrenkoff, Section Chief. Inside was a big office. One wall was transparent; through it you could see grey sky, grey buildings and, far below, grey street. The top of the big desk was chillingly tidy.

Behind the desk was a man. He was narrow, sharp, pale, with black hair slicked back, shiny black eyes. His temples bulged with hardware surgery. He pointed to a chair. The hoarse-voiced man and the wrinkle-faced man sat discreetly near the door.

"We want the girl, Karmade," said the man behind the desk as soon as I sat down. His voice was like him—sharp, hard, shiny.

The first rule in talking to someone you think is lie-detector enhanced is: never give a straight answer.

"What girl?" I asked.

He stared hard at me for a minute, then leaned back, folded his hands on his stomach. He became poetical.

"Karmade, picture yourself in a jail cell. Ten minutes from now. Facing twenty years in the Tombs without parole." He leaned forward over the desk and whispered: "Ever seen the old cons coming out of the Tombs? Seen what they look like?"

"Why should I go to jail?"

He had a chilling smile.

"You don't understand," he said. "We found her DNA in your cabin, in your bunk, in your shower. She's wanted, Karmade. She was wanted—bad—even before she slaughtered the two InterPol detectives tailing her on the flight."

I didn't say anything. I was trying to remember my lawyer's phone number.

Schrenkoff opened a desk drawer, pulled something out. "Ever seen this before?"

I looked at a short, needle-pointed spark-blade. A serial number I recognized was etched on the palm-contoured power pack. I remembered putting the blade in my luggage on Callisto. I suddenly didn't remember packing it on the transport.

"This cut down the agents," said the shiny man. "Found in their cabin on the Titan. You see, Karmade." He put the blade back in the drawer. "We've got you."

"That blade was stolen from me."

"That so? What a coincidence. We find DNA of a hired killer in your bed, and two agents tailing her are slaughtered with your blade. And you never saw the woman, you say, and the blade was stolen. Very strange." He leaned across the desk and whispered: "Think of the Tombs, Karmade."

I thought about them. I looked out the transparent office wall where neon was starting to glow down on darkening streets.

Finally Schrenkoff said: "Look, we don't want you, Karmade. We don't think you helped her work on the agents. Or what if you did? We don't want you. Bring us the girl and we'll forget what we've got on you. Otherwise, we'll turn you over to the prosecutor with a political recommendation. You won't have a chance. What do you say, Karmade?"

My apartment was a standard three-by-three meter, with sanitary cubicle and retractable kitchen, but the living room had something I paid premium rent for—a window. When I got home from visiting Section Chief Schrenkoff I opened it and sat on the foldaway bed I had left unmade 16 months ago, staring down the hundred-story ravine the street made between buildings. The city was dark, and the darkness of it seemed to creep into my brain, as if I was already in the Tombs.

Around midnight I made myself move. I fitted a memory decompression plug into the neural jack behind my left ear, and played back the 72-hour auditory chip. I guessed the chances of any competent killer being caught that way were about zero, but when I indexed the sequence where I had drunk myself to sleep in my cabin, I heard an unfamiliar burst of compressed speech. I played it back slower. There was a clicking sound, and the woman's voice said: "Paradise Corner, New York." It took me about a second to realize that the clicking was my transport cabin console being programmed for directions to Earth destinations.

It was raining when I pushed my way out of the Paradise Corner subway station. Awnings and flashing marquees almost met above the street, making a garish tunnel that people crowded through. Bums and skinny children huddled in sheltered corners, trying to sell broken-down electronics. Far above, you could glimpse the flashing colors of giant signs on buildings that disappeared into dark smog.

The street was lined with neuro stalls, pervodromes, dope bars. Men, women and other types in flashy clothes, or very few clothes, stood outside doors drumming up business. It took me hours of searching meatbooks in the whorehouses specializing in actual humans, and describing the woman to anyone who would listen to work my way to a peep joint at the end of the Corner, near where the neon and glitter give out, and the dark slums resume. There was a floor show going on, featuring a huge sex android with oozing tentacles, and half a dozen dancers. I sat on a hard, crowded bench in the dark, a glass of distilled alcohol in my hand. Slowly I became aware that I knew one of the dancers.

She danced liquidly and well, eyes looking at nothing, muscles rippling in simulated ecstasy and agony. I tried to watch some of the other girls, but I couldn't.

Finally, after many human-machine interfaces, the lights went down. There was applause, drunken cheering. I pushed past people sitting, then people standing, then people leaning at a bar to reach a curtained doorway set below a corner of the stage, which was now blazing with the light of another entertainment.

Beyond the curtain was a dim passage that was a little less deafening than the theater. The floor was bare concrete, the walls plastic curtains with voices behind them. I worked my way down, pulling curtains aside and looking into tiny cubicles where humans and androids were in various stages of undress. At the end of the passage was a metal door, and in the last cubicle before it was the woman.

She was standing with her back to me, zipping up the jumpsuit I had bought her on the transport, looking into a mirror on a broken-down dressing table. When she heard me come in she turned fast.

She looked at me for a second, then started, then looked at me some more.

"Hello," she said breathlessly. "I didn't expect you—that is, I – "

"You expected I'd be in jail. I almost was. But now I'm not going to be."

"What do you mean?"

"Are you going to come quietly, as they say, or do I have to fold you up and carry you?"

Her right hand moved ever so slightly. It seemed to want to be near the hip pocket of her jumpsuit.

"Come where?"

"InterPol Headquarters. Section Chief Schrenkoff. Don't ask me what Section. He wants to talk to you. Something about some dead people."

Her right hand made a flashing movement, but I was ready. By the time the spark-blade was coming toward me I had my gun pointed at the middle of her body.

"No," I said. The blade hesitated. A long second passed.

"Please don't make me kill you," I said. "I don't want to."

"They'll kill me if they get me," she whispered, staring at the gun.

"I won't know about it," I said.

"You'll know," she whispered.

"Drop the rig."

She dropped it. I kicked it and it clattered away somewhere.

There was a faint twitter behind me, on the other side of the curtain, like some electronics booting up.

I hit the floor, her collar in my hand. Then there was a roaring and the room exploded. The curtain flew in shreds, the dressing table dashed itself to splinters, the concrete wall spat dust. I felt my gun kick in my hand. The roaring stopped and something heavy clattered to the floor of the passage. People were screaming behind the ringing in my ears. Smoke billowed. Part of a man was laying in the passage, the missing part splattered on the curtain behind him. I looked at the woman. Blood was oozing from a place on her cheek. I put out my hand to wipe it off, but she was moving, picking up the machine-gun that lay by the dead man, spitting flame and noise back down toward the strip hall as she tumbled across the floor, dragging open what was left of the metal door at the end of the passage. I pushed myself shakily up and ran after her. The door opened onto a narrow alley. It was dark back there, and I was rattled—otherwise, maybe I wouldn't have let her get behind me.

As it was, the last thing I saw was a bright light that seemed to come from the back of my head.

I woke up on a deep, soft sofa in a hushed anteroom with crystal floor lamps, Oriental rugs, and priceless 2-D television sets on real wood stands. I was handcuffed, and my head felt like someone had been driving nails into it. InterPol Section Chief Schrenkoff sat nearby, watching me with cold, shiny eyes. I closed my eyes again and lay still to ease the pounding in my head.

After a while someone said: "Mr. Steele will see you now."

Schrenkoff pulled me to my feet with a hand as hard as a pipe wrench. A bald man wearing tails held a door for us.

On the other side of the door was a carpeted football field with an arched, frescoed ceiling. Soft light came from nowhere. The walls were dark wood, oiled and delicately carved. The air was so still you could hear the blood rush inside your ears. There was something at the far end of the room . Schrenkoff led me that way.

When we got there, I realized we were in an office. There was a massive oak desk, a man in a military outfit standing stiffly facing it. Forty meters away, a fire burned in a huge stone fireplace.

Behind the desk was—something. It had most of a man's head, and the right side was part man, but the left side showed the rigid contours of machine under the silk smoking jacket, and the left hand was translucent plastic. The left side of the neck was metal, and a web of face-contoured mesh ran from it into the bald head. Its eyes glittered wetly under drooping lids. It watched us get nearer and stop next to the soldier. Schrenkoff's hand tightened on my arm. There was silence for a long minute.

Then it croaked: "So, Mr. Schrenkoff, the woman has escaped again."

Schrenkoff swallowed and leveled a finger at the man in the military outfit.

"McEvily – " he got out before the croaking cut him off.

"Major McEvily will be suitably rewarded. He reports losing

four operatives in his encounter with her at Paradise Corner. Perhaps she is more difficult than I anticipated. However, when I buy an InterPol Section Chief—especially at the price I paid for you Mr. Schrenkoff—I expect results. Quick results, Mr. Schrenkoff."

Schrenkoff said desperately: "This man was with her at Paradise Corner."

Major McEvily spun on us with howling eyes. "*My* men captured the prisoner," he snarled. "*My* men engaged in a shoot-out with eight to ten armed – "

"*I* put the finger on him and *I* planted the beeper on him and *I* put the wind up him. You bungled your side of it, McEvily. There were no eight to ten armed anything—just a skinny little striper and this worn-out peeper shooting up your whole task force."

McEvily came a step towards us. "My informants confirm that there were – "

"Be quiet, Major McEvily," croaked the thing, and Major McEvily was quiet.

The thing looked at me. I didn't like that. I wouldn't have liked it even if I hadn't been handcuffed and bruised and far from home. It had ancient, crawling eyes. It said: "Where is the woman, Mr. Karmade?"

"I don't know." Maybe if I was a hero I would have told it to go to hell.

"You were with her at Paradise Corner. Presumably you helped her dispose of the task force."

"I got one of them. I guess she got the rest."

"And where is she now?"

"I don't know."

Schrenkoff stuck a spark-blade into my stomach, set on low power. I tried to make a hole in the floor with my head. When I started to remember who and where I was, Schrenkoff and McEvily were holding me by the armpits and I was vomiting down the front of my shirt.

The thing behind the desk sighed emotionlessly.

"Mr. Karmade," it said. "We are going to persuade you to help us."

I said with difficulty: "Try hiring me."

Schrenkoff slapped the side of my face. "He said he wants to know where the woman is."

"I don't owe her anything," I said in the direction of the monster. "I'm not going to hide her from you. She lied to me, got me in hock for two murders. She tried to cut my throat at Paradise."

Schrenkoff stepped away from me, pulling back his hand.

"Mr. Schrenkoff," said the thing mildly, and Schrenkoff froze. Nobody moved.

"You want the woman? I'll find her. I found her once. I would have brought her in if your cowboys hadn't tried to splash me. All I ask is that you give me some money." I shook my arms up and down. "And take these god-damn things off."

The thing looked at me for longer than was comfortable. Then its mechanical hand touched something on top of the desk.

A minute later there were soft footsteps. Something bumped the back of my legs and someone pulled the handcuffs off, helped me sit down. There was a little carved wooden table next to me, with a glass of water and a cloth napkin on it. I drank the water and used the napkin to wipe puke, sweat and blood off my face. I noticed my hand was shaking when I drank the water.

When I was done drinking and wiping, someone handed me a screen. It showed that my bank account had been credited with a large sum.

"Now," said the thing.

I talked.

※ ※ ※ ※

After I was done, it sat machine-still, death-still. Finally, it raised a hand and flicked a finger at McEvily and Schrenkoff, like someone brushing away a piece of dust. They turned and walked.

After awhile the huge room felt empty. The thing said: "Mr. Karmade, do you know who I am?"

"No," I said. "I can't even figure out *what* you are."

"I am Rexon Augustus Steele."

I stared, startled in spite of myself.

"I will tell you a story, Mr. Karmade. Listen carefully, because your life may depend on it.

"Fifty years ago I was an old man. I was rich, one of the richest men in the solar system, but I was dying. The prosthetic surgeons had done all they could, at great expense. I was told that my body would not stand another organ replacement. My bioelectric kidneys would last three years at most, my heart perhaps five. I was covered with scars and filled with stiff plastic. But I didn't want to die. I had so much money! It was a waste to die when I had so much money, when every day I had more money, and when every day I thought of ways to get more.

"Those were the years when the first mining teams landed on the giant moons of Saturn and Jupiter. The explorations went smoothly; there were no life forms to speak of, and the moons were rich in deuterium. The only failure was the loss of the first Callisto Mission. It landed safely and transmitted routinely for a few hours, then stopped. Contact could not be reestablished. A second team was sent several years later.

"The startling news the second Callisto Mission transmitted was that the first mission had not been lost after all: the first team were safe, but they had abandoned their landing vehicles to go after something their monitors had detected on the moon's surface. By the time the second mission arrived, they had dismantled the landing vehicles and carried the life support systems into some caves. They wouldn't let the second party into the caves, and shot a member of the second team who tried to interfere with them; other than that, they were peaceable. They just wanted to be left alone to worship, they said. What they were worshiping, and what they had found on the moon, they would not say. Some god, or devil, or life form, no one knew. No one knows today. By the time an InterPol military squad arrived from Earth, the Zaghrebs, as the first team had begun calling themselves, had disappeared. Expeditions through the caves found no sign of them or their life systems, just dark greenish frost-rock, ancient and unmoving.

"No one knew what the incident meant. Authorities on Earth decided to treat it as some strange form of space sickness, and went on constructing Callisto mining plants in an orbit close to Luna. That made jobs, and the Zaghreb publicity soon died down.

"Nine years after the Zaghrebs disappeared I got a message from them over a secret communication system I had set up for business communications of an urgent and sensitive nature. The message said simply: 'Eternal Life. We Deliver.'

"I was in a rage: the communication system had cost a great deal of money, and its design was break-proof. My lawyers transmitted to the reply code given in the message, demanding to know who had breached the system and how, threatening legal and paramilitary action. Teams of technicians searched for the source of the message. Somewhere on Callisto, their instruments said, but strangely there was no transmission lag. A new message appeared on the decoding processor in my office. It said, 'You are an old man, Mr. Steele. Do you want to die? Send your lawyers away. Talk to us alone and we will tell you secrets.' I stared at this message a long time. Then I sent everyone away, and sat in front of the console alone.

"'We know you are dying.' the console said. We want to help you.'

"'Why?' I typed.

"'You have something we want.'

"'What?'

"'Take a fast ship to Callisto. Free fall at 20.01.53 north magnetic, 93.11.30 west, 1400 kilometres, and wait for instructions. Let no one know you are coming.'

"'Ridiculous.'

"'In two months your prosthetic liver will malfunction. Then you will come.'

"I had scanning stations concealed on Callisto to monitor covert visits by competitors with possible interests in the mining business. My people checked the 20.01.53 north, 93.11.30 west trajectory. Over the past year three small ships had lain in that orbit—fast, custom-designed ships only a few people in the system could afford. My experts identified them as belonging to three of the richest men in the solar system, old and dying men, like myself. Two months later my prosthetic liver began to malfunction.

"My agents had heard rumors of miraculous improvements

in the health of two of the old men whose ships we had detected around Callisto. Death at close range makes men grasp at straws. Before the rumors could be confirmed, I was heading for Callisto in my private transport.

"By the time we reached Callisto I was sick and delirious. I remember getting into orbit, and a message from the Zaghrebs telling us to wait. I ordered my people to follow the Zaghrebs' instructions even if I was unconscious, and they must have done so, because I next found myself alone in a cave on the surface, wearing a spacesuit, and propped against some rocks. I was too weak to move.

"Then a woman appeared in front of me. I didn't see where she came from, didn't know if she was real. She wasn't wearing a spacesuit or anything else. She was beautiful. She said: 'I am life. Stand up and take Me.' I couldn't move. She knelt down and whispered through my helmet: 'I will give myself to you, old man, but you must pay. After you are healed, something will be asked of you. You must do it. If you go back on your word, you will die. Do you agree?'

"'Yes.'

"The next thing I remembered was waking up in the cabin of my ship, headed back to Earth. I was weak, but no longer sick. Every day I felt stronger. My prosthetic as well as my real organs seemed to be working perfectly. I had a few jumbled memories of what had happened in the cave, but none of them made sense. As soon as I set foot on Earth, post-hypnotic instructions from the Zaghrebs filled my mind. They were not awful or even illegal, merely that I make annual shipments of a certain mineral to a certain location on Callisto. The mineral is neither dangerous nor very rare; my informants indicate that the Zaghrebs attach some spiritual significance to it. I have kept up the shipments. And so, my scanning stations tell me, have at least four other corporations, all owned by rich men who are rumored to be over two hundred years old.

"This—" Steele swept his hand over the mechanical part of his body "—happened in an assassination attempt thirty-two years ago, when People's Food Army terrorists rocketed my rotorcar. The

Zaghreb treatment gave no protection against such injuries. So the Zaghrebs have kept their word. Maybe."

Steele was stiller than a living thing could be. Then he started talking again. "Two years ago, the old men began to disappear: Oscar Angel III, Bukara Ragodan, and Pablo Smircea. Freighters belonging to all three had been observed making secret deliveries to the Zaghrebs. My agents investigated the incidents. Angel and Smircea, and possibly Ragodan also, were with women when they disappeared. Two of the women were traced. Both were Zaghrebs from Callisto. Both had boarded Earth vessels posing as returning miners. Both went straight to the cities where the old men lived, ingratiated themselves with them. Both were alone with the men when they disappeared.

"I stationed agents at New New York port on Callisto, with instructions to identify and destroy Zaghrebs attempting to travel to Earth. I had kept my part of the bargain. I had no intention of being cheated."

There was silence for a minute. Then I said: "You killed every Zaghreb trying to travel to Earth?"

"Zaghrebs are prohibited by law from leaving Callisto, Mr. Karmade. Though primitive and apparently harmless tribespeople, their ancestry and heretical politics offend the System government. You might say I was doing a public service by preventing serious felonies."

"Then if I bring her to you, you'll kill her."

"If you don't bring her to me, I'll kill *you*."

An unmarked robot car took me back to my building. My apartment was silent and close, like a tomb.

I must have fallen asleep in my chair, because when I woke up I was sitting with my overcoat on, my body stiff as a corpse, and a bad taste in my mouth. Dull grey daylight came through my window. Someone was knocking at the door.

I opened it. The woman stood there, a cheap raincoat over her jumpsuit, her hair wet. Her hands were empty. I couldn't think of anything to say. I let her in.

"Want some breakfast?" I asked.

"No, thank you."

I went into the kitchen, poured some breakfast into a cup, tossed it off, filled the cup again, and came out holding the cup and bottle.

"What happened to you?" She was looking at my face.

"You mean after you hit me with the gun?"

"Yes."

"I had a bad night." I sat back down in my chair and looked up at her. "There are men watching this apartment."

She smiled. "They're asleep."

"You're a woman that knows how to put people to bed. I guess you think I look sleepy, too."

She pulled off her raincoat.

"You look worse than sleepy," she said. "Do you have something I can dry off with?"

I waved my bottle at the sanitary cubicle. She went in and the air jets came on.

"What happened to you last night?" she said over the sound.

"I had a talk with a guy."

"Who?"

"Rexon Augustus Steele," I said. "You know him?"

"No."

"He says he knows you. Is it true you're a Zaghreb agent smuggled here to murder him?"

She came out of the cubicle combing her fingers through her short blue hair. "Do you think I am?"

"I don't know," I said. "I don't know who you are or why you're here talking to me when you know this place is crawling with Steele's people. I don't know why I'm sitting here talking to you after you tried to kill me last night."

"I could have killed you last night," she said. "I didn't."

"Why not?"

She didn't answer. She sat on the bed.

"Well, just to pass the time until we both get killed, you could tell me who you are and what you're doing here and why the toughest private police force in the system is trying to splash you," I said.

"Why do you want to know?"

"I'm trying to decide whether to help you."

"Why should you help me?"

"I don't know. I helped you on the transport against my better judgment. I helped you last night without wanting to. It seems to be my fate."

She studied me. Finally she said: "I am no one, from nowhere, and they are afraid of nothing."

"Lady," I said, "I'm tired. My head hurts. Any time now guys with guns are going to come through that door. Don't make my life harder. Please. There's a chance I'll want to help you—a smaller chance I *can* help you—but you've got to tell me who you are and what this is all about."

The woman stood up slowly and stretched, arching her body tautly, like a cat.

"Do you want to know who I am?" she said. Her black eyes felt hot on my face. She pulled the zipper down the front of her jumpsuit, and shrugged out of it. She wasn't wearing anything underneath. Her eyes were burning me like fire.

I was bathed in fire, white-hot and thunderous. I lived in regions of fire, a cocoon that slept in fire. I felt myself stirring, opening, unfolding. I stretched my wings: I flew, expanding, sailing. When I looked back, the fire was a tumbling ball floating in warm blackness. Ahead lay spaces that had no end. I went faster. There were, I saw, balls sailing around the fire, tumbling with deep and sonorous sounds. I passed the track of one and then another, and several more. Their music faded behind me. My wings stretched further and further, so that now they were like gossamer, now like webs, now like dancing fans of light. Now the tumbling balls were lost in darkness, there was emptiness, silence, me spinning, hurtling through it, growing as big as a planet, a sun, a solar system, still touching only silence. Then in that silence I heard a voice, sweet and crystalline and infinitely far away. Others joined it like crystal bells singing, and there were millions and millions of them, and billions and billions of them, calling to me from spaces so wide that not even thoughts could touch them.

I was lying face down in my bed, gasping and sweating. The woman's face was half an inch from mine, lips parted, eyes closed. One of her arms was around my neck. She lay very still. I put my head down on her shoulder. She smelled sweaty, dirty, and sweet. I kissed the corner of her mouth, leaving a little bloodstain there, pushed some stray blue hair off her forehead. My hand looked big and clumsy against her face.

I said hoarsely: "I saw something." She didn't move or say anything—or breathe.

I was up suddenly, standing over her, feeling for a pulse in her wrist, in her neck, feeling for breath at her mouth. She didn't have any of those things. I fumbled the epinephrine inhaler out of my first-aid kit, put it to her mouth, pressed the button. Her chest arched in an impersonation of being alive. Then she was still—no pulse, no breath. I tried again and again. Nothing. I smashed the inhaler against the wall, grabbed her shoulders and shook her. Her head and arms flopped around. She looked very dead, and like she wanted to be left alone, or just didn't care. I stopped shaking her and sat on the edge of the bed. I didn't look at her. I looked at the drops of rain running down the window. I looked at my clothes, caked with dirt and blood, tangled up with her jumpsuit on the floor. I looked at the white scar on my stomach where a chicken-head from Death-Hole Warren had stabbed me, a long time ago, when I had first been a cop. After a while I looked at nothing. After a long time I noticed it was dark.

I sat at the desk and typed a phone number.

After the second ring a hard face said, "McEvily."

"I've got the woman."

"Don't move," he said, and hung up.

It took them eight minutes to get there. Before they came I put on clothes and wrapped the woman in a sheet. She was cold as ice, awkward and uncaring, far away.

✳ ✳ ✳ ✳

I rode in the back seat of a rotor-car filled with gunmen. They took the woman in a different car; I didn't see her when we landed and I was hustled to a cell the size of my shower and no place to look out. I didn't like it in there. I sat on the floor, closed my eyes and tried to remember the vision I had seen while making love to her, of being as big as the sun, soaring through space. I forgot to wonder how and why she had died. I didn't want to know. I was tired of wondering. I just wanted to be away from here.

I was pretty far away when the cell door clanked open. McEvily and two other goons hustled me out and walked me to the football field Rexon Augustus Steele used as an office. As we got within hailing distance of his desk, men dressed in white pushed a metal cart out from somewhere, parked it, and went away. The cart had something lying on it, covered with a sheet. We stopped by the cart, and McEvily and the other two gave military salutes.

McEvily said: "We don't know how he killed her. The medical boys figure some kind of nerve gas that doesn't leave traces. We don't know how he found her or whether he was involved in killing the agents watching the apartment."

Steele flicked his finger. McEvily and his thugs marched away out of sight. There was no one else in the huge space. Steele sat death-still, machine-still, looking at the thing on the cart. He sat that way for a long time.

Finally there was a whir, and his plastic arm lifted up. The hand extended across the desk on a metal stalk, pulled the sheet away from the woman's pale body.

A tremor seemed to run through him. He pulled his hand back in, and sat staring, rocking a little from side to side.

He said, "I didn't want you to kill her." His voice sounded different.

"I'm sorry," I said. "I didn't—I'm sorry."

We both looked at her, Steele still rocking a little bit.

Slowly, I got a feeling. It started at the base of my head and went down my right arm to my hand. It felt like that part of my body was full of something, swollen. Without knowing why, I took two steps and touched the woman on the forehead.

She opened her eyes.

I don't know what Steele did. I stared. I leaned over her and stared into her eyes.

She blinked them, and rubbed them, as if she had been sleeping. She smiled at me, and sat up. She stretched. Then she turned toward Steele.

All the living parts of Steele were trembling. He looked like a trembling man half eaten by machines.

The woman got off the cart, never taking her eyes from Steele. She stood in front of the desk facing him.

He trembled. There was sweat on the side of his face that could sweat.

"Is it – " he choked a little " – is it you?" His voice sounded almost like a human voice.

"Yes," she said very gently. "I've come for you."

Tears started to come out of his old eyes and run down his grey checks. He trembled so much that it seemed the mechanical part of him would have to tear loose, break off.

"Don't be afraid," she said. She started to walk around the desk.

Then she caught fire. I didn't see how, but suddenly flames covered her naked body, white and yellow flames that roared like blow-torch flames. Through their brightness and fury I could see her in a kind of radiant light. I felt the fire's intense heat, but the flames didn't seem to hurt her. She seemed taller, and walked with a stately walk, as though fire were a royal robe. As she came near to Steele she raised her arms, and they were like wings of flame, and the fire got brighter and hotter, so I could hardly see her any more, and could hardly look at her.

Steele raised his arms to her and she stooped and folded him in the fire. Then he was on fire too, the flames enveloped both of them, and got hotter and brighter until I couldn't look at them, had to cover my face with my arms and stumble backward away from the heat. The roaring of the flames got louder, then diminished, so that when I opened my eyes they had almost burned out, and when

I went around behind the desk and looked, Steele and the woman were gone, and there was nothing left of them, not even ashes.

Sunlight

I was coming down the hill road, my split-open boots flapping in the dust, when I heard the clank, like metal hitting metal far off. The night was windless, high clouds throwing a transparent veil over the moon, dry creepers covering the rusted barbed-wire fence along the woods.

It came again – *clank* – metal hitting metal, hard and desperate.

I went down the ravine through dry grass, into deep tree-shade. The stream was almost dry, a trickle of water through sharp-smelling mud and mossy rocks. On the other side four dark figures crouched whispering. I crossed toward them on stepping stones.

"What do you want?" croaked Hol, his skeleton teeth clicking. "You go away." He gestured with a claw finger on the end of a leathery arm grayer and more withered than any of the others, giving him a kind of authority, because he was more eaten by the Virus.

"You after the Resistants again?" I asked them. "You better watch out. That old man's got a shotgun."

"He's dead," croaked Hol, and his fleshless mouth made it a flat, final sound. "All rotten and gone away. Ain't going to shoot nobody. You go away. She's ours."

"If he's dead, she has his gun," I said. "And his lights and gasoline. You let her alone, or she'll shoot you in your tombs come daylight. They're the last Resistants around here," I said to the others, concentrating to remember the importance of it. "Remember the bright Sun – ?"

"Don't fill us up with none of your garbage," croaked Hol. "There ain't no *remember.* Alls there is is—" he made a dry sucking with his black, leathery tongue.

"I'm hungry," whined Toh. "I ain't ate in a long time."

The metal clank came again down the slope above us, and they turned toward it.

"Won't be long," Hol croaked.

"What did you do?" A vague feeling stung through the numbness of the Virus, which had been growing in me a long time.

"I threw a rock into their generator," said Toh dully through the pain of his hunger. "It was a lucky throw."

"She still has all those batteries," I said. The old man had spent years pulling them out of rusted-out cars in the daytime when the Viruses were in their tombs.

"They'll run down," Hol predicted flatly.

As if in answer to his words, the faint beams over the top of the hill flickered and went out.

Hol gave a rasping scream of triumph and fierce hunger, and they all ran.

The Virus ran me after them.

At the top of the hill the land sloped gently into meadow, and I caught the smell of her like perfumed meat among the tall grass and trees. As we got close, flying silently through the grass, I *saw* her, saw the taut, small shape squatting over the metal generator housing, white hands moving in jerky panic in the machinery. She had cut off the battery cable trying to fix it.

Hol hit the old man's twelve-foot chain-link fence with a crash.

The girl spun around, eyes and mouth wide open, hair splayed in the air.

The shotgun in her hands roared blinding fire. Buckshot tore hurtlessly through me.

I could smell her sweat, her fear, the sweet blood pounding inside her.

She dropped the shotgun and spun back around onto her knees. Something clicked.

Light erupted from a hundred car headlights mounted on poles, the roof of the low wooden house, the water tank and shed, white as diamond, sharp as knives, hot as fire. I writhed backward, burned. I felt the ground hit me roughly, stumbled to my feet and ran.

Up the meadow cool darkness closed over me.

But the smell of her had made the Virus hungry. Now it tore me into the thick woods beyond the meadow, whipping through underbrush, smashing branches away, damp, heavy air rushing, taut leathery legs blurring, until I smelled a wild dog upwind.

Then all my senses converged, darkened, narrowed, and the woods roared past like a storm, until I numbly overtook the black running smear howling in terror, crushed it under me, fighting its flailing legs, burying my teeth in its soft underbelly where a fountain of hot blood rushed, and the Virus sucked and drank deep...

I came to myself on the hill road, staggering drunkenly back in the direction of my tomb, moon floating low over the hills on the other side of the valley. As soon as I remembered the dog I stumbled to my knees and retched, but the Virus wouldn't let me throw away all that precious blood, oozing through me now with its exciting warmth. Someday soon I wouldn't wake up after feeding, I knew; when the Virus finished eating my brain I would be a puppet like Hol, a bone frame to carry billions of them and their networks of feed vessels, with just enough of a nervous system to find more blood. It would be better that way: never to wake up, not to remember the tangled mess of the dog...

I lay in the narrow basement crawl-space of a rotten house, eyes I couldn't close anymore staring at gray dirt walls, with sometimes a worm or insect to keep me company as the long daytime passed. When the gunshot sounded I was trying to remember the time before the Virus came, straining to focus the blurry outlines of an emerald orchard rippling in a brightness I thought must be sunlight, and a little white house –

The gunshot cut off a distant shriek. I rolled over in the narrow space. Two more gunshots came close together. I knew that gun. Either the old Resistant man was alive after all and back on his daytime rounds hunting out Virus tombs, or else his daughter had finally come out to do it. I guessed it was the daughter—the old man wouldn't use three shells on a Virus when it only took one to sever the head. I listened to the distant buzz of locusts and the hoot of a mourning dove, the occasional patter of a squirrel in some part of the house.

Hours later, when the hot smell of dust and rotting wood was strong in my tomb, feet crunched on gravel, then thumped on the sagging boards of the porch. The front door squeaked. Footsteps creaked above my head, too light and scared for the old man's.

An intoxicating whiff of the girl wafted through the cracks in the trapdoor.

She climbed the groaning stairs, the precariously-leaning house shuddering under her. A vague anger came over me. Her father would have known that the house, with its broken windows and gaping boards, was too bright for the Virus, that you had to poke around in the basement and dark, inner rooms. What had he taught her?

The footsteps came back down the stairs, came closer. The trapdoor opened, showering dust.

Light blinded and burned. There was a fearful cry.

I huddled against the dirt wall, arms over my face. The Virus quivered, seeing its death in the long black barrel that extended from the light, and it shrieked in my throat, but I was numb.

There was a faint noise, like someone gasping.

The trapdoor fell with a boom and it was mercifully dark again, and I heard footsteps running away.

Something had fallen on my leg, a little patch of wet on my tattered overalls. I sniffed at it. The smell shocked me, bringing forgotten memories of ancient, clean sorrows, of flushed face and blurry eyes that passed like a shower of rain in the cool, strong air of long ago—the smell of tears.

The next night the moon floated silver-bright and serene over quiet hills. I went slowly along the hill road, trying to pretend I was taking one of the aimless rambles the Virus allowed me when it wasn't hungry. But as I came over the rise there was only darkness instead of the Resistants' light behind the ridge, only silence instead of a gasoline generator running.

I hurried down under trees where crickets and a hoot-owl sang, on stepping stones over sharp-smelling mud, up the dry grass slope beyond. As I got to the top, the bright stench of gasoline covered every other smell.

The lights were still shining in the compound halfway across the meadow, but so dim orange that the four black figures creeping close to it barely had to shield their eyes. The old man hadn't taught his daughter to repair the generator, either. The fool.

Now two of the figures were climbing the fence.

There was a roar of thunder that lit the night blinding yellow. The compound was a fireball, a mushroom of smoke boiling into the sky. A roaring crackle came in a wave across the meadow.

I jumped away from the burning glare, fell, then stumbled to a clump of trees in the shelter of the hill, leaned there to let the stabbing pain go out of my eyes.

Running feet and harsh breath came over the crest of the hill. A pale figure pelted down the path.

The girl.

I wondered how she had set off the gasoline, how she had gotten out of the compound without Hol and the others smelling her, and then the Virus caught up with her and knocked her unconscious to the ground, her flashlight and shotgun tumbling away into the grass.

It seemed a long time later that I woke again, but it couldn't have been more than a few seconds. The girl lay twisted on the path in a circle of darkness that throbbed like a heartbeat, the Virus's pounding, the lustful contraction of its million feed-vessels shaking my body. I watched numbly, as in a dream, as my withered, Virus-driven body bared its teeth and knelt over the pulse rippling in her milk-white belly--

In that second I saw her face.

A little fair-haired girl swung on the oak that arched over the orchard track under a blue and white summer sky, wearing a blue and white Sunday dress with limp ankle socks and lace-up shoes, and I could see her face, smiling shyly as I came along the track–

I gasped. The memory was clear and steady, full of sunlight.

—the tie around the waist of her dress had come undone and fluttered in the orchard air, cool and breezy and smelling like dew though it was mid-morning, as she pushed forward and backward on the swing, smiling shyly –

The girl on the path stirred, hands moving down to her sides to push against the ground dizzily, trying feebly to push herself up. Her eyes opened, squinting, one at time, and saw me, and closed, and heavy tears spilled out of them, her mouth twisting in a terrible sorrow.

Then a strange thing happened. The salt smell of her tears came to me, and in a minute I realized that the Virus was silent, it's throbbing stopped, as if the sunlit memory of this girl from long ago had routed it from my brain just as the real sun sent it lurking into dark holes. Maybe it wasn't hungry: it had eaten a dog last night; maybe there was no reason for it to interfere if the smell of tears gave me back my nerves for a little while.

The girl sat up, looking into my face with horrified fascination, wiping a streak of dirt across her face with the back of her hand. She was shaking hard.

I turned and pointed into the night.

"There's some others," I croaked, and my horrible voice made her jerk back. "You can see their lights on the other side of the valley. Go there."

She struggled up, disturbing the dust of the path, trembling and staring; then she turned and stumbled in the exact direction I pointed, holding her torn clothes together with her hands, staggering off the path into big rocks and briars, trying to stagger through them with mindless effort.

"You can't go that way," I croaked. "Go around along the path, and then across the valley by – "

She would never make it, I knew. The valley was full of Virus tombs, in caves, rotten shacks, ruined wells. And if she stayed here the others would get her.

✳ ✳ ✳ ✳

My legs like pistons in the dark of the valley woods, trees and vines, bushes, rocks, stars and blue night air roaring by like a storm, moon like a silver pennant flying, cold smell of the woods, power of the Virus flowing.

But not to catch a dog or deer or rabbit. The girl was tied to my back with strips of her clothes, and I was taking her across the valley toward the speck of light that Hol had licked his lips at and told me was another Resistants' compound, full of hot blood the Virus wanted to drink.

I ran until in the dark I smelled and heard and finally saw two shadows rush level with me in a shallow copse of young trees. They put their black claws on me and dragged me down, tumbling in mud, dust and grass.

They were the burned remains of Hol and Toh. Hol had one arm, leathery flesh burned off the side of his face to scorched bone, and Toh was blackened and crisped.

"You share her," Hol croaked. "There's enough."

I crouched between them and the girl.

"No," I said.

"I'm hungry," croaked the Virus from Hol's mouth. "I'm hungry as the hills' old bones; hungry as the emptiness between the stars."

Then I felt the Virus hanging on my skeleton hear him and wake up and start to throb, and I moved numbly aside from her.

Hol knelt down crooning, and Toh sobbed and screamed from his blistered lips. Hol rolled her over so we could see the pulse of her belly. Then I throbbed, and the madness of hunger burst in me, and I didn't care what happened as long as I could eat her.

She was gazing crazily at the stars in the misty blue-black sky as if none of this was happening, as if she were far away.

She said: "Terrel, when will I see my ma?"

Her voice, soft but clear and ringing as a bell, cut the night to slivers around me, sawed through the pounding in my body. Terrel had been my name, I realized, when we had played in the orchard long ago. But there was nothing left of Terrel now. How had she looked upon the Virus and seen a man long ago devoured? And what she said was crazy too, I suddenly remembered: her mother had died years before the Virus came.

And then I remembered her *father,* old Mr. Willow, dressed up in a black Sunday suit with his long, red apple-farmer's face, coming back from the cemetery where they laid a handful of flowers from the meadow, his daughter's profile serious and clear next to him in the old car they drove along the black-top road past the store and gas station where Hollister Gautraux and Tommy Robbins worked, and the sun shone –

"I heard her calling in the orchard when I was swinging," the girl went on thought-fully, "and I ran, but I couldn't find her. And Pa told me she wasn't coming back."

Her words trailed away.

With trembling effort, I wrenched my eyes from the darkness around me to the sunlight in my head –

Hol's dry teeth touched her stomach.

I was no Virus –

I kicked Hol in the face with my split-open boot.

Then I was crazy with hatred, bellowing and flailing, smashing Toh's head with a brick-sized rock, clawing and smashing against Hol's greater strength until he ran screaming, panicked by the uncanniness of a Virus raising its hand against another.

Silence fell. Toh lay in the grass holding his head, grey and white ooze coming between his fingers.

We flew again across the valley toward the light twinkling too bright to look at near the top of the hills beyond. After a while the land sloped upward, getting steadily steeper, and soon I could see the glow from the Resistants' compound over the tops of the trees. My body ran nerveless, effortless, the girl barely weighing on my back, until I seemed to float numbly in slow motion, in blue spaces near the moon.

Gradually a deep chill crept over me, as if something floating above me gave off a radiation of deadly cold.

And then I felt the Virus; not as a throbbing hunger or an irresistible lust or a numb motion of my body, but as a living spirit, cold and cruel and incomprehensibly old. And somehow I knew that this was their Soul, the Old One, the One that came to crush rebellion, to freeze the hearts of the brave.

It had crept through the endless emptiness of space in frozen spores, I saw, driven by its nightmarish hunger over the billions of years, gnawing itself and shrieking soundlessly to the void. It had hungered too much to now be denied any food, any sacrifice; it could let no warm flesh be snatched from its icy teeth.

And this was to be my punishment: that I felt it pouring into me with exquisite slowness, like black oil, devouring all light like liquid darkness, all warmth like the coldness of Hell.

The girl tied to my back began to caress me, her hot throbbing flesh to fill me with exquisite vibrations. The smell of her filled my head.

No, I thought like a drowning man.

But my body stopped running, tore the strips that held her to my back, threw her to the ground, feed-vessels pounding, vision dark and narrow.

"Run," I croaked before the Virus strangled me.

She screamed. She struggled up and ran.

Her white shape throbbed like molten pearl in the darkness. I caught her in three steps and nuzzled her, breathing in the maddening smell of her panicked blood –

She screamed and ran again.

I had my gray claws in her, feeling the swaying of her muscles like wind swaying in the trees, the thumping of her heart –

There was a faint shout, clear and bell-like in the dark.

The girl screamed once more.

I let her go once more to see her squirm through the dark in her tender, sloppy flesh before I caught her, drank deep –

Footsteps pounded and a big man appeared through the trees. He was a Resistant. He carried a stabbing light and something else, that jumped toward me and cut me with deafening fire. The woods and air and moon and the deep, deep blue beyond did crazy somersaults until they jerked steady again, and I was looking up at the girl clinging to the man, and he dragging her back up the hill, shining his light around as if to ward off ghosts, the barrel of his shotgun smoking.

His clear voice said, as if from some great distance: "You're all right now – you're all right. Hurry, now, we have to get inside. But where did you come from? How did you get here?" And her sobbing and holding on to him as if she would never let go.

They disappeared through the trees. Soon another figure stumbled into view: a withered, headless body clawing at the air, stumbling blindly and falling, then crawling frantically, wagging its severed neck. The sound of its crashing through bushes slowly diminished, leaving the night quiet and empty.

It would crawl until in a few hours the last of the dog's blood oozed through the feed-vessels, and then it would lie down and die.

And the same would happen to me, propped against something that gave me a view of dark trees and sky, the full moon now floating down toward the west in the eldering night, smell of moss and dust and dew coming to my breathless nostrils in the stillness.

A coldness hung in the air, as if the Virus-spirit floated nearby, contemplating the loss of its prey. But it had no more interest in me: I was free. I watched the moon slowly set, peacefully remembering the sunlit world, and imagining a race of Resistants spreading from this hilltop to reclaim it.

The Shining Place

Five hundred kilometers from where the Manned Heliopause Probe orbited its fusion pulse booster on a Kevlar tether, I stood on the brick terrace construct in my observational software and gazed at a faint speck of light.

I punched magnification; the speck became a bright amoeba swimming through a dark ocean, a star-flower blooming in a charcoal field, then an octopus flailing through inky water, then a vast whirlpool, its hundred billion star-voices singing thunderous cacophony.

Another punch and the galaxy fell behind me like sparkling dust, its roar fading. The Bootes Void yawned ahead, hollow and lightless, a vacuum desert a hundred million light-years across. Soon I was floating in crystal stillness, celestial voices of faraway galaxy clusters tinting the emptiness faintest blue, like rarified water. I rushed on, not seeming to move in that vastness.

A red light blinked. The Probe communication link crackled, making noises I was not now able to understand. I ignored it. After a while it went away.

The galaxies were a sigh echoing faintly in the dark. In the subtle blending of their voices, was that music? Delicate harmonies of praise, of awe? Was it the Pattern at last, audible only in this place of silence? If I could get closer to the middle of the Void, where only the purest tones penetrated—

I punched magnification.

Nothing happened.

Then, screaming, I slipped backward, the oceans of measurement and computation I swam in draining away, drying up, leaving me gasping like a fish on a dry seabed.

Lustrous depths faded to dark, humming hardware banks. The leaden weight of my body strapped to its machine sagged around me. An animal howled in the tiny observation chamber.

An Adi-series military clone stared down at me with wide, ice-green eyes, a narrow beam of ceiling light glinting from her braided silver-gold hair.

She said: "Dr. Hawk, your observational allocation has been pre-empted by emergency order. Research Director Stone requires your presence in his chamber immediately."

Neural jacks clicked out of sockets in my quadriplegic walker. My body shook with transition shock, tears running from my old eyes. The clone's face was like exquisitely sculpted metal, full of gene-programmed indifference.

"You've been listening to that machine music again," I willed the walker's synthesizer to accuse her. Its flat voice cut through the whimpering I could feel coming from my throat. "I told you not to. You'll end up as fertilizer on some government farm."

She didn't answer, but fear flashed in her eyes. That and a cool dose of endorphin from the walker made me feel better: soon I could will it to lift me and stamp jerkily into the gangway, the clanging of its ambulators like dissonant chords in the Probe's endless hum, the long-contracted tendons of my legs burning as the walker stretched them. The Adi followed me along the dim, electric-smelling defile between pipes and cables, then slowly up the ladder to Stone's observatory.

At the top of the ladder was a vast dome of simulated starlight glowing on banks of hardware vined with wires that converged on a gilded chair. In the chair sat a huge, white-robed figure, hood thrown back to show many wires plugged into its naked head, massive hands resting on its knees. A murmur of sound swirled around it, and its face was obscured by a shifting haze of holography.

A holographic bubble erupted from the white figure, expanding as it approached. Stone's face smiled from it, his body still wrapped in the murmur and fog of inputs. A dozen faces hung around him in other bubbles like a pantheon of gods: the rest of the Class A scientific team. Whatever it was must be important if they had all been pulled off their mission activities.

Stone's timeshare face said politely: "Dr. Hawk, thank you for coming. Can you tell me, what is *that?*"

A bubble bloomed with static in front of me, then cleared. In it smooth metal glared under a black sky. On the metal hunched a gray barnacle shape. The picture zoomed in, until I could see tiny impact-craters in an ancient surface wrinkled like congealed scum or morbid, frozen flesh.

"A rock," I said, the synthesizer's flat voice covering my anger.

"It's stuck to our hull," said Stone.

"A magnetized rock. Stone, I have no time for this. I'm in the middle of an urgent observational program on the Platform."

"It's talking to us," Stone went on. "Network heard it an hour ago, at 1420 megahertz, repeating every quarter second."

There was silence. I stared at the rock. All the Class A personnel were watching me. Suddenly hair prickled on the back of my old neck.

"Saying what?"

The Probe Network's cool voice answered: "According to my data the signal corresponds to the Prelude in G major for clavier, BWV 902, written in 1719 or 1720 by the German programmer Johann Sebastian Bach. This musical pattern is also known to correspond to a sequence from the default human genetic code, junk DNA: chromosome 17, codons p-804 to -1247."

My heart pounded.

"Then it's not coming from that rock," I said. "You're getting it mixed up with my Platform transmissions."

"The object is emitting the signal at regular quarter-second intervals, Dr. Hawk," said Stone. "I have personally checked for faults."

I stared at him, blind with sudden, feverish thoughts.

"But I share your astonishment," he went on. "A rock in the Heliopause Cloud broadcasting obsolete Earth music? How can it be?"

"I note again that it is clearly a case of recordation," said Network. "Dr. Hawk has been transmitting this music into the Cloud. The object has obviously recorded his transmissions by some unknown mechanism."

"You have been broadcasting this—Prelude from the Observation Platform," said Stone. "Why?"

"My observational software translated some galactic cluster patterns into a sound pattern resembling it." The synthesizer turned the uncomprehending stutter of my thoughts into a strange, flat staccato. "It has already been found in DNA and the natural music repertory—it may be a fragment of the Pattern. I broadcast it to—to talk back to the stars." A sudden chill of exultation took me. "Play it," I told Network. "Play the music."

There was a few seconds silence, and then it began, quietly, simple as a child's music-box song; but patterns quickly built: intricate, abstract, formal, yet full of the smell of grass and trees, sunlight, wind, and clouds, things found on a speck of dust floating in the darkness some 35 billion kilometers away.

"Turn it off," snapped the timeshare with a flash of fear and revulsion at the unapproved music, the "junk" pattern that coded for no known traits. It stopped abruptly.

"I do not understand your methods, Dr. Hawk," Stone went on after a minute, "but somehow you have provoked a reply. We are constructing a decision tree. I suggest you plug in."

✳ ✳ ✳ ✳

At the bottom of the ladder the clone blocked the gangway, the walker's shadow falling over her.

"Bach," she said, staring up into my face. "That is one of the programs you gave me."

"Move! Don't you understand what's happening?" The walker's claws snapped agitatedly.

She tried to smile, but licked her lips fearfully. "Research Director Stone doesn't want to hear Bach."

"You want to end up like him? Like the rest of them? A walking refrigerator?"

Her eyes flickered away from mine.

In jealousy and desperate impatience the walker grabbed her wrists and squeezed until sensors said her bones would break. "You do what I say," the synthesizer croaked, "or you'll be clone meat for the rest of your life. I've risked my career teaching you. If I say listen to Bach, you'll listen to Bach. Understand?"

She didn't cry out, but the pain in her face made me let her go.

Back in my observation chamber I screened the object and Network's preliminary data. It was a discoid two and a half meters wide and one thick, estimated mass 2,000 kilograms, hanging magnetically onto the Probe outside some pump bays. The Platform transmitter's wave signature came clearly through its quarter-second broadcasts of the Bach Prelude, but whatever had recorded the signal was beyond the reach of Network's instruments, inside the gray, rotten-looking rock.

Network and I debated how to proceed. The other Class A personnel were arguing with it, too, while it integrated the results of all the arguments on a decision tree that grew like a sparkling multidimensional icicle. Stone had suspended all scheduled mission activities and put our data on an urgent feed to Earth.

"Patterns in the stars, in water, the ebb and flow of civilizations, neurons—the same patterns code the whole universe at different scales, like an endless fractal. And this rock sings what my be a basic pattern, part of the Pattern."

"Your religious beliefs are fascinating, Dr. Hawk, but we are here to formulate a crash research program. The Artifact has obviously *recorded* this signal from your own transmissions; it would certainly be odd if a rock in near-interstellar space could independently generate human musical patterns."

"Odd! Isn't it *odd* that the galaxies 'independently' resemble swirls of water? That synaptic connections in the brain look like trees? That the human embryo takes the shape first of an amoeba, then an amphibian, a reptile, a bird, a monkey? That the melodies of human composers are found in DNA coding sequences? But One Pattern governs the whole; all these are its fragments, its harmonics. The Prelude is apparently one frequently recurring fragment that a human somehow heard and wrote down four hundred and fifty years ago. Who knows what it may signify? I demand that we intensify our observational effort to ascertain the significance of the Prelude pattern in large-scale space structures! I demand that we devote a major computational effort to analyzing the structure of the Prelude itself!"

The decision tree was closed a few minutes later, and I found that my eloquence had bought me an almost invisible node, corresponding to the task of playing Morrison Context-Neutral Communication Codes—in memory on every Probe in case of ETI contact—to the Artifact, one of the lowest-priority research projects. I raged at Network, tried to get Stone on link, finally gave up and watched sullenly while Network broadcast the codes at the rock, from simple to complex, at varying wavelengths, amplitudes, intervals, and transmission rates. It was ridiculous. The rock paid no attention to us, never varying its quarter-second transmission of the Bach Prelude even when we broadcast the Prelude back at it.

I kept it on visual in my darkened observation chamber, light from the holoscreens glowing on hardware and the low metal bulkhead. EVA robots passed back and forth in front of its hideous bulk like giant metal spiders in the glaring arc-lights and the blue flare of welding machines building a cage over it, prodding and scraping and drilling tiny holes, gauging its field strengths, mapping its surface, trying to scan its insides. Research results accumulated in interlocking data collation windows: the rock appeared to be an amalgam of long-chain silicates and magnetic heavy metals; thermoluminescence showed it had been cold about 4.5 billion years, roughly the age of the solar system, it showed no signs of surface or internal dynamics. The window listed not a single research task investigating the structure of the Prelude it was singing.

I opened a deep purple restricted-access menu in the air, flicked through passwords and clearances for the Class D Personnel Surveillance Channel, and gave the Adi clone's designation number.

She appeared life-size, taking a shower, atomized water beading on her muscular ivory body, making her hair a river of gold. Her wrists were cut and swollen.

My old heart pounded.

She dried herself in the airjets, taped a transcriptase precursor medication patch to her arm, and pulled on a disposable nightshirt, rolling down the cuffs to hide her wrists. Then she climbed up out of the shower stall into a dark aisle between banks of sleep-chests where clones lay stiffly in their gene-expression programming cycles. Vacant-eyed clones passed her in the aisle; I saw with pride that only she looked lonely and vulnerable.

She climbed a ladder to her sleep-chest and opened the transparent cover. Gene-expression music wafted out like cheap perfume, saccharine, catchy, and soulless, carrying selected DNA sequences to be absorbed by her sleeping subconscious and turned into expressed traits by the transcriptase now flooding her cells. As she climbed into the chest, her fingers sought a tiny slit in the plastic sleep-mat and pulled something out with a motion so slight anyone not watching for it would miss it. She turned her head from one side to the other, seeming to search for a comfortable position, deftly slipping the pea-size receivers into her ears. Then she lay stiffly, waiting fearfully for the unapproved music I sent her every sleep period to replace the machine drivel.

I sent The Bach Prelude. If Stone wouldn't spend any of Network's precious capacity researching it, I would do some research of my own. The clone trembled once as the notes started across my secured link to her receivers, then slowly relaxed in the flow of the music.

Watching her sleep, the music pouring over her like a lazy summer brook, I fell into a deep drowsiness.

How could they not see? It wasn't a rock, not a rock at all, but the mummy of some ancient space creature, its noisome, frozen smell penetrating even the video signal to my chamber. As I watched, it raised a pitted, vacuum-rotted trunk and trumpeted a nightmare scream to the stars. An EVA robot approached on some mindless scientific business; its effector cut the mummy open, exposing blind maggot-creatures chewing a horrible decay.

But behind it, beyond the arc-lights and robots, above the Probe's gleaming hull, was something even more terrible—not the playground of crashing pinwheels flying in sonorous vacuum I visited in my observational software, but the Void, the yawning eternity that made of anything finite a charnel thing like the Artifact, in which a man would die before reaching even a tenth of the way to the nearest star.

A hand touched me. My body jerked against hard metal, and I opened my eyes. Another strange sight hung before them. A man was strapped to a metal crucifix, itself a caricature of a man, with blockish feet, pipe-wrench hands, piston muscles. It embraced the man with wire tendrils that seemed to suck the life from him: he was old and withered, face gaunt, arms and legs shrunken. An angel leaned over him.

My body jerked painfully again, and the man on the crucifix jerked like a beheaded chicken, a ghastly, reflexive jolt that splayed his fingers and made his face grin like a death's-head.

The clone surveillance channel was still open, and I was watching the Adi leaning over me in my observatory.

She wore only a gray nightshirt. Her face was wild, intent.

"He talks," she whispered. She put her hands to her head and looked upward, as if words were coming out of the air. "In the music. Can't you hear?"

I had left the Bach Prelude playing over and over on audio.

She swayed to its rhythm.

"The Shining Place," she whispered. "The Shining Place." The Artifact's exhausted lump still sat behind its bars like a dead zoo animal in a cage. Above it hung the decision tree; below, a countdown was running. Its title block said ARTIFACT PHYSICAL DISAGGREGATION SEQUENCE.

"My God. They're going to cut it." The walker whined up from the reclining position it had taken when I had fallen asleep. "Decision tree-analysis summary, Artifact Physical Disaggregation," I snapped at Network. "What the hell is going on?"

Behind me, the chamber hatch whirred open and the gangway grating rang faintly as the clone went away down it.

"Based on the Artifact Task Groups' research results and value assignments, I have computed an eighty-seven-percent probability that the object contains a natural crystal structure that records and reemits electromagnetic signals by some process," said Network's precise, unhurried voice. "The second most probable option, at six percent is that the object is an accretion of frozen Cloud material surrounding a transceiver of unknown— "

"But it's only been a few hours— Why aren't we waiting for Earth Control input?"

"Signal lag to Earth is nearly three days. On direction of Research Director Stone, I am tracking approximately ten thousand objects in the region of the Cloud where we found the Artifact. Elapsed time increases their dispersion, making them more difficult to track. If we find a transceiver when we disaggregate the Artifact, the Class A Staff places an almost infinite value on being able to recover these objects, on the chance that some of them are pieces of an alien construct, perhaps a ruined ship."

"Tree input request."

"I'm sorry, Dr. Hawk, the tree is closed. As you can see, the decision is about to be implemented."

On-screen, an EVA robot stalked toward the Artifact's cage.

"Get me Stone."

"I'm sorry, Dr. Hawk, he cannot be disturbed."

The robot locked itself onto the cage. Readout windows swarmed into the air around an insert showing Dr. Tarsus, mission EVA specialist, in crimson robes, wires from her head plugged into a transducer panel. She twitched an exquisite gene-programmed shoulder; the robot extended a spinning circular saw. The countdown reached zero. The saw sank into the Artifact, gray dust pouring from one end and slithering away along the hull like a snake in the vacuum.

Suddenly there was someone in the insert with Tarsus. A wild figure in a nightshirt. It yanked a handful of wires out of the transducer. Tarsus's body jerked, and her beautiful face twisted convulsively.

A burst of horrible, dense music came across-link.

The clone clawed at her head and screamed.

My body arched backward against the walker, teeth clenched, hands clawing, eyeballs rolled up in their sockets.

"Thank you, Network," came Stone's patient voice. "Dr. Tarsus, may I suggest that we proceed with the cutting sequence as soon as you can reconnect. We are several minutes behind schedule."

As soon as I could see again, the robot's saw was sinking back into the Artifact.

The observation chamber flipped over. Unsecured furniture crashed down the floor to the wall, the quadriplegic walker leaping over them to grab the edge of the chamber hatch, now on the ceiling. The lights went out, and there was a metal howl I could feel through the walker's arms.

Blank, turbulent darkness shuddered and rattled around me.

"Network," I said.

A small emergency screen popped open in front of me. It showed the Artifact's cage stretching upward like spaghetti, the Artifact straining against it a meter off the hull.

"By some unknown means of propulsion – " Network began.

A cage bar snapped with a bang, and the Probe lurched sickeningly.

"Transmit the Corrente from Bach's Partita No. 1 in B-flat major for clavier," my synthesizer droned.

I was still Artifact Communication Task Coordinator. Music sounded through the blare of alarms and howl of metal, like a breath of air from a summer day on Earth, quiet and pensive.

The Probe shuddered. Weight and direction evaporated, junk clattering back and forth in the dark chamber, but the shrieking of metal had stopped, and the Artifact was resting back on the hull among the twisted and broken bars of its cage. Bach's music floated down serene and bright, like sunlight through trees.

At the end of a gangway with only the black glare of emergency lights, a clone stepped out of the shadows.

"Class A personnel are confined to life-support areas," he said.

The walker banged his head into the wall. He slid onto the floor.

I fumbled down a long ladder, crackling blue of a welding machine below sending shadows and acrid smoke up the narrow shaft. The groan of saws and bang of riveters on the hull came through the metal. At the bottom, the welder jerked away from a twisted beam to let me pass. A hatch opened into a dark bay with humming refrigeration units on both sides. On the metal decking the clone lay on a disposable pallet.

"Adi," my cold machine voice said.

She turned toward me in the flickering shadows of the welder. One of her eyes was dark with blood.

The hum of the refrigeration units ate up silence.

"Searching," she murmured, ". . . lost."

The words brought something over me—a vision again of the Void, endless chasm of night through which a being ran in terror and loneliness, looking for a glimmer of light.

My body stirred on the walker, whining like an animal.

"What is it?" I asked her. "The Artifact?"

But her eyes were closed, and she seemed not to hear.

With a faint whir, a module floated into the bay. White static cascaded from it, hardening into Research Director Stone's robed figure standing like a colossal angel in the dark.

"Dr. Hawk," it said. "I need you."

Its light showed gently floating clouds of blue smoke from the welder.

"It *moved,* Hawk," Stone went on with sudden incredulous awe. "It actually jumped up off the hull. It's *intelligent,* Hawk, or at least interactive."

"This clone is damaged," I said.

"Of course it's damaged," said Stone. "They are gene-programmed to respond to Network's security music with massive cerebral hemorrhage. Network says you sent the music that ended the Artifact transient."

"I played the Prelude for the clone. It put her into some kind of telepathic or empathic contact with the Artifact," I said.

"You talked to it," said Stone. "How did you know – "

"She needs emergency surgery for the hemorrhage," I said.

"Dr. Hawk, we are wasting valuable time. I will send you another Adi-series clone at once. Now – "

"I want this one. Fixed up, right now. *Now.*"

Stone studied me. "I will have her transported to the autosurgery bay as soon as you tell me how you talked to it."

I thought about that. Then I said: "Imagine you are roaming through space, searching the endless static for an intelligent signal, roaming for years—millennia, maybe. One day you hear a signal— you rush toward the source, shouting it back into the darkness, but now there is only static and the echo of your own shouts. Then someone you can't see or hear tries to cut you open. . . .

"When the thing moved, I remembered that all the patterns that code the universe are harmonics of the One Pattern. *The thing can only hear our music,* Stone, simply because it is coded out of the same basic patterns deep down, just as everything is. To it our other, less primordial signals are just static.

"So I sent it more music. I sent the Corrente because it has the same feeling as the Prelude, of quiet joy, release, but is different enough that it could not be mistaken for an echo."

Stone's face froze, so that I saw I was talking to a timeshare. He came back: "Your analysis reminds us that we possess an excellent tool for encoding information musically—I refer to the Probe's gene-expression music software. If your theory is correct, this software could be adapted from its function of packaging DNA sequences in melodic forms to encoding Morrison Context-Neutral Communication Codes in musical sequences perhaps recognizable to the Entity." He froze again for a minute. "We note that such an adaptation will likely require Network's full capacity. I regret that, in the name of science, I must withdraw my offer of surgery for the clone."

The walker smashed the transceiver module into the wall, Stone dying in a shower of sparks and shattered plastic. But his voice still issued tinnily from its remains.

"Be reasonable, Dr. Hawk—surely you knew that months of feeding the clone that junk-DNA music garbage would unbalance it. Yes, we were monitoring you. I told the others to leave you alone, that you've been an eccentric from the first, brilliant but mad. You were the one who was never going to listen to 'machine music,' even to prevent nerve damage from your neural interface surgery." He sighed. "Have you ever regretted that decision?"

Hanging over a precipice of black in the glaring arc-lights, the Entity and the clone now huddled together, the clone's face calm and intent, as if listening to music in a dream, her cheek pressed against the Entity's noisome bulk.

A metal creak woke me groggily from the doze of old age. It was dark. A refrigeration-unit door was open and two clones leaned over the Adi, getting hold of her limp legs and shoulders, lifting her.

"What is it?" I droned, heart pounding. "Are they going to give her the surgery?"

"She's brain-dead," said the clone carrying her legs as they shuffled her into the unit. "She's going to refuse compaction."

Her face was calm and intent, as it had been in my dream.

I went up onto the Platform. I had no observational allocation. The brick terrace construct I had installed in the observational software to keep me from transition vertigo was dead silent. I looked up into frozen heavens, at wheels of light so distant their unimaginable speed was immovable stillness. Below them a time series display showed the Adi clone's EEG, serrated lines gradually flattening into the repose of death.

Hours or days later, Network said in the dark: "Dr. Hawk, we are having a substantive exchange with the Entity using our modified gene-expression music program. It is asking illogical questions about your Bach music. We have had to abandon our decision tree. Research Director Stone asks in the name of science that you assist the Ad Hoc Committee on Entity Communication."

In the name of science. . .

Looking up at the stars, I saw again the Void, cold endless desert of night through which a being searched, alone.

Her cheek pressed against its noisome bulk –

After a long time, I said: "All right."

The hideous hump of the Entity appeared, glowing eerily against the terrace brick. Alphanumerics below it spelled out: Thank you/Q: Existence [Music] Co-spatial location Co-time Existence [?]/ Go Ahead.

"The Ad Hoc Committee is on link with it," said Network. "We are trying to determine what it is saying."

The message on the screen was replaced by: Thank you/ Restate [Q: Existence [Music] Co-spatial location Co-time Existence {?]/ Go Ahead.

"'Music' refers to the Bach Prelude," said Network.

Thank you/ Q: Spacial Location Present-time [Music] Specify/ Go Ahead, said the Entity.

"The Ad Hoc Committee is proceeding under the assumption, based on various tests, that it has properly assimilated Morrison Code grammar. If that is true, it seems to be asking us to identify *the present location of the Bach music.*"

The Ad Hoc Committee said: Thank you / Q: Spatial Location Present-time [You] Specify / Go Ahead.

"If it specifies its own location, we may obtain a reference for what it means by that term."

"Let me hear its raw signal," I said. "Its music."

There was a pause, and then the Entity's transmission came, a strange fugue form, echoing, deep, unearthly sad. I knew what it meant even before Network's computers translated it into the Morrison message: Thank you / A: Spatial Location Present-time [Self] Unknown / Go Ahead.

Lost.

Searching, the Adi clone had said.

"Ask it what it is searching for," I said.

There was a pause while Network cleared the message with the Ad Hoc Committee.

Thank you / Q: Substantive identity [?] Search [You] / Go Ahead.

Network's computerized music signal was compact, elegant, formatted in the style of Bach, but superficial, sterile, like all their machine pablum.

Thank you / A: [Music] = Precursor [— The rest of the Entity's answer was incomprehensible to the computer, but the music of it spoke to me: distant as mountains at the purple edge of vision, as the memory of a childhood home, strange and yet familiar as a dream of the next world.

The Shining Place. The Shining Place, the clone had said.

The Ad Hoc Committee sent: Thank you / Q: Time duration Search [You] Specify / Go Ahead.

The Entity's answer made me sick, the devouring maw of Time, the Void's monstrous bride, yawning before me.

There was a long pause.

Thank you / S: Source [Music] = Substantive identity [Entity [Derivation [Ourselves]]] = Definitional identity [Bach] / Go Ahead, said the Committee.

"Since the Entity evidently values the Prelude, the Committee feels that identification of its source as a human should instill a sense of our importance," said Network.

Thank you / Q: Spacial location Present-time [Bach] Specify / Go Ahead, said the Entity.

Pause.

A: [Bach] Interface [Self] / Go Ahead, said the Entity.

"It wants to speak with J. S. Bach," said Network.

The Committee transmitted: Thank you / A: Affirmative / Stand by.

I was staring over the edge of the terrace at the stars glittering below when feet chafed stone steps in the silence.

Across the terrace came a plump man in a dark, archaic suit with breeches and high stockings, many small buttons down the front of his long, plain jacket. He had a double chin and thick lips, a high forehead and a large, fleshy nose.

"Excuse me, sir," he said. His voice was strong but restrained, proper, hard to read. "I am Cantor Bach. Are you the person who wishes to speak with me?"

He had been ginned up out of two billion Bach stylistic rules from the Probe's gene-expression music software, tied into an AI personality simulation programmed with all known Bach biographical data.

I said nothing, but Network overrode, and I found my nondescript observation-body answering: "The traveler who wishes to meet with you will be here in a few minutes."

The simulation nodded. Its eyes were grave, abstracted, as if thinking about things far away.

It glanced toward the edge of the terrace. "You have a commanding view here. May I – ?" It went to the low wall and stood looking over doubtfully. This mountain is so high," it said finally, "that some of the stars appear to be below us."

There was absolute silence.

After a while it raised a hand and pointed to a faint constellation.

"Look there," it said.

In the middle of the terrace Network had electronically placed a clavichord. The Bach simulation walked to it absently and touched the keys, hesitantly at first, then more quickly, a simple, echoing melody forming under its fingers, strangely familiar, like something I had heard snatches of in the chaos of the stars.

"They have been set in a joyous dance," it murmured as the music died away.

I kneaded my hands to get rid of a sudden chill. "Yes. Yes," I said hoarsely. "The One Pattern. She has gone into it, to merge with it." Then the terrible thought came, the one I had been hiding for so many years. "But why—why is it that when you listen for it, you hear only chaos, only entropy?"

The simulation studied me gravely.

Feet chafed stone steps, and a figure was coming slowly across the terrace, wrapped in white robes. It was a thin, old man, bald, hawklike face wrinkled but eyes huge and clear, like a baby's eyes. If the Committee's programming had gone right, it was the Entity's communication channel tied into a human body construct that would not look too strange to the Bach simulation.

"The young girl," I shouted to the old man construct in desperation. "Where is she? Where has she gone? To the One Pattern?" But Network changed my words to a quiet: "This is Cantor Bach, the source of the music about which you inquired."

The Bach simulation put out its hand, murmuring something polite, but the construct just looked at the hand, then slowly raised its eyes to study the face. It brought its own knobby hand up to its chest. "Lost," it said, staring into the Bach's eyes. "Lost."

The Bach returned its look curiously and intently.

"Searching," said the construct, hand still on its chest.

"It's a trick," I told it dully. "They're distracting you with this phony meeting while they strengthen your cage and decide how to get you back to Earth." But my voice said to the Bach: "A piece of music you wrote fascinates him. He believes you can help him find something he is looking for."

"Ah," said the simulation. "What piece of music?"

"A prelude for clavier." Network hummed a few bars.

"Yes," said the construct, eyes still fixed on the Bach.

The Bach sat at the clavichord, and the glittering music flowed from its fingers like the sun rising over the terrace.

The construct broke into excited, garbled speech in which I caught the words "Shining Place."

"Shining Place," repeated the Bach simulation.

"Yes." The Entity construct stared at it expectantly.

Network cleared my throat. "The Prelude appears to resemble something he has been searching for. He seems to regard it as some kind of *precursor* to this other thing."

The Bach simulation touched the keys again and a gentle music grew, like flowers bobbing in a breeze.

"That is the next Prelude I wrote, if that is what you mean," it said. "I wrote if for the birth of my daughter Elisabeth."

The construct leaned forward, hands squeezed together hard. "Precursor," it said.

The simulation's eyes burned at it, as if trying to read its thoughts. Finally it said hesitantly: "There is a sound one hears sometimes, when one is very still—like the seed of music unfolding in the mind. Like the precursor of music itself, if that is what you mean. It is as though the mind attunes itself with the Thoughts of some great Mind, which are the patterns that make this world."

The Entity construct just stared.

"No one can play that music for you, my friend," the simulation told it. "You must listen for it yourself, with an inner ear." It glanced at me. "If you cannot hear it, perhaps you are listening for the wrong thing. Perhaps you are expecting something grand, mighty. But this music is simple, as simple and familiar as grass and wind and sunlight. It is the music at the basis of your own being."

There was absolute silence.

"Listen for it now. Listen!"

In the silence, at the very edge of hearing, I imagined there was a sound, very faint, like my own thoughts stirring.

And out of the corner of my eye I caught a tiny movement, as if the flat EEG readout of the Adi clone had ticked up ever so slightly.

The Entity construct moved first. It went toward the stone steps. After a pause, I followed curiously. The Bach came after me. Over the edge of the terrace, the steps faded into deep, silent vertigo. I could hardly make myself put my feet on them, but the Bach was behind me, and the construct leading, and as soon as we had climbed down a few they were gone, and we stood on rocky, slanting ground near a mountain's top, cloud mist blowing in a fresh wind, lit pearly bright. I stared, amazed that Network had simulated such a place.

The music seemed to waft up the mountain from somewhere in the mist. The old man was hurrying stiffly down the slope. We followed.

When we reached it, I saw that the music came from a deep, fast-running brook with rocky banks, bubbling and gurgling, sparkling with light of all colors.

Bach helped the old man into the water, holding him by the hand as his bony legs cautiously felt their way down the bank, white robe pulled by the fast current, more and more of his shape diffused and scattered by the water, until Bach leaned far over, and the old man's head went under in the middle of the brook.

Bach let him go. He was swept quickly away downstream into the bright mist.

Looking down into the rushing water, I saw that another shape lay there, a lissome shape white and golden, one rippling arm stretched out, holding precariously to some root or water plant as it slept.

Bach helped me into the water. I stretched my free hand toward the shape, trembling with fear and eagerness, because now the EEG readout hanging in the air spiked clear and strong in time with the music of the brook.

As soon as I touched the water I remembered that none of this—the brook, the mountaintop, the mist, Bach himself—was real; it was all a mirage, an image constructed in my brain from the patterns fed me by the machines of the Probe. The only real thing was the music itself, the raw signal, now dancing and shimmering around me, tingling and cold. *But it's not the Probe signal,* I realized. *I've somehow gotten plugged into the Entity's signal.*

I went under the rushing water, and as the stream of signals flowed through me, I realized more than I had before: I saw that the machines of the Probe, the Probe itself, the spaces it wandered through, the stars, my body, the Earth, were all illusions, images constructed in my mind like twinkling reflections on the surface of deep currents. The only thing real was the signal that coded them, the patterns I interpreted as--

Music.

All the rest was washed away.

Alarms blared. The metal of the walker was hard and cold, the observation chamber dark. A confusion of voices babbled on-link.

On-screen, the Entity lay tumbled against the bars of its cage, no longer clinging to the hull. Readouts showed its electromagnetic field strengths registering zero.

An insert showed strongly spiked EEG waves.

"He's gone," said a croaking, bubbling voice in my ear. "He touched the Pattern, and went free." I turned my head with difficulty to see who was talking—and banged my cheek on the walker's head brace.

Something was wriggling in the corner of my vision. It took me a minute of staring to see that it was my hand—my hand!— struggling to be free of the walker's straps.

"Network." My atrophied voice scraped my throat, "Open Refrigeration Unit 19. And get some med techs to me and the clone if you want samples of activated DNA sequences responsible for global central nervous system regeneration.

"And put Stone on-link; put them all on-link. I have seen the end of our search! The One Pattern resonates *inside us* as music! We don't need to fly through space! We can find the Pattern now! We must build machines to amplify it, chemicals to quiet our minds so we can hear it! I demand that we initiate a crash project! I demand – !"

The Lord of Sleep

In the middle of his shift, Alex Stane's eyes started to close. A whirlpool of darkness opened at his feet, and the dingy airport departure lounge roared around him.

He heaved himself out of one of the hundred plastic chairs and lurched toward the men's bathroom, hoping no drug runner stoolies or airport security people were watching, banged into the doors of two occupied toilet stalls before he found an empty one, slumped onto the seat heavily, and snapped the lock with trembling fingers.

Somnophobia, they called it: aversion to sleep. It and the resulting psychoses were why they made sniffers retire after five years, to nice desk jobs where you could dodder away the rest of your career dreaming of the jolt, the high singing in your brain, the incredible waking –

Stane's trembling fingers drew spray disinfectant and the tiny, precious canister of rhinoneurotransmitter from his jacket pocket. The disinfectant stung the roof of his mouth as he doused his implanted catheter, then popped its outer cap with a fingernail. He opened his mouth wide enough for two dentists and snapped in the neurotransmitter canister, feeling the sinus pressure as it fired into his rhinencephalon. Then he snapped it back out and capped the catheter again.

At first there was nothing.

Then there was everything, the smell images of all times and places blindingly superimposed.

That faded like a sunset and waking came, expanding in the way you never get used to, like a wide, rippleless lake glowing the evening, opening up within and around him so that he seemed to sense the things going on beyond the walls, the abundant life outside the bathroom, in the airport, the vast evening beyond, all over the vast planet Earth.

The man he saw in the bathroom mirror coming out of the toilet stall was tall and thin, with large, bony hands, hair slicked back from craggy, stained features, feverish eyes.

That man strode down the airport concourse now with vigorous steps, carrying the empty briefcase that made him look like a business traveler. He would lose his job if airport security caught him falling asleep in the middle of his shift; that meant he wasn't getting his mandatory eight hours per night, which meant the somnophobia was getting him, the rhinoneurotransmitter interfering with the buildup of gamma amino butyric acid in his reticular activating system, where sleep came from. He was sure some of his coworkers suspected; everyone knew stories of sniffers faking their papers to keep going after the mandatory retirement period, which was the main safeguard against the somno. He didn't care what they thought as long as they left him alone. Alone to work in the clarity of the rhino, far from their murky, petrified world.

The vast, worn smell of the terminal came to him now finely disaggregated, the cracked, greenish marble floor, the stuffy, echoing space up to the vaulted ceiling three stories above, half-dead plants in their tubs by the tall windows bluish now with dusk, candy and sour newsprint in the newsstand, rotten teeth and nicotine lungs of a janitor slowly sweeping cigarette butts, puffs of oily jet fuel smoke –

In all those smells something stood out. Something distant yet crystal clear, a cold, electric smell he had been trained to recognize years ago, wafting down the C concourse.

Stane waited in line for the metal detectors, then strode hungrily down the endless, jostling corridor roaring with voices, flight announcements, footsteps, fixing now on the frayed smell of a flight attendant on NoDoz, the high, ever-present buzz of caffeine, the sour, flaming smell of alcohol, the bitter spoor of tranquilizers. But the electric snowflake smell got stronger until he got to the crowded, breath-heavy air of Gate 12. In one of the rows of seats a small, tense man in a dark suit sat with a briefcase and overnight bag. The cocaine spoor fairly sparked around him.

If they could get you to shadow a suspect smeared with cocaine cologne strong enough to attract all the police dogs and novice sniffers in the airport, the real smuggler would get through. Stane walked casually back to the concourse. This was what they paid him for, and why the airport security people closed their eyes to all the little signs that he was a non-sleeper: because he could distinguish smells a novice would confuse, and knew the drug-runners' tricks.

Sure enough, at Gate 19, departing for Chicago, a dumpy housewife type stood in line for economy class with just a twinkle of snowflake scent around her fat carry-ons under the heavy, orchid smell of her perfume.

Stane walked away down the concourse, speed-dialing a number on his cellphone.

When it answered, he said: "Gate 19, female, 5'6", brown, blue, 190, red flowered blouse and black stretch pains, two sky blue bags," and hung up.

He didn't wait to see the plainclothes detectives go into the departure lounge. He had smelled something else, very faint.

Heroin, it said to him first, then opium. But it wasn't either, he realized as he breathed the potent calmness of it in the crowded concourse; there was a warmth to it, an aliveness the opiates didn't have. He walked in the direction of the higher-numbered gates only to have it fade, went back quickly toward the terminal, fascinating whiffs twining through the thick spoor of the airport. For a minute he was sure the excitement in the smell signaled methamphetamine, then LSD; but the screaming tension of the stimulants and hallucinogens was missing, replaced by a flowery calmness, the calmness that had made him first think of opiates. A designer drug? But there was a wholesome, almost sweaty smell to it, a smell you didn't get from the laboratory; like something that grew out of the ground in the sun and rain.

He went down a narrow escalator to a small ground for floor departure lounge whose worn burgundy carpet was patched with duct tape. Two dozen people waited for a flight to Twin Forks, delayed by snow. The spoor was so strong there that it made Stane dizzy.

He was sure now that it was something new. It was coming from the row of seats by the wall, near the embarkation door. He slouched over and pretended to look at flight booklets ranged on a stand.

A woman sat near the embarkation door. She had the kind of long, straight blonde hair that had been out of style for decades, with bangs that crept into blue eyes wide and fascinatingly blank, as if she were blind. She wore a short white dress, and her legs, rounded but long and lithe, were crossed, and her hands crossed over them, knotted together.

With a shock Stane realized that the spoor came not from the woman's small suitcase, but from *her*, out of her pores, on her breath. The few parts per million of it in the air made him drunk; he tried to imagine what it must be doing to her.

He strolled over to the check-in counter where a beefy ticket agent chewed gum and went through a list on a clipboard. Stane showed him his Narcotics Detection & Interdiction ID in an airline ticket folder.

"You have room on this flight?" he asked. The agent nodded. "Lady in white," Stane said. "Give me her information when I board."

Out by the escalator, he called airport and ND&I. "Emergency surveillance, Northwest flight 962, Twin Forks, departure immediately."

The flight announcement came before they could ask too many questions. He could have requested a surveillance detail or called her in to Twin Forks, but already he didn't want to let her out of his sight. And he had a perfectly legitimate reason to follow her; it was part of his job to identify new drugs.

The lounge was almost empty when he got back, the open embarkation door letting in the shriek of engines and the choking stench of jet fuel over the high, far scent of winter. He studied the

copy of the woman's ticket the agent handed him along with his
boarding pass. Her name was Suzanne Telse, and she was going to
be late for her Twin Forks connection to Minneapolis.

Stane was the last person off the plane in Twin Forks. The rhino
he had snorted was wearing off, space closing in so that now all
of him seemed cramped inside the modern, new-smelling arrival
lounge, shapes of things around him torpid and dark. Snow fell
heavily outside the windows. The Departures screen inclining
from the ceiling showed only two flights, both delayed, the one to
Minneapolis listed at Gate 6. When Stane got there, half a dozen
people were arguing with the agent at the check-in counter, waving
their ticket folders. The woman was sitting in an empty row of
seats, staring out at the snow.

Stane needed a snort, but the sight of the woman – her smell
was almost hidden from him now – fascinated him. He sank into
a chair and watched her.

Soon the agent announced over the intercom to the nearly
empty airport: "Ladies and gentlemen, we are sorry to announce
that flight 714 to Minneapolis has now been canceled due to snow.
We regret any inconvenience this may cause you. If you would like
to make overnight arrangements here in Twin Forks, please see
me at Gate 6."

The woman in white didn't move, made no sign she had heard.
Soon she and Stane were the only passengers in the lounge.

Stane went to the ticket counter. He felt heavy as lead, old as the
rotten stones of ancient cities. He licked his dry mouth. "Is there
an airport hotel?"

The agent was quickly tallying tickets against a list. She didn't
look at him. "Yes, sir, but I'm sorry to say it's filled up."

The hotel connected to the modernistic terminal building
through a glass atrium. After Stane flashed his ND&I ID, the front
desk man canceled somebody's reservation and put him in a room
on the fourth floor. Back at Gate 6, the woman was alone in the
brightly lit departure lounge; the agent had taken her pile of tickets

and gone. The Arrival and Departure screens were blank. Stane sat directly across from the woman. She gave no sign that she noticed him.

Behind her the lounge suddenly multiplied itself, abruptly stretching out in all directions, row after row of vinyl seats on gray carpeting as far as he could see, as if mirrors had been set up on the walls, reflecting the lounge in unending perspective. An infinite-regress hallucination, a kind known to be associated with somnophobia. Stane had had them before, but it was still disturbing. His hands gripped the chair arms and he concentrated on the woman in front of him, on the paleness of her hair, the solidity of her shoulders turned so she could look out the window. In a few minutes the far rows of seats got hazy, then disappeared, bringing the lounge back to normal.

He took a deep breath. "Miss?"

She didn't answer, didn't move.

"Miss?"

He stood up awkwardly, took two steps and touched her shoulder.

She looked at him, blue eyes unexpectedly steady.

"You're going to Minneapolis?"

"Yes." Her voice was soft, husky, maybe from tiredness.

"The flight is canceled. Are you going to sit here all night?"

She shifted her shoulders then, to face him. "Do you have a better idea?"

✳ ✳ ✳ ✳

The hotel lobby was empty as Stane carried her bag into the elevator. She didn't look at him as they rode to the fourth floor, or look away. He might have been the bellboy.

The room was small, with one bed and indirect lighting. Stane put her bag on the low dresser. The room and hall outside were very silent even though it was before midnight.

She went into the bathroom and locked the door.

Stane sat on the bed and snorted. As he put the disinfectant and rhinoneurotransmitter away and the room got big as a football field, darkness and silence outside flinging away to endlessness, he woke up enough to realize that the woman hadn't seemed surprised to be offered a bed in his room. Was she that used to being picked up? Or was she some kind of newfangled decoy? Had a few hundred pounds of cocaine or heroin gone through his airport after she had made him drunk with her smell?

It was creeping under the bathroom door now, twining sinuously through the hotel odors of dust, cleansers, and stale cigarette smoke like a tendril of jasmine. It was *alive*, Stane's freshly primed rhinencephalic synapses told him, the smell not of a drug but of a metabolic process. Something was going on in the woman's body, something incredible.

More tendrils joined the first, spreading and flowering, filling the room thick as a jungle –

– turning to tongues of flame, licking him, whispering with hot breath of lavender sweat and jasmine blood –

He stumbled to the bathroom door and leaned against it.

"Hey." His voice was a faraway drunken sob. "Hey. . ."

The door opened, almost spilling him onto the floor.

The woman stood in a bright background of white tile, naked. Her pale hair fell over milky shoulders, plump breasts, her body smoothly curved, palms of long fingered hands facing him like a Madonna's. Her eyes were empty blue tunnels of infinite regress.

His trembling hands reached for her.

Then it was strange.

She retreated from him. She slipped sideways in a direction he didn't recognize, and the shift made her body seem flat, as if a movie of her was being projected on a tilted sheet of rock crystal.

He stood dumbfounded. He put out trembling hands. They touched the cool tile of the bathroom wall.

She was still an arm's-length away, her body like glass filled with light. An angel's body, more beautiful than any human's, hands held out to him, face lustful and mocking, burning him with its insane smell –

He didn't wake up; he hadn't been asleep. Static cleared enough for him to realize he existed, and gradually to remember who he was, and finally where he was. He lay naked on a disheveled bed, sheets damp with sweat, gray light leaking around the edges of heavy curtains. He was alone. Leftover static made grainy the outlines of the lamp, a table, a low dresser. The bed under him felt grainy as sand, and his ears hissed. It was like a bad rhino hangover.

Had he snorted that much? He couldn't remember. His head spun with confused memories, trying to separate reality from what must have been somno hallucination.

He went into the bathroom and splashed water on his face, and in the mirror it looked wild, skeletal, like the faces of the old-time sniffers at the airports where he had done his apprenticeship, before the regulations got tight, when you could work as long you wanted without sleep, go on snorting and waking until –

What had finally happened to them? he wondered. Most had dropped out of sight sooner or later, no one knowing exactly how or why, or much caring. The old-timers had joked about old Telsa coming to get them, taking them away one by one –

Telsa –

He stared at himself in the mirror, thunderstruck. Susan Telsa, the first and most famous experimental sniffer, who had built up an enormous sleep deficit and disappeared while on surveillance, apparently after going into somnophobic psychosis, who had raved about somnophobic sensory distortions being "transition phenomena" leading to a "deeper level of reality" – But it was just a fairy tale, a joke, at best a metaphor: the old lady who comes to take the old sniffers away to the land beyond sleep –

The names – Suzanne Telse and Susan Telsa – had to be a coincidence.

Yet wasn't there a resemblance between the woman in white and Telsa's early pictures?

The airport was full of people again, and plows had the runways mostly cleared of snow. The woman's spoor was cold, but still faintly detectable.

It was strongest at Gate 8.

Stane flashed his ND&I ID at the agent behind the check-in

counter. Suzanne Telse had been on the last flight out of Gate 8, to Des Moines.

The four p.m. flight to Des Moines was almost empty. Stane sat by a window with his eyes closed, body exhausted but brain wide open on a bright, silent space, the roar of the jets, buffeting of the plane, even it's harsh, recycled smells distant and vague.

The woman had done something to him last night, he was sure, though he could remember almost nothing. It was hard to describe, like a hole punched in his brain through which something poured, something strange. Was that why he was following her again instead of turning her over to a surveillance team? he wondered vaguely. To find out what she had done? Or was there more? Had his pursuit of the drug runners – and especially of her – taken on in his rhino-deteriorated brain the trappings of a bizarre courtship, the only substitute he could now experience after having held human intimacy at a distance for so long? But it was strange – he had never had an appetite for women before, or for anything in this world except the rhino.

The Des Moines airport was small and rundown. The woman's smell was there, but faint, almost undetectable, and on the cracked sidewalk outside the 1950s terminal building where the taxis lined up under a gray sky, it was gone, scattered over the town by a cold, fitful wind.

But she was there, in Des Moines.

Stane got a room at a rundown motel and called Washington ND&I. Sam Martinelli, the day supervisor, was a sniffer himself, retired six years, his catheter surgically removed in accordance with the law. "Where are you?"

"Des Moines. I forgot to check in last night. Sorry."

"Come in, Stane. We're sending you a replacement."

"That won't work. This is some kind of new designer drug, and someone who hasn't smelled it before could miss it."

"Your auth is suspended, Stane. We're going to do a neuro on you. Come in."

An ice flower blossomed in Stane's stomach. "Why?"

"Erratic behavior. Don't worry. If you're clean – "

Stane hung up. After a few seconds his cell rang. He ignored it, ignored it when it rang again a few minutes later.

He lay on the hollow motel bed. The room smelled of oil and car exhaust almost as strongly as the parking lot. So it was the end of the line, suddenly, just like that. If he went in for the neuro test they would scrape enough rhino off his synapses to fill a 55 gallon drum. If he didn't go in he would be cut off, without even the step-down program to keep away the withdrawal psychosis. And if he got through withdrawal there was nothing on the other side but the foul, half-lit hell of this world without rhino, and at the end of it death.

He weighed his rhino canister in his hand. It had been almost full at the beginning of his shift the night before; good for about two dozen more snorts.

At his current rate, he had enough rhino for three days.

Maybe enough time to find the woman.

✳ ✳ ✳ ✳

"Drive around," he told a cabbie. "I want to see all parts of the city."

"Don't talk," he said when the cabbie started to give him a travelogue in his friendly Midwestern twang. After that they drove in silence, Stane's window open, his head singing with a recent snort, through the winter-brown shrubbery and cooking smells of residential neighborhoods, the cold, clean wind of an expressway, the echoing concrete of a business district, perfumed office workers like plastic flowers stuck in Styrofoam, the overpowering wild spoor of a cattle-yard. By evening Stane had paid the cabbie $500 in hourly installments.

His government-issue sleeping pills were back in Washington, but by this time he shouldn't have needed them. He'd been awake almost 100 hours; even the somnophobia didn't let you fight the neurochemical changes leading to sleep forever – at least not until you were a hopeless psychotic. But the hole the woman had left in his brain seemed to be growing bigger, more and more of the strange wakefulness streaming in, bringing now one and now another of his senses into sharp focus. He lay all night and studied the topography of the low motel ceiling, listening to harmonics and overtones he had never heard before in the boom of the TV in the next room.

Until, without warning, long past midnight, he remembered something.

– the woman's wet, satin skin flickering unsteadily on his hands, her straining face and sweat-tangled hair, sweaty lips moving, talking intensely –

Whispering: "I come for those who reject sleep."

His heart pounded. He tried to pry his subconscious open further, to remember more, but it slipped away, the sudden sensory image fading.

All the next day and late into the night he rode, sniffing, and when he got back to the motel he'd been without sleep for five days. Static hissed quietly like drizzle from the ceiling. He lay on the bed and tried to close his eyes but they opened again, moving restlessly around the room. Then suddenly the static went away as if shut off with a switch, and he lay in an infinitely regressed space, the cigarette burnt dresser and peeling mirror, room door with the plastic disclaimer notices, the tiny dark bathroom repeating themselves as far as he could see in every direction.

And the woman astride him, whispering through swollen lips: " . . . the next world . . ."

Then she and the infinite regress were gone, replaced again by static.

The next night he caught her smell.

He'd been riding all day. His rhino was almost gone. The static was much stronger now; a fog of it blew outside the cab, obscuring everything. But through hissing darkness her spoor came.

What is this place? He asked the cabbie.

Convention Center, the cabbie said. Sure you're all right, buddy?

Take me closer.

The light was deep, dusky blue, and stretching away on both sides was asphalt with streetlights and hedges. Parking lots.

Stane got out onto still, new-smelling sidewalk. A huge shape grew up beyond. The woman's spoor came from it in faint snatches mixed up with other smells.

There was a glass door in an endless concrete wall. He pushed through it.

Pinkish arc lights a hundred feet up made underwater daylight for thousands of people milling in an ocean of sweat, breath, food, plastic, metal, wood. There was a roar of voices, music, PA system announcements. The woman's smell pierced it all like lightning.

He tried to be careful, following the smell blindly through roaring pink soup, but he stepped on toes, blundered into people, tables, and booths. Somewhere in the midst of it all she stood, her blind eyes the only things he could see clearly in the static and pandemonium. He felt the round firmness of her arm.

Somehow he found a door. Out in blue night he pulled her along a sidewalk, then out into the parking lot. The sky was clear now, the full moon floating low above streetlights and hedges like a huge Chinese lantern. Everything was suddenly quiet and clear, the static gone.

"I found you," Stane said hoarsely.

She laughed mockingly. "Congratulations." Yet it flashed on him that finding her in Des Moines and among the camouflaging smells of the Convention Center had been some kind of test.

"Who are you?" he asked her. "What did you do to me in Twin Forks?"

"What you begged me to do."

"And what was that?"

"I waked you. Did you like it?"

"Meaning what? Why can't I sleep?"

"You yourself rejected sleep."

In sudden fury he yanked her toward him. "Explain it to me so I can understand it."

Her head went back, mouth a little open, eyes relaxed and empty, without malice or excitement.

Later he remembered her saying: "You were already a little awake because of your artificial sense enhancement, awake enough to find me. You were weary of the epiphenomenal world, begging for the Waking. I helped you because once I was like you, and one of the Awakened Ones helped me.

"Once you are Awake there is no more unconsciousness. When the epiphenomenal world is shut out, as in sleep, you live in the underlying world, which mortals see only vaguely, in dreams. There is no more sleep, not even death. In Twin Forks I withdrew a little into the underlying world; to touch me, taste me, you had to follow . . ."

They were resting on a bench under the greenish radiance of a streetlight as dawn tinted the horizon pink and yellow, in a part of the lot far from the Convention Center, where there were no cars.

"There is no death in the underlying world," said the woman. "Death is the tool of the God who rules the epiphenomenal world, who creates the pageant by means of forgetting. Think of what you could see if you didn't have to die, if you were so free of sleep you could go to your next life remembering the last, keep going without ever forgetting, until eternity for you was one long day. There are those who are so free from sleep that they never die. Our refined metabolisms can be detected by sufficiently awakened senses, such as smell. We go from life to life without forgetting, and awaken others who are ready, who come to us, who reject sleep . . ."

There was a discrete crackle of tires on pavement as a long black limousine with mirrored windows turned the corner at a hedge and came slowly toward them.

The woman stood up. "You're on your own now," she said.

Stane stood up too, uneasily. "What do you – ?"

The limousine slowed, almost stopped, and the rear door opened. Hands extending from the dim interior helped the women in; Stane caught a last flash of her long, lithe leg before the door slammed and the car was gliding away.

Panic hit him. "Hey!" He jumped toward the door, missing the handle.

The limousine began to pick up speed.

"Hey!" Stane screamed, his voice flat in the vast lot. He sprinted desperately, getting close enough for his hand to slide off the trunk, then tumbling on asphalt. When he struggled up, hands bleeding and suit torn, the car was a hundred feet away, gliding off with maddening aplomb, mirrored rear window glinting in the strengthening yellow light. He watched until it was a tiny black spot between the hedges that telescoped into the distance. Then he turned back toward the Convention Center.

There was no Convention Center.

He looked around.

A mild dawn breeze rustled the hedges, and a streetlight near him swayed a little, creaking. There was no other sound. There was nothing in sight in any direction but benches and hedges and streetlights.

Stane fought down panic. He moved carefully toward the nearest bench and sat down to wait until the infinite regress hallucination when away.

It didn't go away.

In an hour the sun was warm, the sky clear, cloudless blue. There was no sign of the static that should accompany the transition back to normal perception.

Stane was trying to think. His ND&I training said infinite regress hallucinations were temporary. But apprehension was growing in him, and a strange excitement at what the woman had said. He had always thought Susan Telsa insane, but now something he had read about her was coming back to him: her explanation of the infinite-regress hallucinations. They were a trick the mind played on first entering another world, she had said; in that world space did not exist, so the mind supplied its own "space" in the form of the endless repetition of remembered immediate surroundings

If the woman in white was Telsa, perhaps he was in that world right now.

Or perhaps this "world" was a hallucination, stable only because he had gone into acute somno psychosis from prolonged rhino use without sleep.

Either way, he had to find her again. If anyone knew what was happening to him, she did.

Trembling, he started to walk in the direction her limousine had disappeared.

✳ ✳ ✳ ✳

He walked for hours on quiet, sun-warmed asphalt. A few times he shinned up streetlights to scour the distance, and every time saw nothing but benches, hedges, streetlights, and empty parking spaces to the horizon. The sun was getting toward mid-afternoon when he saw the man.

He was sitting on a bench as if waiting for the parking lot shuttle bus. From a distance his glasses blanked out his eyes: round, wide-rimmed glasses that matched his perfectly round, bald head. The bald head and his robes made him look like a Hare Krishna, except that the robes were mud-brown and had big buttons down the front. He was old.

Stane ran to him and stood over him, gasping, heart pounding. The old man just stared at him.

"Welcome," the old man said finally. His voice was dry, dusty, as if the mud of his robes had dried up inside him.

"How can I get out of here? Is there a bus?" Now that there seemed to be a chance of escape, Stane's agitation had come back.

"How did you get in?" asked the old man.

Stane stared at him. "Who – ?"

"I am the guardian of this place." The old man waved a wrinkled hand.

"What place?"

"Where do you go when you go to bed?"

Fear was coming over him. "Sleep."

"Yet here you are, wide awake. How did that happen?"

"The – the woman – "

"Your kind are not allowed here. Not awake."

He studied Stane coldly.

"Your *woman* and the others like her think they have escaped the fetters that bind everyone else. They are free. They have all the time there is. They are awake." The word was full of weary sarcasm. "But what do you think made her meet you, for example, come to where you were at the right time? What made her bring you here, where she thinks she has her perfect freedom, only to meet me?" He stared into Stane's eyes with his black, somehow numbing eyes. "It was *appointed*, that is what. She has no more escaped her fate than you have."

"She may not sleep, and she may see into this place, but she has not escaped all the things that come upon one unawares, and so she is still unconscious of many things, and I still hold sway over her. Would you like to help me in a certain matter?"

Stane licked his lips.

"Would you like to get out of this place?"

"Yes."

"If you look behind this hedge you will find a conveyance. With it you can catch her, exit the same way she does − wait a minute before you go." His eyes pulled Stane back with their numbing force. "All I ask is that you deliver something to her. Something very small."

It lay on his palm, a tiny sack of mud-brown cloth tied with a black string.

"Open this and show it to her with my kindest personal regards," he said wearily. Stane took it with trembling fingers. It was heavy and slightly cold.

"Now," the old man said.

Behind the hedge was a brown, engine-bound motorcycle. And it was almost as if the old man had *become* the motorcycle, because when Stane wheeled it back around to the bench he was gone. Or had he walked off behind another hedge while Stane was getting it?

Stane knew how to ride a motorcycle. Soon he was crouching behind the windshield and rushing through a collapsing, telescoping perspective of hedges/benches/streetlights, feeling the powerful vibration of the cycle and the small bumps under his wheels, trying to calculate how long it would take to catch the limousine, assuming it had kept on all this time at the same speed and in the same direction.

Three hours later, Stanes's arms were cramped from holding the motorcycle's handles. But when the sun touched the horizon, sending pools of blue shadow across the asphalt, he thought there was a black dot at the very limit of his vision. He gunned the cycle forward, and in a minute the rear of the limousine was rushing toward him as if it were standing still. His heart pounded, wondering what they would do when they saw him, but the limousine just kept floating along at a constant speed, until Stane had to brake sharply to keep from running into it.

There was no sign at all from the limo. Stane couldn't see through the rear window. He pulled alongside. The mirrored glass reflected in curved distortion the vast, pink sunset, wispy clouds low over the horizon tinted pink and purple.

He pounded on the driver side window. The car continued to cruise along obliviously. He tried to cup his hand over the glass and put his face close enough to see in, but the glimpses he got leaning far over and wrestling the cycle with the other hand told him nothing. Finally, after a few tries, and almost falling off the cycle, he popped one of the rear doors.

It stuck half unlatched. He yanked at it again, before whoever was inside could pull it shut. It came open, showing a swatch of blue carpeting and upholstery. He nosed into the lee of the door and dived in on his stomach, hearing the clank and scrape as the cycle went down. He wriggled his legs into the car and slammed the door behind him.

The woman was there. But not as he could ever have imagined her: barely human, even. In the radiance of her he realized also that he was not inside a car, that there was no car, no motorcycle, no endless parking lot, that these had been illusions, or rather symbols; that there had been no distance between him and the woman all this time, opening up as the illusory limo drove, that there had never been any distance between them at all; that if only he could have risen to the task, woken up a little more, he would have realized this instead of using the delusive device of the dream-motorcycle to give himself the illusion of chasing her – the dream-motorcycle that had been pandered to him before he had had a chance to waken further. And he saw more, wrapped in the woman-creature's membrane of light, which pulsed, as if she lived on a blood of light, her veins reaching to the sun and all the other spheres, a tiny capillary going even into his own brain: he saw that everything he had thought was real – the airports and drug-runners, the cities where he had lived, his dingy apartments, his coworkers, the rhino, his body, even the subtle world he had entered with the woman's help – were unreal in themselves, merely symbols projected by the deep Real to signify Itself to those who slept, perceiving It only vaguely in shifting dreams. In an instant of incinerating clarity he comprehended it, the vision he knew now he had always sought: everything, the whole universe a play of light and shadow glittering from an abstract, perfect diamond of infinite facets, infinite clarity, infinite light –

In his side something began to throb, heavy and cold. A dry, dusty voice came from it like a radiation of darkness, a black gas. "Give this to her with my kindest personal regards," it croaked, giving off a bad smell.

Fear pierced him. He had brought into this light –

"Give it to her," croaked the thing with a cloud of black gas. "Unwrap it and hold it up to her. Shake her and make her look at it."

Suddenly he could vaguely feel again that he was wrapped in flesh. He fumbled blindly for the pocket in which he had put the brown-wrapped thing so he could throw it out of the car, which too had become vaguely visible –

The thing was heavy, cold in his hands –

"Give it to her," croaked the thing. "Give it to her." Its black gas seemed to disturb her; she trembled, and her brilliant tendrils turned sickly gray where the gas touched them.

"Unwrap it," chanted the croaking voice. Unwrap it."

His shaking hands unwrapped it.

It was a chunk of darkness.

Dead black, like a hole in his hand, which sucked at his attention, drew him into itself like water down a drain, whirling and vortexing down into the darkness of –

"No!" croaked the voice, fading from his hearing. "It's not for you. Give it to her. To *her*. Give it to ..."

Sleep.

※ ※ ※ ※

His shoulder ached and his face hurt. He was cold: his ears stung with cold, hands numb with it, feet burning with it. For a long while he was unable to move, unsure where he was or if he was dying –

With an effort he opened his eyes.

There was unsteady ground, glaring dark light, stark shadows –

Hardness under him – he was lying –

He scrabbled his arms and legs suddenly, and pushed – His face peeled painfully away from asphalt –

He was in the Des Moines Convention Center parking lot, and it was night, and cold, and he was sick.

He scrambled up desperately, leaned on a bench. The effort made him retch, again and again.

When he could, he looked around, straining his streaming eyes into the darkness.

The vast concrete bulk of the Convention Center rose 200 yards away.

He sobbed, leaning on the bench, the somno hallucinations swirling not far away, but temporarily diminished by his recent unconsciousness, his merciful sleep.

It had gone too far, he realized dimly through his nausea and sleep-revulsion and sudden, sharp rhino hunger. He had to go in, give himself up, take the step down program, and after that the ND&I desk job if they would still give it to him –

He breathed deeply, steadied himself, and started hobbling shakily in the direction of the Convention Center, where there would be a telephone –

His right hand was clenched on something. It hurt to open it, the muscles spasming.

In the greenish streetlight glare a black hole lay in his palm, seeming to absorb light and consciousness, sucking him dizzily down like water down a drain –

With panicked strength he threw it from him, as hard as he could.

Just a black rock, he told himself, trembling, an asphalt-coated pebble from the parking lot that he had picked up to play a part in his hallucination.

But strangely, he didn't hear it fall. There was no distant clatter as it hit the asphalt; only silence, as if it had disappeared in the air, diffused into the darkness above him.

He started again toward the Convention Center, a coldness creeping over him now as he thought of his life to come.

The Dakna

Theodore Janus came out of stillness sweaty and trembling, his hands cramped on the 3-space mouse grips of the audience response register, evening light softening the ruins of Washington, D.C. outside his glass greenhouse walls.

Must have been a tough debate, he thought, unlocking his legs from lotus and switching off the register console with its miniature TV screen, on which political commentators were now starting to babble. He stood up shakily, stretched, wrung his hands.

When the phone chime rang half an hour later, he was getting out of a hot bath. He tied on a robe and touched the Answer key. The bald head of Sheldon Frye of the Committee to Re-Elect Senator Smith appeared on the bathroom monitor.

Frye looked at him mournfully. "That's what I should be doing," he said. "But I have to call and compliment all the volunteers so we can sucker them into helping next time around too."

"How did we do?" In meditation Janus had felt the ebb and flow of the TV audience's emotions, but he could remember little of the debate itself. His job was not to evaluate substance, but merely to feed back real-time audience reaction to help channel the Senator's performance.

"The media people are opening champagne and writing acceptance speeches. The Senator says you deserve much of the credit."

Janus grunted, toweling his hair.

"Can we count on you for the press conference? We'd rotate to someone else, but there's nobody with your sensitivity."

"You can count on me. Listen, Sheldon, I have to go. I have an appointment."

✳ ✳ ✳ ✳

In Janus's office monitor, Roland Lord Morph-Andrew put back his black hood to show a bare head bubbled with socket-shields, a gaunt face drawn into a half-grimace – probably due to nerve damage from the deep-brain penetrations, Janus guessed. Morph-Andrew's dark eyes burned with saturnine intelligence. A short, stupid Type C clone—the kind that was still legal—stood behind his chair.

"I wish to engage your services, Mr. Janus," he said.

"I'm flattered."

"I am a collector, as you may be aware. There is an—object I wish you to find. My informants indicate that though you choose not to avail yourself of modern technological enhancements, your investigative work is of high quality."

"I use a more organic approach to enhancement."

"Yes. I understand also that you have been active in the reactionary movement. But that is no impediment to a business relationship. You have heard, Mr. Janus, of Carl Von Hellinger."

"Of course."

"What do you know of him?"

"What everybody knows. He was a designer and composer, of the so-called Washington Decadent School. A notorious degenerate. Highly 'technologically enhanced' for his time. He died in an accident twenty-five years ago. Some of his music is very beautiful. Some very ugly."

"Like life itself, perhaps."

Janus smiled politely.

"He was one of the geniuses of the New World, Mr. Janus. No doubt you have heard how he composed his great masterpiece, his most famous piece of music."

"There are various theories."

"But only one is correct. With these," he gestured at his head, "I can understand Von Hellinger. Without neural link you are exiled from the meaning of his music. The audial tracks he recorded are mere muddy echoes of the neural tracks, their passion, their power. I *know* he created 'The Dakna' in link with a woman, that it was her voiceless sorrow and pain he distilled through his art. In link I can *feel* her loneliness, her sweetness, her shining beauty. It could not be his—he was a madman, a pleasure-impulse addict—it was hers, the Dakna's.

"I want you to find her," he said. "I will pay anything to find her."

"Excellency, people have been chasing this 'Dakna' for decades. For awhile, as you will remember, it was a fad. If she ever existed, she has been found and hoarded. Or she's dead."

"She has not been found," said Morph-Andrew. "I have made inquiries over many years. And if she is dead, I want to know. I must know.

"I have run search analyses on her. The results are inconclusive—too many variables, too many unknowns. Locating lost items is one of the few functions apparently performed better using the 'techniques' of your Party. I understand this is because randomness, signal-to-noise ratios, and proliferation of variables are not constraints."

"Correct. However, other constraints exist."

"I will double your usual fee, which I understand is exorbitant in itself. I wish you to start immediately."

Next afternoon, Janus went through glass doors off his living room into the close, dry-grass smell of his greenhouse. It was built onto what had been a large second-floor balcony when he had bought the building from the Chamber of Commerce for one dollar and a commitment to renovate. Most of his plants were East Asian, a few South American: vines and cacti, grasses and climbing shrubs with tiny white flowers. It looked like a greenhouse full of weeds.

Janus put a stone mortar and pestle on a grass mat. Then he

went to the plants, looking them over carefully, gently taking from each kind leaves or berries or blossoms and putting them in the pestle.

Finally, as the sun was setting, Janus sat on the mat and began to grind.

He chanted softly in rhythm with the mortar, the chant the ancient texts said was to consecrate the plants, but which modern practitioners theorized helped to calm the mind. By the time he was done grinding, the hypnotic hum and lull of the chant had opened a quietness around him that held the ruined buildings of Northwest Washington and the deepening blue dusk, the cool air coming gently through the greenhouse windows.

The pestle now held a quarter cup of greenish paste. Very slowly he ate it, the bitter, cinnamonish, deliquescent taste filling his throat, head, and soon his whole body. By then he could feel the pull of it at his nervous system, not the overwhelming jangle of a synthetic isolate, but instead a seductive stillness as the neuromodulator analogs in the leaf paste tucked into the synaptic activation sites he had cultivated through many years of meditation.

He had downloaded "The Dakna"; he tapped the stereo remote to turn it on.

A synthesizer wash coalesced from the silence. Slowly, rhythmically, a melody built itself, sweet and clear, like the voice of a girl. Gradually it became sensual, as if she grew to exquisite womanhood. Her face seemed to form in the cool dusk: young, strange, beautiful.

Then the darkness came.

At the end of it, Janus was shaken. His heightened perceptions told him Morph-Andrew was right: the Dakna was a woman that some awful thing had destroyed, and the music was her despair. It was an allegory of the Whitedeath plague, he knew, its near destruction of the human race.

Sitting in lotus on his mat, he touched the mantra sleeping in the center of his forehead. With his last scrap of thought before it pulled him down into the absolute stillness of meditation, he asked: "Where is the Dakna?"

When he emerged, night air and the whir of crickets were coming gently through the windows. The lights of the two other renovated buildings on his block were islands in the darkness. He felt groggy, but two scenes were vivid in his mind. In one, he was standing in bright daylight in an empty lot, looking at a plaque. In the other he was looking up at the address on a dilapidated building, storm clouds piling in the sky behind it.

Next morning he drove his ATV to Georgetown, skirting the wild neighborhoods. He wound through the narrow lanes of Memorial Park, whose wooded hills covered the incinerated rubble of much of the old downtown, then jockeyed in heavy traffic on M Street. Almost as soon as he turned from M onto Spring Street, the city bustle ceased and the asphalt became elderly and potholed.

After a few more blocks bushes grew up through cracks in the asphalt, making the street look like a strip of savannah. He parked. He was at the edge of a wild neighborhood, big trees shading buildings tumbled into thickly overgrown hills and cliffs, with here and there an intact wall with hollow windows and rusted fire escape ladders. Birds sang and locusts made their electric buzz. A sign warned of dog packs and poisonous snakes.

The plaque he had seen in his search vision was a famous one, and he had been able to look up the address online. Soon he was standing at the empty lot where the plaque was, an overgrown patch of ground littered with old bricks, rubbled concrete, and shards of rusted metal. Two shoulder-high wall segments were heavily shrouded with ivy and bearberry, a few birds pecking at the red fruit. The heating gas explosion twenty-five years before had almost leveled the building, and weather had done the rest.

It was 151 Spring Street, site of Carl Von Hellinger's death. Janus absently read the plaque on the stone pedestal. The fact that his vision had brought him here, to the best-known place connected with Von Hellinger, and hence with "The Dakna," confirmed what he had told Morph-Andrew about the futility of trying to find her. Such false leads occurred when the search object had never existed or was gone from the planet—then the searcher's subconscious tended to hunt through its own theories and memories to supply an answer to the search question.

Janus sat on a chunk of concrete in the sun and became very still. A lizard flickered across the ground by his feet. A breeze fluttered the leaves on a wisteria bush. Finally he stirred, sighed. It was no use: the place was a jumble of impressions, confused and unreadable. Investigators, professional and amateur, souvenir hunters, and tourists had been over the lot in droves, turning over bricks, poking into every hollow. Their babble almost submerged a burning scream now faint with age, perhaps the explosion that had killed Von Hellinger and most of his entourage. Ironically, the Dakna-hunters had probably wiped out the last traces of the Dakna.

He got up to leave. The walls of the next building on the street were whole almost all the way to the top. In a window on the second floor Janus saw a face.

Then it was gone.

"Hello," he called. A crow cawed back.

He pushed through arrowwood leaves to a doorway choked with blooming sumac. Inside, ceilings had collapsed so that blue sky showed over mounds of rubble grown with coarse grass, shrubs, and creepers. Grasshoppers jumped around his feet. Further back the ceilings still held, and a slope of rubble led to the second floor.

He hesitated, then climbed it.

At the top, a few pebbles were rattling down crumbled concrete steps leading to the third floor.

He climbed the steps. The third floor was roofless. At the far end of a big space with rubble for floor and sky for ceiling, next to a hollow window, crouched a wild, ragged figure with matted grey hair. It wore a greasy overcoat over other coats, rags wrapped around its feet.

"Don't be afraid," said Janus. Holding his empty hands out by his sides, he walked slowly forward.

The person jumped out the window with a fluttering of overcoat skirts.

Janus ran to the window. The person lay face down on the ground below.

The person was a woman. Her breath made red bubbles in the blood oozing from her mouth as Janus sat with her in the back of the ambulance he had called, trying to guess how old she was under the dirt and stinking, castoff clothes. At George Washington Hospital an emergency room nurse cut off some of the clothes with scissors.

"Sorry, we don't do these," she told Janus. "There's a veterinary hospital on 20th Street."

She held up the woman's filthy arm. Clone identification numbers were tattooed near the armpit.

The veterinary hospital had a stuffy waiting room with dusty plants crowded on the windowsills. Janus sat on an ancient, lumpy sofa.

After several hours a young man in a lab coat came into the waiting room. "Mr. Janus? She's all right. Sorry it took so long. She's an unusual model." He led Janus through a narrow hall with worn linoleum and a musky smell. "Where did you get her?"

"I found her. In a wild neighborhood, living in a collapsed building."

The vet nodded. "They isolate themselves sometimes if they're abandoned or lost. Their socialization usually doesn't cover that kind of situation. They may become afraid of people or feel that they don't deserve to live. Like abandoned children."

He led Janus to a small grey room with a sink. The clone lay unconscious on a scratched metal table, two medication patches on her neck. There were dark bruises on her face, arms, and chest. Clean, she was shockingly young, her hair cornflower blonde.

"I've never seen anything like her," said the vet. "Of course she's a Type A. They aren't allowed to make these anymore. But she's also highly engineered."

He pulled the clone's legs apart so Janus could see her crotch. It was smooth and hairless, without a trace of sex organs, nothing but a urinary sphincter tucked into the fold of flesh.

The vet held an X-ray negative up to the light. It showed a nightmarish skeleton, heavy and anthropoidal, ribs fused into solid armor, skull a lumpish mass of bone, hands and forearms like blades. "That's why it took so long to check her out. Without this armoring, though, a three-story fall might have killed her. As it is, her injuries are minor."

On the outside she was slender and shapely, face delicate.

"My guess is that she was designed as a bodyguard," said the vet. "Her muscle configuration is more like an ape's than a human's, making her about three times as strong as a man. The breasts are nerveless: window dressing. She must have cost a fortune." He studied her, hands on his hips. "If she's legal, she must be at least twenty years old, but she must have been in her growth tank most of that time because she doesn't show any of the cancers they get after that many years active. The only other things I know about her is this." He smoothed blonde hair away from her neck. On her occipital lobe was a small socket shield. When he touched it she moaned and rolled her head away. "She's sensitive to any touching of it, even under heavy sedation, so I assume it's some kind of negative reinforcement thing. But you can see – " he held her head so Janus could look "—the area around it is inflamed, as if it's been used recently–overused, in fact. If she's been living in the wild, I wonder . . ."

"Can you wake her up?"

"Sure. And you can take her home, if you'll watch her for signs of concussion."

He took two pairs of metal manacles out of a cabinet and fastened her wrists and ankles to the metal table.

"A precaution," he said over his shoulder. "Occasionally they're disturbed when they wake up. This one could do a lot of damage."

He peeled the sedative patches off the clone's neck. In a few minutes she started to move, and then her eyes opened. They were lovely, large, and blue. She lay still for a minute.

Then she saw Janus and the vet and she screamed. Her arms

and legs strained at the manacles, her muscles and veins bulging grotesquely, making the metal creak. Her face twisted in a snarl, showing the ape-like bones of her skull.

"It's okay," the vet said gently. "Don't be afraid. We're friends." He took a chocolate bar from a drawer and held it near her face. "Look. This is for you. Poor little thing." He tried to stroke her hair, and her teeth snapped at him. He gently touched her stomach and she urinated, screaming convulsively. He shook his head then, smoothed two new patches onto her flushed, metal-hard neck. In a minute her body jerked, then a few more times with lessening strength; her head lolled to the side and she was unconscious, her muscles relaxing slowly.

The vet kept shaking his head. Finally he said wearily: "Her socialization is gone. It's cruel. I'm glad they can't make these anymore." He looked at Janus bitterly. He opened a cupboard and took down a box. "I'll have to destroy her."

"No," said Janus.

In blue dusk Janus carried the clone from his ATV to his outside basement stairs. Her slender, unconscious body was incongruously heavy and hard. He lugged her into the basement, put her on a wide Oriental couch he was storing.

He covered her with spare blankets, pulled the tab on a self-cook dinner and put it next to the couch. Then he peeled the two sedative patches off her neck and left, locking the heavy metal door behind him. The windows were barred in the faux Victorian style of the house; they and the metal door should hold her until he found out whether she was what his search vision had led him to.

That night he had a dream. He was standing once again at the overgrown lot on Spring Street, but as he watched there was a waver, a movement, as if the whole scene had tilted. The scene was reflected in a mirror, he realized, held by a hand he couldn't see.

Next day he drove to the second address from his search vision.

This one was unfamiliar to him – just someplace in Northeast that he had never visited. As he navigated the potholed and overgrown—and occasionally smooth and busy—streets, he was deep in thought. Last night's dream troubled him. Dreams frequently conveyed information in symbolic form; a hand holding a mirror showing his search vision scene could mean that someone had interfered with his search. But who, how, and why? He told himself for the tenth time that he shouldn't have taken the Roland Morph-Andrew job; it was like consorting with the enemy. But maybe it was precisely his ambivalence about the job that had given rise to the dream.

The Northeast Washington address was on a street lined with four-story brownstones, half of them deserted, the rest rundown. The one Janus wanted bulked against the still noon sky of gathering clouds, some of its windows boarded up. He rang the bell three times before the door opened.

The female that opened it was identical to the one Janus had found in Georgetown, but looked twenty years older. She wore only boxer shorts and a dirty camisole that had once been pink, and he could see the serial number near her armpit. Her skin was blotched with melanomas and a cataract was starting to grow in one of her blue eyes. A jack wire dangled from her occipital socket. A cigarette hung from her lips.

"What do you want?" she asked flatly, studying him with lethargic curiosity. "They're all upstairs partying. You want to see Rabenz?"

"Yes.

The stairs creaked and the banister was blistered and rickety. A lone clarinet played the blues somewhere above them. On a dim third floor landing the clone frisked him expertly almost before he knew what she was doing.

He followed her into a loft with a vast, dusty floor, where two dozen people hung from the ceiling in harnesses at various heights. Their faces were vacant, some cross-eyed or drooling. They were all metalheads, modified with the heavy, intrusive hardware of twenty years ago, bundles of jack wires taped to bracing lines and feeding into a bank of dusty black cases along one wall. A small, bald man rocked convulsively in his harness; one of his wires was connected to a synthesizer, from which the sound of the clarinet came. None of them paid attention to Janus or anything else.

The clone walked to a man hanging near the middle of the group and shook his leg. His eyes slowly woke up.

"A meathead wants to see you," she said.

The man looked at Janus.

"Yeah, baby," he said wheezingly. "What is it that is?" He had a narrow, elderly, dissipated face with a few wisps of shoulder-length hair growing from his socket-studded head.

"I'm looking for some information."

The man looked blank.

"Is she yours?" Janus asked, nodding at the clone.

"Who wants to know?"

"Theodore Janus, Investigator, Locator of Lost Persons, Objects, and Information." He held out a card. The man's bony hands made no move to take it.

"And what Lost Persons, Objects, and Information are you looking for today, sweetheart?"

"The Dakna."

The man ogled him, then laughed wheezingly. His eyes went blank and a ripple of amusement ran through the room. Some of the harnessed people smiled faintly, others rocked slightly, a few came to life and turned their heads toward Janus.

Rabenz's eyes came back on. "No Dakna around here. You can buy the download."

"Where did you get the clone?"

"Hell built her. When Hell blew away, I kept her."

"Von Hellinger? You were part of his group?"

"Long-long ago, baby. Long-long ago." His eyes got distant, and there was a hint of sadness in them. "We was out of town when he blew; she was with us. We kept her. End of story."

"Von Hellinger designed her? For himself or on commission?"

The man studied him. "You bore me, Locator-man. All this ancient history. I've spent too much time on your planet already." And his eyes went blank. Some of the other hanging people started swinging, as if he ran among them, the neural ghost of a young man.

Janus repressed an urge to tear him down, slap him awake. But it wouldn't help matters to get arrested. Instead he stuffed his card into the pocket of the man's loose overalls, making him swing slightly on his wires.

Then he had another idea. Following the clone down the stairs, he touched the wire hanging from her single socket. "What's this?"

She looked sideways at him, hesitated. Then her breathing seemed to pick up.

"You want to play with it?"

She had a tiny, windowless room off the first floor hall, with a bare, stained mattress in the corner. She pulled off her slip and lay on the mattress. Her skin was loose, but the muscles underneath were hard. A large, discolored lump showed in one of her breasts.

She jacked the wire from her head into a worn little box next to the mattress, put Janus's hand on the control knob.

"Go slow," she whispered. "It hurts if you go too fast."

Squatting next to her, he turned the knob a little. She sighed and stared at the ceiling. A little sweat showed on her face. Thunder boomed distantly through an open window somewhere in the hall.

"You belonged to Von Hellinger before Rabenz?" Janus asked her.

She shook her head quickly, concentrating on the impulses from the transducer. Janus turned the knob a little more and her lips swelled with blood, her face flushed. Wind gusted suddenly outside; the faintest breath of it, tinged with electricity, reached them in the tiny room.

"Who, then?"

"Missy."

"Who is Missy?"

She shook her head. "More," she breathed.

"As soon as you tell me who Missy is."

"I—I come from her."

"She's your seed-mother?"

She nodded with difficulty. "Give me more."

He put his hand on the knob, but didn't turn it.

"What happened to her?"

"They said she died." Tears came out of her eyes, ran down the sides of her head. "She got sick. I wasn't there—they took me away. If I'd 'a been there I wouldn't've let her *die*." Muscles bulged and tendons stood out in her neck.

Janus studied her sweating face, then turned the knob a little more, and she gasped and arched her back.

He turned it by slow degrees as far as it would go in the guttural boom of thunder, the hiss of rain from the hall window, the old clone clinging to him like a child or lover. When she had peaked he turned off the machine, left her sleeping.

✳ ✳ ✳ ✳

It was still raining when Janus, carrying a spark-blade set to stun, edged into his basement, locking the door behind him. Only a little grey light came through the barred windows, making the room dark, sleepy with the sound of rain. There was no one on the sofa. The dinner pack he had left last night was torn open and licked clean, but there was no other sign anyone was down there.

"Hello?" he said.

Only the sound of rain.

"I want to talk to you," he tried again, squinting toward the crates piled in the back of the room, where someone might hide.

A sledgehammer blow threw him against the wall, the spark-blade clattering away across the floor. When he came to, steel hands were frisking him, a desperate pale face gasping over him in the dark.

He forced his trembling lips to move. "M-Missy. I know about Missy."

The hands stopped abruptly. Then he was yanked up so his face was an inch from the clone's sweating face. Her lips worked.

"You know—where Missy is?" she asked finally, her voice thick and clumsy.

"Did someone hurt you? Is that why you're afraid?"

Slowly she let go of him and stood up. He stood up too, much more slowly and leaning against the wall, breathing painfully. He looked into the clone's dilated eyes.

"Where is Missy?"

"What's your name?"

She shrugged. "Where is Missy?"

Something flashed on Janus, something about imprinting techniques used with Class A clones—

"You haven't been named?" he blurted. Panic blazed in her eyes, but before she could move, he had given her the first name he could think of: "Theodora! Your name is Theodora!"

Her eyelids fluttered and she shook like a malfunctioning machine, sank kneeling to the floor as if in a faint. When she looked up again, her expression was complicated, a mixture of relief and fear, hate and worship.

She had been made for Missy; her world was to have revolved around Missy. Though she had never seen her, she had woken up knowing her and her family; she would know them now if she saw them or heard their voices. She didn't know when she had woken up from the growth tank, or who had woken her, or how she had gotten to the wrecked building in Von Hellinger's old neighborhood. Janus didn't think she was lying. In "Missy's" absence, Janus's' christening had made her his property in her mind, and clones were hard-wired to obey their owners. Janus guessed the memory loss was due to some trauma, maybe her fall from the window.

He talked to her late into the night, sitting at the kitchen table and giving her bread, cheese, and apples, nursing his bruised face and shoulder and aching head and trying to make sense of her monosyllabic answers. Other than her devotion to Missy, the only thing he learned was that she was afraid of some "bad men" who had hurt her. As she stuttered incoherently about them, her trembling hand touched her occipital socket over and over. Finally he went to bed, but not to sleep. Questions surrounded him in the dark, guesses chasing them.

Around 2 A.M. he got up and walked around the dark apartment.

The rain had ended, and mist shrouded the moon and the lone streetlight on the corner. He looked out over a wild landscape: ruined buildings leaning among the trees, here and there electric lights, but mostly jungle darkness. The message light on his living room phone was lit. He keyed the monitor to show the guest room where he had put the clone. The sleek lines of her sleeping body appeared on the screen. With surprise he felt himself grow aroused. It had not happened in a long, long time; the meditation seemed to do that after a number of years, moving the body's energy to different centers.

It was strange. He made himself remember the nerveless breasts, featureless loins, the armored monkey's skeleton, but oddly that only seemed to arouse him more.

To distract himself he played his phone message. It was a well-groomed young woman from the Committee to Re-Elect Senator Lazur N. Smith inviting him to an exclusive fundraising reception. After awhile he went back to bed and slept.

He had the search vision dream again, and this time he clearly caught the flash of a mirror held in front of him by an unseen hand, and he knew his Dakna search had been blocked by someone, probably another psychic operator.

Regina Lady Welley had a great mane of black hair hiding all but her two temple sockets, feed wires wrapped into a long braid that hung down her shoulder. Her eyes blazed with deep data access and rapid analysis capability. Her voice was supple, vibrant.

"My friends, our civilization is at a turning point. The human race must in this generation decide whether to continue to mount the ladder of knowledge leading to our high destiny—" Welley's media technicians kicked in and she stood, tanned and vigorous, on a cliff overlooking blue mountains, gesturing upward at stars that glittered like jewels in evening blue "—or retreat from the challenges of our time into superstitious self-delusion. Already, the fearful have begun to cringe from the demands of the future." Filthy Cro-Magnon savages backed away from a crackling fire with terrified bellows, hands before their faces; one of them looked remarkably like Senator Lazur Smith.

Janus, sitting on his living room couch next to Theodora, laughed nervously. He remembered now the skillful buildup of emotion during Welley's opening, the rapid alternation between exhilaration and anger that had filtered into him from the city viewers.

Theodora was eating a bowl of popcorn hungrily. She seemed always hungry. Janus had decided to watch a recording of the debate in case he needed to say polite things about it at the Smith campaign reception.

"After overcoming the terrible odds of the past century, as well as over the whole twenty-five thousand years of mankind's ascent on Earth—" a flash of Welley's brawny figure, sweat-stained and muddy, leading a band of handsome warriors over the crest of a hill, a banner flying in the breeze "—it would be ironic if our downfall came of our own lack of will, our own fear.

"But come it might. The past decade has seen a slump in agricultural productivity for the first time in hundreds of years. Fifteen years ago, our nation's fields were tilled by highly independent Class A clones." Strapping, happy-looking men and women operating harvesters and trucks worked at evening in a field where tall, green corn stretched to the horizon; silos overflowed with grain. "Today, because of policies supported by Senator Smith, Class A and B clones are all but illegal, and agricultural work must proceed using the Class C variety." Hordes of short, stupid-faced creatures trampled tender shoots into the mud. "Clone replacement organs are no longer available." A young woman wept by a gravestone. "Whole industries have been destroyed by the restrictions on genetic engineering supported by Senator Smith.

"My friends, a vote for Lazur Smith is a vote for the Dark Ages. And they may soon be upon us." A ragged family in a filthy hovel grubbed food from a broken bowl.

Lazur Smith was twenty years older than Welley, his white hair cut short to show a skull without sockets. There was a quiet confidence about him, and he had smiling wrinkles around his eyes.

"My fellow citizens, her Ladyship's party dates back decades, to a time when the United Sates was obliged to grant hereditary governorships in parts of our nation to combat the anarchy and famine of the Whitedeath plague." Smith's technicians flashed a frame of a sneering Welley in a crown and purple robes, holding out her hand to be kissed. Janus remembered with a jolt that the audience had had a negative reaction to this beginning shot of Smith's, perceiving it as too personal, too cynical. He had fed this back to campaign headquarters as fast as he could, then watched Smith's remarks veer away from Welley's aristocratic background. Even the live debates featured only computer-montaged recordings of the candidates, of course, hundreds of orations and rebuttals constructed in media laboratories months before to hopefully cover every contingency, every point the opponent might raise. These were sequenced based on real-time audience feedback during the debate. The Technological Democracy Party took its readings from samples of viewers it paid to watch the debates hooked up to brain field monitors; the Evolutionary Progress Party used psychics like Janus. Judging by recent elections, the EPP's technique was more effective.

"Lady Welley has reminded us of the techniques for tampering with nature upon which our society has become dependent. She has reminded us of the clone slaves that slowed the development of labor-saving technologies and brutalized our young people, but she has forgotten to mention the dark side of this 'revolution,' with its cruelty and perversions, its malfunctions and monstrosities." A roomful of bloody bodies from one of the most notorious clone malfunctions flashed on the screen, followed by nauseating pictures of some of the deformities coming out of the growth tanks. "The present Congress has begun to phase out this immoral and dangerous technology without impairing existing property rights. I am proud to have been one of the leaders of this change in the law.

"The tampering with genes necessary to build the clones and championed by Lady Welley's party has also been a mixed blessing in another way, as the citizens of this nation will remember." A nearly subliminal flash of a Welly-like corpse covered with the white, fungus-like growth of the Whitedeath plague flashed on the screen. Theodora spilled her popcorn with sudden, silent terror, and Janus's heart pounded in spite of the knowledge that it was an audacious cheap shot. Yet it was the thrust that had won the debate, he realized, just as shots like it had won many debates—and many elections—for the EPP. The idea had begun to creep into popular culture that recombinant DNA research had produced the Whitedeath virus, though no one knew if that was true.

Theodora said casually: "That's Missy's daddy."

"What?"

"That man." She pointed at Smith.

". . . alternative technologies more attuned to life on this planet. Already, ancient mental techniques allowing us to locate natural resources and heal many diseases are being revived and studied . . ."

"Missy is his daughter?" Janus asked her carefully.

She nodded.

"You're sure?"

She nodded.

Janus sat back, dumbfounded. When he could pay attention again, Welley was storming: "--outrageous lie! The new technologies were used to *defeat* the plague, and without them we would not be here today!"

But the damage had been done.

Theodora didn't seem nervous at the reception, even when applause spread through the ballroom for Janus's entrance; she held his arm and smiled radiantly. He bowed, shook several dozen hands, watched people look her up and down. The short, canary-yellow dress she had chosen from the online catalogue was perfect for the occasion, he saw, stimulating but not undignified, and it amply covered the serial number at her armpit. The party function was part of her programming, he realized: she talked hardly at all, but held a glass of something gracefully, listened interestedly; but when anyone got less than a few meters from Janus, she kept an eye on them. The perfect bodyguard, her slender figure and innocent blue eyes giving no hint that she was three times as strong as a man, armored and combat-wired.

A touch on his elbow made him turn, and he shook hands with Sheldon Frye, Smith's campaign manager and political confidant, short and bald, with a benign squint.

"Glad you could come, Janus," he said. "You alone?"

"I brought a friend."

"I didn't think you had any." Frye guided Janus around groups of people in the direction of the bar. "You 'developed' types worry me. Our side touts these mental techniques as the New Technology, but some of you guys are like cold fish."

"Even the Senator?"

"You bet. It's his biggest liability in a race with a charismatic candidate like Welley. We coach him for hours, but he's still too aloof."

Fye ordered Scotch and water, Janus orange juice.

"But he's still going to win," said Janus.

"Sure he's going to win. He may be aloof, but he's sane. That's what's kept him winning all these years against those nuts."

A table-sized crash tore a hole in the hundred conversations in the ballroom. There was an animal howl. People turned and stared.

"Excuse me," Janus said to Frye, and pushed through the crowd.

An hors d'oeuvres table had been overturned, food and dishes shattered on the floor. Theodora crouched next to it, holding the socket at the back of her head, whining and staring up at two men. Janus squatted next to her, put his hands on her arms.

"Theodora."

She was shaking. She didn't seem to notice him.

Somebody said: "Hey, is that your slave meat?"

He looked up. The two men Theodora was staring at wore tuxedos, held drinks. Waiters were setting the table back up, sweeping up the mess. The ballroom began to fill with conversation again.

"Cootchy—cootchy—coo," said one of the men, leaning forward

and tickling the back of his head with his finger. He was short, pudgy, and very drunk.

The clone snarled like an animal, her face showing its ape-bones.

"Whooo! Ugly!" said the man, rocking back on his heels.

His friend said urgently: "Come on Broward, let's get out of here."

"She your slave pussy?" the drunk asked Janus again.

Janus stood up. "Did you touch the socket in the back of her head?" he asked politely.

"Not recently," said the drunk. "But she remembered me."

"What do you mean?"

"I mean that's my little playmate you got your hands all over, buddy. I had her long before you even met her."

The other man said: "Broward, *shut up*." He pulled at the drunk's arm.

"Me and Dade here wore her out," the drunk hooted. "Dumped her when she malfunctioned. Know what that little electrode on her head does? Sixty hertz box, have her bucking around moaning as long as you want. Me and Dade here, we wore her *out*. Got pictures make you—"

The other man walked away quickly.

"I'm coming," Broward said to his back. "Sixty hertz box," he winked at Janus. "Get her going. You'll have fun."

He turned to leave, but Janus's hand yanked him back. "You raped her?"

"What are you, a Techno?" the man screeched. "She's a *clone*, you fuckhead. Twisted genes, not even human, you—" Janus shook him just once, so hard it cut him off.

"Where did you get her?" Janus asked.

"You fucking--!" screamed the man. Janus shook him again, so hard his head snapped back.

"Where?" The ballroom was silent again.

"She was a present," gasped the man.

"From who?"

"A – a friend." The man seemed to come to his senses finally, to realize that he had said the wrong thing.

The other man who had been with Broward pushed through the staring crowd, Sheldon Frye at his heels.

"Janus, what in God's name--" started Frye. Then he caught sight of the clone. His shocked eyes stayed riveted on her.

It was raining again, a soft, warm rain, hissing in the brush around the parking lot, wrinkling the reflections of streetlights in the puddles, bringing out the smells of pavement, dirt, and growing things.

The clone wouldn't get into the ATV, wouldn't talk, wouldn't look at him. She stood trembling with her arms wrapped around herself, staring at the ground. Janus felt the rain running down his neck, watched it wilt her hair and dress. He put his arms around her, feeling her massive, blockish skeleton. She raised her face to him. He kissed her hot, sticky woman's mouth. When he closed his eyes he could imagine he was holding a suit of armor.

At dawn the street below his bedroom was full of mist. The phone chime woke him.

Rabenz's thin, anxious face appeared on the screen. He studied Janus doubtfully. "Are you Janus? I found the card you left. Hey, I—what you asked me about a few days ago. There's something you might want to know."

"What?"

"Not on the phone, man, not on the phone. You come out here. Now. Bring your money card."

Before he went out, Janus leaned over the clone sleeping peacefully in his bed, gently smoothed a lock of blonde hair out of her face.

The mist was thick in Northeast too, seeming to absorb the sound of Janus's pounding on the street door of Rabenz's building. After five minutes, in a rage, he threw his shoulder against it and it burst inward, a piece of metal jingling along the floor. He climbed the stairs to the third floor, where Rabenz and his friends had been before. The loft was empty except for harness hooks in the ceiling and walls. He went through the whole building. Except for a couple of rooms with sagging cots, the place showed no signs of occupancy.

When he got back to his apartment and opened the door, Theodora was lying nearly decapitated in a pool of blood.

He was standing over her, one of his hands white on the door jamb, he saw as the darkness cleared from his head. Everything was spinning sickeningly. He looked down at her, tried to see her through the spinning. Her face was wax-grey, coarse. Her hands lay stiff and blade-like near her shoulders, covered with gore. She had torn out her own throat. The phone console near her was switched on, the line dead. He turned it off with a numb hand. He was standing at the window. The street and sky were empty.

As he left the city, church bells were ringing, ringing as they still did every noon for the dead, the two-thirds of the human race the Whitedeath had taken. Janus drove into the wilds of Maryland, hulks of frame houses grown with vines and moss leaning on grassy hills and in stands of trees. Far out in this deserted country he took a dirt track up a hill. In a glade near the top he dug a hole, working until late afternoon to make it deep, deaf to the songs of the birds and numb to the breeze, a bundle wrapped in sheets lying nearby on the grass. Finally he climbed out of the hole and lowered the bundle in. Then he filled the hole and packed down the earth.

He sat the rest of the afternoon and the cool evening at the foot of the grave, barely breathing, his mind deep in fields of light, searching for her.

But as is the case with the dead, he couldn't come to her. She had gone too fast, too far.

His cell phone ringing roused him in cool purple dusk.

It was Sheldon Frye. "Ted, can you come down to the office this evening? It's important."

"No."

Frye studied him as if trying to read his mood over the link.

"Well, let's at least get secure," he said finally. There was static while he switched on scramblers, then he was back, a little staticky.

"The Senator's off making TV ads, otherwise he'd speak with you himself," said Frye. "You know how he values your contributions to the cause. If I didn't know how dedicated you are, I'd be ashamed to ask another favor of you."

Janus sat silent in the cricket-trilled dusk.

"To be frank, Ted, a matter you're apparently involved in could embarrass the Senator. The clone you brought to the fundraiser last night—we found out she was a clone from Dan Broward, who was—is on the Senator's staff—"

"The clone's dead, Sheldon," Janus cut him off.

Frye looked at him curiously. "I'm sorry."

"She killed herself. Cut her throat with her hands."

"My God. A malfunction?"

"I don't think so. I think someone gave her her deathcode. Called on the phone and said it to her."

"But—who would do a thing like that?

"Normally only a clone's owner would know it's deathcode."

Frye waited.

"Did Smith ever have a daughter, Sheldon?"

"May I ask who you're working for on this, Janus?"

"Confidential."

"Is it someone who could be interested in hurting the Senator politically? A Techno political operative like Roland Lord Morph-Andrew, for example, who could be using you—manipulating you—for that purpose?"

"Maybe."

"And you'd go along with that?"

"Maybe."

"I don't understand. You, of all people."

Janus said: "Do you believe that campaign stuff the Senator gives out, about clones having human attributes?"

"Of course I do."

"Then I'll leave it at this: Someone was killed. I'm going to find out why and by whom."

"You don't think the Senator—"

"I don't know."

They stared at each other, and then Frye let out his breath. "You're a dedicated man. I'm glad you're with us and not against us. Look, I'll tell you what we know about the clone. Then you'll understand why we're so sensitive.

"Janus, over the past few years the Party has started to make a difference, slowly but surely—first with the clone restrictions, then the environmental regulations, soon the DNA research restrictions and the funding for paranormal research. We're beginning to break the metal-heads' hold on the country. In the early days—back before your time—that had seemed impossible.

"But things are at a delicate stage. We need to win this election to keep our agenda on track. We think we can win it, but the margin is small and the least breath of scandal could blow up in our faces."

He took a deep breath. "Yes, the Senator had a daughter, a long time ago, named Melissa. The clones—half a dozen of them—were a present from the Senator for her twenty-third birthday. They were seeded from Missy, so they looked exactly like her. After she died they were sold off.

"Missy got some viral strain—an offshoot of the Whitedeath, I guess. Such things were still floating around back then. She had been keeping—bad company. It almost killed Lazur. She was his only child. Of course, she was immediately quarantined and euthanized, in accordance with the law. By the time Lazur heard about it, she was gone." He sat silent for a minute. "Look, the clones were a foolish indulgence by the Senator before the Party's clone rights platform had really developed. But do you think the voters will understand that? That bastard Broward admits that Morph-Andrew gave her to him, and that he – abused her. He didn't seem to realize he was being manipulated, that he had put the Senator in a very deep hole indeed. It made me sick to listen to him. The Senator wanted to fire Broward, call the police, make a clean breast of everything; I was just barely able to persuade him to wait until after the election. To keep Broward quiet, we're keeping him on the payroll and letting him believe we're not too upset by what he did, but his day is coming, believe me. You understand why we're worried about this coming out?"

Roland Lord Morph-Andrew's enormous concrete castle stood in moonless blackness on Sugarloaf Mountain, thirty miles north of Washington. An aging Type B clone opened metal gates for the ATV as if Janus was expected, and a human or Type A butler led him down a high, echoing hall with carved stone walls and an arched, frescoed ceiling, into a dark, churchlike place. All around was the quiet hum of supercooled circuitry. Janus felt an attention sweep him, part human, but huge and chill.

The only light came from a dais near the middle of the darkness. A man sat on a throne atop it, linked to the banks of processors through hundreds of wires running from his head and neck; tubes of liquid ran to nozzles in his arms and legs. A naked woman slept at his feet, her face in shadow.

As Janus came closer, a voice, deep and amplified, boomed from the ceiling: "Good evening, Mr. Janus. I have been expecting you." Morph-Andrew's lips didn't move, but his eyes blazed down at Janus with unearthly intelligence. "You have a question to ask me. I know what it is. I have computed it. I have computed all of your actions, your thoughts, your whole life. It took a small part of my capacity." He laughed thunderously, though his lips only smiled. "Finding lost trinkets and curing psychosomatic diseases may gain your Party popularity, but in the long run we will win, Mr. Janus, because we have Intelligence. We are expanding knowledge and technique beyond anything you can imagine. With these implants I can travel to other worlds aboard a space probe. I can solve tenth-order differential polynomials in seconds. I can make a simulation model of a man's life, know his thoughts."

Janus let his eyes close, his breath relax, the ocean of silence rising within him. He could see Morph-Andrew's aura, throbbing and yellow, shot through with needles of black.

"You're ill," he said tiredly, his voice flat and small in the huge space. "If you keep using that machinery, you're going to die."

"I am more alive than you will ever be," boomed Morph-Andrew, but Janus thought he felt a chill of fear. "Do you not want to know the answer to your question?"

"Yes."

"Then listen: no, I did not kill her. Yes, I did give her to your Senator's aides, who tortured her and threw her away. Beautiful, isn't it, the regard for life your Party observes? Why did I arrange for you to find her? That will become clear as events unfold. You have been my tool and you will continue to be my tool."

"Don't bet on it."

"You have no choice. You will act according to your nature. I have computed it.

"But look. I have a gift for you, before you return to your hovel. Look."

The sleeping woman stirred, then slowly sat up, golden hair falling about her shoulders. Janus's heart pounded. It was Theodora. But as she turned to face him, he saw that this one had a woman's genitals.

"I bought a batch of them years ago, in their growth tanks," said Morph-Andrew. "Not all of them were engineered like the one you had before. This one has genitalia and a human skeleton. She is physically indistinguishable from her seed-mother. But in every other way she is identical to her clone-sister. You are lucky, Mr. Janus—few men have such a second chance."

✳ ✳ ✳ ✳

A light was burning in the second story of the Capitol Hill mansion Janus and the clone pulled up to an hour later, the clone now wearing Janus's raincoat. A faint smell of roses hung in the still air. Janus rang, and in a minute the door was opened by Lazur Smith himself, in slacks and a dress shirt though it was nearly 3 a.m.

He was even more impressive in person than on TV: very tall, still handsome despite his sixty-odd years, with a quiet magnetism—what in politics they called "charisma," but which Janus knew was the palpable field of a nervous system cultured by over forty years of meditation. Unlike Janus, who had spent his career experimenting with the ancient techniques for clairvoyance, Smith had focused on the projective techniques—rapport, communication, persuasion.

And the day they learn to broadcast that on TV, thought Janus, there won't be a Techno left in Congress.

He said quietly: "Hello, Lazur," trying to keep his pride in the man out of his voice.

"Hello, Ted," said Smith just as quietly. Come on in." He didn't seem surprised to see him. It was as if he had been expecting them, though he didn't boast as Morph-Andrew had.

He led them through a dark hall on soft carpeting, up a wide staircase, and into a big, comfortable study lined with antique paper books that gave it a faintly musty smell.

As soon as he had shut the door, Smith turned and held his hands out to the clone. "Come here, young lady."

She hesitated, then walked to him. He took her hands and stared into her face

"So beautiful," he breathed. "Just like your seed-mother." He sat her in an armchair, sat in another himself. "Von Hellinger was a genius, whatever else he was."

"What else was he?" asked Janus.

"A seducer and a corrupter. And a murderer."

"Who did he murder?"

"My daughter." Smith looked slowly from the clone to Janus. "But you know this."

Janus thought fast. "An Akashic search I ran in connection with an inquiry—"

"Yes," said Smith. "Sheldon thought we could divert you by telling you half the story, but I knew differently. You're good, Janus. I ought to try that leaf-muck you eat. My constituents would never understand, though, if it got out. They'd think I was on drugs."

He laughed. Then his face became slowly grave. Janus felt himself being drawn into the man's mood; he hung on his words as Smith began quietly to talk: "Melissa met Von Hellinger at some Georgetown party when she was in college. I should have taken better care of her. She was wild after her mother died, and I was busy with politics, trying to break the metal-heads' hold on the country.

"He was all the things fascinating to a young girl: an artist beginning to be famous, a pleasure impulse addict with strange friends, a depressive bursting with existential self-pity. And, of course, he was a metal-head. We forget how fashionable that was once.

"She began living with him and his entourage in a tenement in some artists' neighborhood. I tried to keep it quiet, especially the set of bodyguard clones she persuaded me to commission him to design. Even with the income from his compositions he always needed money to support his sick habits.

"They lived together for several years, and I rarely saw them. I was busy, and Von Hellinger and I detested each other. Then one night my daughter appeared at my door, crying. I took her in my arms, and something brushed my hand. To my horror there was a deep-brain hookup in her head—just like that one." He pointed to the clone, who sat blankly, as if she wasn't hearing any of this.

"I told her to get out and never come back.

"She never did. Von Hellinger infected her with a Whitedeath viral mutation one of his depraved followers managed to isolate, linked himself to her deep-brain penetration, and wrote a symphony."

"The Dakna," Janus breathed, and the horror in his own voice surprised him.

"Yes." Smith sat brooding, his feelings settling like a heavy blanket on Janus and the clone. "When he was finished with her, he called the Health Department police, pretending he had just found her. I suppose by that time she couldn't tell them what he had done. Because it was a low-infectivity mutation, only she had to be incinerated. They quarantined Von Hellinger and his people for a few weeks, then let them go. I sold the clones several months after her death, some still in their growth tanks."

There was a heavy silence after he was done talking, that Janus finally broke with an effort.

"I think I can tell the rest of it," he said slowly. "The clones you sold fell into Roland Morph-Andrew's hands. He must have run across information about your daughter and Von Hellinger, and calculated that the clones could be used to embarrass you politically. But he knew that if the Technos released the information, it might not be believed, or you might get a sympathy backlash. So he planted the clone on a couple of your aides. That didn't get the story public; they just tortured her and threw her out. So he called me with a phony story about the Dakna, got me to run a search that led me to the closest still-extant links to her, one of which was the clone. Very clever.

"But there are still two loose ends I can't figure out. First, when I ran my searches on the Dakna, I was apparently blocked or diverted. There are probably only a couple of dozen people in the country who have been meditating long enough to do that to me, and most of them work for security firms. Why would any of them be interested in the Dakna?

"Second, someone killed the clone Morph-Andrew led me to." Smith looked at the new clone. "No, this is a replacement. The first clone died yesterday. Somebody gave her her deathcode. Over the phone. I was lured out of the house by a call from an informant that turned out to be a decoy, and when I came back—" his voice shook, cracked. "Who could have done that? Deathcode information is private; only a clone's owner would know it—or former owner. Maybe the same owner who might have some connection to an old Techno beatnik named Rabenz, a strong enough connection to convince him to call me to get me out of my house. A connection from years ago, maybe, like having used Rabenz as a spy to get inside information on Von Hellinger and his daughter."

"You're not accusing me, surely, of—" said Smith slowly, his brow knitted. "Are you in league with the Technos now, Ted? The metal-heads?"

Janus could feel the hypnotic concentration of the man's brain on him. "You know I'm not. If I had been, I wouldn't have come to you with this. I would have had Morph-Andrew get me phone records to see if you made calls to Rabenz and my apartment yesterday. Well, I can still ask him." With an effort, he stood up. "I'm sure what I find will clear you. I'm sorry, Lazur. I shouldn't have come. I guess I was hoping you could give me some magic answers that would clear everything up—"

But Smith was looking at the clone. "Do you know Missy, my dear?" he asked her gently.

"Yes." At the name she sat up, face alert.

"And you would recognize her and obey her anywhere, wouldn't you?"

Eagerly: "Yes."

Smith said: "Melissa."

One of the bookshelf-covered walls slid aside, and behind it was a room, a small bedroom crowded with medical machines, one wall a holographic window of a beautiful summer day. Next to the bed was a wheelchair.

In the wheelchair was a nightmare of twisted bones and eaten flesh, hairless skin mottled scar-pink. Tubes and wires from the machines ran to its skeletal limbs.

Smith said again, very gently: "Melissa."

The thing's skinned-over eyes rolled in their sockets. "Ahhh," it croaked, a moan of pain as much as acknowledgement.

"I took her from the euthanatorium myself, in my own arms," said Smith dreamily. "My subcommittee oversaw the Public Health Department, and I knew the Washington Director, and I bribed him to let me take her, then made sure he was inspecting Von Hellinger's building when the explosion came. It was a mild case, low-infectivity. She got better—"

"The explosion that killed Von Hellinger and his group—you arranged—"

"Melissa," Smith said gently to the thing in the wheelchair. "One of your clones is here, and a man named Janus who wants to take you from me. You must tell your clone what to do. Tell her: 'Kill Janus.' Tell her: 'Kill Janus.'"

The study door was locked, immoveable against Janus's panicked hands.

"Kill Janus, kill Janus," parroted the thing in a piping voice.

The clone's head was cocked, listening for the voice she was hard-wired to recognize.

"Tell her again, Melissa."

"Kill Janus, kill Janus," piped the thing.

The clone shivered. "That's not Missy," she said tightly.

There was a silence that seemed endless, though it lasted only a few seconds.

Janus laughed then, with a note of hysteria. "Morph-Andrew. Morph-Andrew's hot-wired her, Lazur."

"A malfunction," said Smith. "A dangerous malfunction, though not the kind I would have told the police made her kill you." He took a spark-tube from his pocket. "I'm sorry, Janus, I'll have to kill you myself. You were sent here by Morph-Andrew to attack me—"

He turned to the clone, who was looking from him to Janus in confusion, and said loudly and clearly: "Missy is dead. Long live Missy."

The clone jerked back as if hit and her hands sprang bladelike to her neck. But before they touched it she froze, began to tremble, then slowly relaxed.

"Missy is dead. Long live Missy," Smith thundered. *"Missy is dead. Long live Missy."* The room was suddenly filled with searing anger like invisible flames.

Again the glassy-eyed, reflexive jerk, the bladelike hands, again the hot-wired interruption of the deathcode response.

But from the room behind the wall a sound came. A rasping, choking gurgle like the laughter of Death, a heavy spattering of liquid—

They turned to see the figure in the wheelchair, withered hands like blades covered with thick blood, head hanging from a spit of bone, dark blood soaking white hospital clothes—

✳ ✳ ✳ ✳

"--a political season like none in history," exulted the news analyst on Janus's living room screen. "The Lazur Smith scandal, in which a prominent Evolutionary Progress Party Senator has pled guilty to arranging the bombing death of his daughter and her lover, then hiding a clone infected with a Whitedeath-like disease in the mistaken belief that *she* was his daughter, is only the beginning. In fact, the scandal, which initially dealt a serious blow to the EPP's showing in the polls, now appears to have actually improved the Party's chances in November's elections. This because of the incredible discovery that the inspiration for composer Carl Von Hellinger's famous symphony "The Dakna," *was a clone.* Scientists using brain tissue gathered in an autopsy now say conclusively that Senator Smith's clone was the source of the neural tracks recorded by Von Hellinger as part of the symphony said to embody the quintessential humanity of the twenty-first century. Suffering from a Whitedeath-like viral mutation, the clone's anguish produced some of the most hauntingly human music in history.

"Coming only a month before the Congressional elections, this revelation has turned many voters toward the EPP, whose platforms have long included a clone rights plank—"

Janus hit the Off button and rainy, deep grey dusk filled the apartment. He went to a window, opened it. A cold, wet wind gusted fitfully, hissing through the trees and bushes around the ruined buildings on his street. He filled his lungs with it to get the smell of police stations and courtrooms out of them, then turned around abruptly, willing himself to see Theodora in the lithe, blonde figure on the couch.

The clone Morph-Andrew had given him, newly out of her growth tank, still unnamed, almost experienceless, looked blankly back at him.

He pointed to the guest room.

"You can sleep in there," he said.

Black Memes

Ransom made his mistake out of impatience.

The robot excavator repairing the broken sewer under Thomas Square on his shift had run into a problem it couldn't solve or describe—one of those things it takes human eyes to see and a human brain to understand. After twenty minutes of trying to make sense of its reports, carefully filtered through his apartment's AI network to remove possible infectious memes, Ransom slammed his hand on his desk.

"Put it on direct feed," he said.

"Countermanded," said Network's soft voice. "Regulations require – "

"Cut off," Ransom snapped. If he could just see what the robot was babbling about for a second without Network's paranoid abstraction software turning the signal into antiseptic text and stick diagrams – . Network fell silent, its AI circuits closed down.

The holoscreen bloomed with dark mud and shattered concrete flowing with water filthy from the infected crowds milling on the Square, heavy plastic pipes snaking into the hole to feed the excavation machines. Ransom's hungry eyes scanned. Then without warning he was looking at something else.

A naked woman writhed on the screen, wearing only a narrow plastic bracelet on each wrist. The roar of a crowd thundered around her. Above her nose she had no face. Her head was burst open, skull peeled away, enlarged brain swelling out of it like a huge cauliflower, purplish as dried, wrinkled liver. Her shriveled eyeballs dangled from the brain by their optic nerve fibers. And she danced with lust, swollen, distorted head wagging, thin, shapely mouth open and gasping, her lithe, sweaty body writhing while the crowd roared—

Ransom jumped backward, knocking over his chair.

He knelt on the carpet, eyes squeezed shut. The roar of the crowd still came faintly from the screen.

"Network," he rasped.

The sound was immediately cut off.

Do Not Attempt To Describe Your Meme Contact, Or Your Call Will Be Terminated, said a blue opening screen at the City's Emergency Psychological Infection Clinic number. That screen stayed a long time, as if many other calls were being answered before his, until Ransom was afraid there was no one there, that the government too had finally fallen to the epidemic.

But at last the screen spelled: "An operator has answered your call." That was the Clinic's response filtered through Network's abstraction circuits to ensure that no infectious material penetrated the clean interior of his mind. Only now it wasn't clean anymore.

The screen listened neutrally to his panicked words, then paused while his message was processed by a filter on the Clinic's side. Finally it spelled: "The operator inquires whether you violated Department of Mental Health Emergency Regulations requiring AI preview of all transmissions to exclude clandestine broadcasts containing infective memes."

It listened coldly to his stumbling apology and explanation and plea. In a while it said: "The operator states that forty-eight hours' dosage of thorazine will be sent to you by messenger robot under Emergency Regulation 4332.7. The operator instructs you to take it as indicated and watch Sanity TV until a physician contacts you. The operator asserts that this should be late in the day tomorrow."

Pause. Then Network's red override screen said: "Questionable message, with emotional overtones; Danger Level 2."

Ransom flicked a shaky finger through the Release window. Level 2 was a routine risk, an artifact more of AI security systems' paranoia than any real danger.

"The operator states that you should not be apprehensive. The operator observes that you contacted the Clinic immediately after your infective episode, just as Regulations require. The operator asserts that cure rates under these conditions are high."

Thinking back to the days when he talked to real people instead of AI systems, Ransom translated that into: "Don't worry, we'll fix you up." Tears of gratitude ran down his face.

"Memes are not *alive*," said Dr. Christian Solomon, seated in the clean, square, sane studio of the government broadcasting facility located somewhere in a downtown bunker. "That is a persistent myth springing from the fanciful descriptions used by early researchers to describe them." He had a graying goatee, a bald spot, metal-framed glasses, a light-colored tie, and he gestured with large, hairy hands at the lovely, healthy Michelle Rayne, who hosted the twenty-four-hour Sanity TV talk show. "When you think of it, it's rather obvious—how can ideas, images, concepts, and the like be thought of as *alive*? In fact this discussion of the memes as being alive was simply meant to dramatize their tendency to reproduce themselves, figuratively speaking, by spreading from brain to brain through the process of communication. As you can see, however, in this process obviously it is *humans* who are the active, living participants—the memes are merely communicable mental constructs. As such, they cannot really threaten us—they are tools created by the human mind, and which therefore can be controlled by the human mind."

Michelle's concerned, beautiful face filled the screen: "Yet I think the point is worth making, because many of our viewers may have gotten into the habit of thinking of the memes as almost living organisms, like viruses or some other *active* cause of mental disease, and, as such, may have despaired of ever overcoming the epidemic of communicable insanity that now – "

The figure of Network's mobile unit walked silently though the bedroom, a load of washing in her arms.

"Where is the thorazine?" Ransom asked her dully, the words stirring a cold, dull dread in his chest that several hours of Sanity TV had numbed. The light in the apartment's holographic windows—the real ones had been filled in years ago, when the memes were still just a nuisance—was turning long and yellow.

She paused gracefully, a lock of blonde hair falling over one eye. "There is a riot outside the building," she said softly. "The delivery robots can't get through. The grocery delivery is being held up too."

The large rooms of the thirtieth-floor apartment were as silent and serene as the nineteenth-century Sicilian landscape the windows showed. Ransom looked back at the holoscreen. Sanity TV was the only place you could safely see a live human face; the programming was carefully counterinfectious, so Network didn't need to abstract it, though the picture blanked out now and then as the preview filter caught some pirate transmission trying to override the government's coded, secured signal.

"*--can* be brought under control, sanity and stability *can* be restored," Michelle was saying seriously to the camera as she did every day, "*if* the Regulations are followed. As always, the paramount duty of every uninfected citizen is: stay uninfected! *Take* the precautions, hard as they may be, lonely as they may be. If you have an information-tight place to live, *stay there*, tough it out, and sign up for a remote-social-services job. If you do not have a place that is meme-secure, come to one of the government bunkers . . ."

The windows gradually faded to black, until the only light was the holoscreen. Ransom slouched on his low king-size bed watching it. As if summoned by darkness, stray thoughts began to stir inside him. He caught himself thinking of the burst-head woman.

No. He jerked his mind back to the screen.

" – if you look at the situation in pseudo-evolutionary terms, the memes have sealed their own death warrant," a large, handsome woman who was an evolutionary biologist was saying to Michelle Rayne. "Most of the people they 'inhabit' fail to take precautions for their own livelihood or safety, and some even purposely injure themselves – "

— like the dancing woman. No matter how much gene engineering she had bought, she couldn't live more than a few days or weeks with an exposed brain before a biological infection or injury killed her. And yet she danced –

No.

"—at this rate, all the carriers will die, and the earth will be inherited, so to speak, by the uninfected and resistant."

– her lithe hips thrusting hungrily –

A throbbing started in Ransom's body.

"But also, through government psychoanalysis techniques that are becoming increasingly refined, specially trained doctors – "

They would have had to inject growth hormones into her brain, cut her skull away, re-engineer the tissue so it developed the dry, protective skin. And all so she could become hideous and blind and probably insane from the drugs, and die in a little while of some horrible infection. Yet she danced –

There was a rustling, and Ransom turned away from the screen. Network's mobile unit was lowering herself gracefully onto the bed, her slender, shapely form wearing a white lace teddy. Her large eyes were fixed on his.

"I hear your heartbeat," she said softly. "You mustn't think about what you saw. I'll help you."

She rolled onto her back and arched her body, hands by her ears, eyes closed, delicate lips parted.

She had no real passion, Ransom knew. He had seen her repaired, standing in the closet off the kitchen that was her "room," torso swung open to show circuit boards and gears, her delicate, intelligent face frozen. She was made of metal and plastic, warmed glycerin pumped under an organic sheath that was the exquisite sculpture of a woman.

She clung to him with small, sweaty hands that could easily crush his bones, rubbing her face against his side, legs twined around his legs.

" – fortunately, the City's robots and remote-controlled machines can continue to provide services and food distribution indefinitely. There should be plenty of time to let the memes kill themselves off as long as we have a continuing supply of dedicated sane individuals to operate and oversee the machines in return for guaranteed food, health care, and – "

The burst-head woman's lust was real, he could tell even from his split-second look at her. She had at great expense and maybe great pain deformed herself—*to make herself into a meme image to infect the sanes,* he realized; *to become a means of meme reproduction.* Was that what filled her blind, perhaps insane body with passion?

The mobile unit knelt next to him, looking into his face as if she could hear what he was thinking.

Her hot, lovely eyes were dead plastic.

She raised a small hand and carefully smashed his head into the wall, and as he lost consciousness he saw her getting out of bed to go stand in her closet.

✳ ✳ ✳ ✳

She woke him later. Light was bright in the fake windows. He had a splitting headache.

"I'm sorry," she said. "The meme was taking root in you. I could tell by your autonomic functions. The doctor is on link."

Anger, fear, and relief followed her words into Ransom's brain. He struggled up past her to his desk, squeezing his eyes shut to ease the pain in his head. She went quietly out of the room. The government-blue holoscreen spelled: "The doctor requests that you describe your meme contact."

Ransom ran a shaky hand across his face and blurted out what he had seen. At the end of it he was sweating.

Pause. Then: "The doctor wishes to know what aspects of this image disturb you."

He stuttered: "It—it made me wonder, how—how anyone—or why they would be so – "

"The doctor wishes to inquire whether the image attracts as well as repels you."

"No! Of course not!"

Network's red override screen said: "Questionable message with unanalyzed conceptual content; Danger Level 4."

Ransom felt cold, as if the blood had left his hands and feet. "Release," he stuttered. After all, a general-purpose AI system like Network would not understand psychoanalysis.

The blue screen spelled: "The doctor speculates that you are suffering from a 'booster-meme' infection. The doctor explains that this occurs when an earlier, covertly implanted meme takes root in the mind without the knowledge of the host. This meme by itself is not harmful, nor even noticeable until another infectious meme is introduced. But when the second meme is introduced, the first 'boosts' it, that is, magnifies its effect. The doctor states that this is a device becoming common in meme-proliferation strategies."

Pause.

"Questionable message with unanalyzed conceptual content; Danger Level 6."

He released eagerly. It made sense—the meme seemed to have infected him so fast; there had been no resistance to the images, the throbbing in his mind and body –

"The doctor speculates that you have absorbed a Covert Isolation Meme Complex (CIMC), and that this has greatly enhanced the effect of the Libidinous/Irrational Meme Image (LIMI) you were exposed to yesterday. The doctor explains that LIMIs are fast-implant but normally low-infectivity memes. The doctor explains that LIMIs are effectively boosted by CIMC because CIMC creates an excessively paranoid fear of contact with other persons, causing the host to isolate himself, usually in the care of an automated household AI system; but this exclusive interaction with a completely rational companion after a time creates a strong subconscious craving for contact with the irrational aspect of the human personality; this craving can then be exploited by a LIMI. The doctor deduces that this is why the LIMI is apparently taking root so quickly."

"But—but the Regulations say to stay away form everyone, even over link," Ransom stuttered. His heart banged suddenly. What if this wasn't a doctor at all, but a disguised meme transmission? But it couldn't be—the government security systems that constantly scanned the broadcasting frequencies destroyed meme transmissions within seconds.

A red override screen said: "Highly questionable message with potentially damaging content; Danger Level 10."

Ransom curled up in his chair, panting, chewing his finger, eyes riveted to the screen.

"Shall I terminate contact?" asked Network softly.

He didn't answer. After another minute, the red screen spelled: "Questionable message with unanalyzed conceptual content; Danger Level 4."

Trembling, he released.

"The doctor takes as an example your unquestioning acceptance of the LIMI as a real rather than a computer-simulation image. In the absence of an unconscious yearning for and vulnerability to this type of image, you would almost certainly have entertained the conjecture that it was a simulation."

Ransom stared. Of course. It had to be. Wasn't it silly to think that anyone could live as mutilated as the burst-head woman? Or that they would be *celebrating* if they did? The memes weren't *that* powerful, for God's sake. Cool relief washed over him.

"Examples of what?" he asked. "I missed your last screen." He was still trembling convulsively.

"Highly questionable message with potentially damaging content; Danger Level 10."

"Release."

"The doctor suggests that this interface proceed without security abstraction. The doctor believes this will weaken the CIMC."

Network's warning screen was white on black: "Government Regulations Require – "

Ransom was suddenly sick to his stomach at the thought of being trapped with this machine for one more day, being wrapped one more night in its plastic arms. "I'm invoking the emergency exception to the Regulations," he said with forced calm. "For emergency psychoanalysis. Switch off abstraction function. Maintain preview filter for pirate transmissions."

The black screen flickered away, and Ransom was looking at a human face; the face of a woman. She looked a little like Network's mobile unit, with blonde hair, high cheekbones, fair skin. But this one's eyes were deep blue-green with tiredness in them, her skin spoiled a little by long-ago acne.

"Welcome," she said. Her lips twisted in a wry, angry smile.

Ransom gawked. He couldn't say anything.

"As I was trying to tell you before your valiant home computer stopped me, the Regulations you see on TV are put out with the expectation that people will cheat a little. That's healthy, even though we have to frown on it officially because of course it can result in infection. But an isolation meme makes you too paranoid even to cheat, setting you up for the irrationality meme. You end up thinking like your AI security system."

"What should I—what should I do?" His voice sounded clumsy, clogged, all the words pronounced a little wrong. He stared in fascination as *feelings*—irritation, sympathy, disgust, protectiveness—crossed her face like sun and shadow. A knot of warmth blossomed in his chest as he realized that they were directed at *him*.

"I'm going to recommend—and now don't switch off on me, understand? – a home visit. I'm going to be in your neighborhood," she studied something off-screen, "later this afternoon. Don't switch me off," she commanded angrily, reading his horrified face. "I don't have time to screw around. Your complex is going to make this seem like murder, I know."

"A *home visit*," he rasped. "But how can you – "

"I'm a resistant," she said simply, her mouth twisting as if the word had a bitter taste.

✳ ✳ ✳ ✳

"Cut off!" he told the black-and-white screen that warned him it would be obligated to inform the authorities if a home visit was attempted. Then he sat paralyzed, curled in his bedroom armchair, listening fearfully to the tiny, unfiltered sounds that now came into the silent apartment—the metal ticking of heating elements, a faint rush of water in a pipe, a distant creak, as if someone had stepped on a stair. His thoughts were a jumble; the terror of going through the isolation zone to his front door throbbing against a suddenly unbearable craving to be with a real human; a wondering how he would look to the doctor, who was even more beautiful with her fluent eyes than Network's mobile unit, which had been customized to his subconscious wants back in the days when such services were available.

The forgotten chime of the doorbell sent him rushing in panic to the bathroom to gawk at himself in the mirror and desperately try to pull a comb through his shoulder-length gray hair, his bushy beard, run his hands over his face –

The bell chimed again impatiently.

He ran through the living room to the heavy metal door, punched the release code with trembling fingers, dragged it open. The two-meter isolation space around the apartment was gray with dust, humped with ancient furniture and junk, dim with service lights. Small footprints in the dust showed where the mobile unit patrolled it to make sure nothing and no one got in.

Another metal door had lock lights on it. He coded it and dragged it aside as the bell rang a third time.

The passage outside was pitch-black: only delivery robots roamed the building anymore, and they didn't need lights. Standing shadowed in the blackness, holding a flashlight, was the doctor. She was slender, of medium height, wearing gray fatigues and carrying a heavy square bag on a strap over her shoulder.

"I thought you weren't going to open it, and I was going to kill you," she said angrily. "I don't have time to play around." And after a few seconds, looking carefully into his face, more gently: "Can I come in?"

Ransom was staring at her eyes. Compared to the Network mobile unit and the sober talk-show guests on Sanity, they were wild, liquid. She might be meme-resistant, but the memes had done something to her, he saw.

He backed up and pushed the heavy doors shut behind her, against the fearful blackness. As soon as they were in the airy stillness of the apartment, colors of Oriental carpets, potted plants, and upholstery around them, she relaxed slowly, letting out a long breath and looking around.

"This is nice," she said simply.

"I—I used to be a lawyer," he heard himself saying with surprise. "Before."

She nodded. Then she said softly: "There's a baby asleep in the foyer of your building. Wrapped in dirty rags." For a moment there was rage and sorrow and helplessness in her eyes, and a single tear rolled down the curve of her cheek. Before he could stop himself, Ransom had put out a trembling hand to touch it. The liquid on his fingers caught the light, like pearl or diamond.

"Now I run heavy excavation machines for the Emergency Sanitation Department," he said, as if to cover over the image of the sleeping baby. "I've been doing that, oh, years now."

She laughed suddenly. "Sit down," she said, pointing to his blue couch. She lowered the bag from her shoulder and sat next to him, facing him. "We'll have you back running heavy excavation machines in no time. But I want you to listen." She was grave again. "The first thing you have to know about the memes is: *they're alive.*"

He stared at her clear blond face in horror. "They are not *alive*," he said. "The TV – "

"They put out that stuff to keep the sanes brave. It's good enough for people who just go along doing what they're told. Who don't have to fight for their lives." Her eyes clouded, like water when the wind blows on it. "The memes are *alive*. For millennia people thought they were products of our minds—epiphenomena" – she waved a hand—"but it was a symbiotic relationship from the start, the same way our intestines are full of microorganisms. We used them, they used us."

"Are you really a doctor? Are you?"

"Yes," she whispered, taking his hand, holding his eyes with her beautiful eyes. Her hand was ice-cold, sweaty. He could smell her, a sweet, sour smell that made him dizzy. "As we evolved, the memes evolved, getting more complex, more sophisticated. Christianity, Islam, Marxism, were early epidemics, where successful strains reproduced into billions of brains."

"You're not the doctor," he said. "You're – "

"*Listen!*" Her wild eyes paralyzed him. "Twenty years ago,

the memes' evolution started to accelerate. We gave them the means with our neural networks, telespace nets, communications systems. They started to evolve independently of us, for the first time taking forms not useful or life-supporting for us. Remember the outcries about 'information sickness' and 'future shock'? You probably put in the first parts of your information security system then. The memes were starting to leave us behind. It was as if the microorganisms inside us had started to use our intestines not to help us digest food, but for their own purposes. And soon – "

The electricity of terror coursed through him.

"You're not a doctor." He was standing, his body hunched taut over her. "You're infected. You're – "

She leapt to her feet too, face blazing. "Don't you understand?" she shrilled. "*They* are the organisms of the future. They don't have bodies to drag in the mud, to drag their evolution out over millions of years. They can evolve in an instant, the time it takes you to *think.*"

Ransom started pushing her desperately toward the metal door. She struggled, hissing into his face.

"We are their reproductive organs, don't you understand? That is our purpose. We are their *genitals.*" Suddenly she tore away from him and yanked the zipper down the front of her fatigues.

"I plant this meme in you," she said through lips and tongue swollen with lust.

"Network!" he screamed in the darkness of his eyes.

The woman's breasts and stomach were mutilated, fresh cuts overlying scars on top of scars.

Light running feet padded, and then the mobile unit had the woman by the arms, pressing her irresistibly toward the door. The woman's left arm twisted backward horribly and snapped out of its socket, and Ransom saw that it was a prosthesis, under it a jagged stump.

The mobile unit grabbed the woman's shoulder and twisted her backward with tremendous strength, until she screamed, just once, an insane scream of pain and joy. Then the unit had the metal door open and they disappeared into the isolation zone, the woman struggling wildly. The door closed behind them.

❋ ❋ ❋ ❋

Ransom couldn't tell how much time passed before the unit leaned over him huddled in his bedroom armchair.

"I have ejected the infected woman from the building and informed the authorities of the security penetration," she said calmly. "Also, the thorazine has arrived." She held out a glass of water and a capsule. "I've contacted the Emergency Psychological Infection Clinic. They will be placing an emergency physician call within the next hour. They are also conducting an urgent security investigation; they believe their transmission code has been penetrated by – "

"Cut off," Ransom said.

She stood frozen over him holding out the pills, like the statue of a ministering angel, as the fake afternoon light turned long and yellow. He knew he should take the thorazine and lie down to watch Sanity TV until he fell asleep or the real doctor called, but he couldn't. The memes were taking root in his mind, sending their tendrils deep, the images they had planted—the two disfigured women, the exegesis of their evolution, even the image of the sleeping baby—growing and merging in some strange way as they ran again and again through his mind. Soon he saw an ocean of people with their faces turned upward, millions of them, hushed with a common purpose, a common thought; and out of their minds rose a great, shining meme, wobbling upward like a bubble, a single organism of thought formed from the ocean of minds. The people moaned in worship and ecstasy, raising their hands. Ransom felt himself among them, throbbing with the deep, irrational lust that is the force of evolution.

The light in the apartment was blue and transparent as shallow water when he finally moved. His holoscreen blinked with an official Emergency Message. He coded the metal doors in the living room and the dim gray isolation space. The passage outside was black and silent, smelling of machine oil and dust. The apartment door closed behind him with a dull boom.

He felt other armored doors at intervals as he groped along the wall. The elevators seemed farther away than he remembered. The button he fumblingly pressed in one of them blooming with sudden light showed dimly that its mirrors were all smashed, its brass rail bent and blackened, its walls and floor scratched and dented as with great violence. At the bottom, as the doors rolled aside, dim light from the exterior windows covered with bulletproof plastic scratched almost opaque showed a ragged bundle lying against the wall of the dirty, littered foyer. It was a little child, a baby almost, with a baby's big, round head and thin hair, a baby's dirty, calm, sleeping face. It wore rags, with rags tied around its feet for shoes. Its small hands rested calmly on the filthy carpet.

Ransom knelt and gently touched it. Its lips and one of its hands stirred, but it didn't wake. Ransom got up and went toward the massive, solenoid-bolted entrance door. Outside in the dusk a singing voice echoed crazily and seductively in the empty street.

He could still go back, he knew; he had the codes for his doors, and the government psychiatrists might still be able to cure him. But he had lost the desire to be cured, he realized. It would be death. Outside were the woman with the blue-green eyes, the tides of evolution, life itself, clamorous, hideous, gorgeous, always in motion. To hold back, to refuse to sire evolution's next creature, the one who would replace him, would be to die.

He touched the worn solenoid release and the door clicked open a crack, letting in a breath of air, blue and deep with evening, its coolness surprisingly delicious.

He pushed out into the evening-blue street. His way was clear. All doubt dropped from his mind. He chose the memes. He chose Life.

Sleepers Awake

It all started with a flash.

It had been a mild October Sunday, yellow leaves fluttering down against a blue sky, barking of a neighborhood dog and the tang of wood smoke coming faintly in the still air, warm enough to sit on your back deck all day. I had sat on mine till evening, reading, dozing, and watching the light turn long and yellow, then blue. Even when it got chilly and too dark to follow my spy book, where a beautiful girl in a parking garage was begging the hero to help her escape from terrorists, I didn't want to go in. I was leaning my chair against the cool brick of the house, listening to the trilling of crickets and an occasional car down on Thayer Avenue when it came: a split-second of flashbulb blue piercing the neighborhood like an x-ray.

My chair thumped down on four legs. Another chair scraped back in the kitchen. Vicky slid the glass door open, a magazine in her hand. "What was that?"

We went and stood by the deck railing. The evening air was still and deep, two early stars shining through the branches of our backyard oak.

The screen door next door slammed and Mrs. Roemer's old, hoarse voice said: "Going to rain, I imagine."

"There aren't any clouds," said Vicky.

"What?"

"There aren't any clouds. It wasn't lightning," Vicky yelled.

"Maybe an electric short in the circuit box down the street. Big one. Somebody ought to call the electric company," I told Vicky.

I got her to go in and call. I stood looking up into the darkness, crickets rippling the silence softly. Three houses down, Cindy Lippmann stood in her back yard holding her baby, her face a white blur looking up into the air.

"You can bet it's some kind of bad weather, anyhow," said Mrs. Roemer sourly, and went back inside, screen door slamming behind her.

Looking up through the branches of the oak, I thought I heard, very faintly, the ringing of tiny bells blending with the crickets' song.

Vicky came back out. "The line's busy. Probably a lot of people --"

"Listen," I hissed.

"What?"

I strained my ears. The ringing seem to have retreated back into my imagination.

But that night, on the edge of sleep, I thought I heard it again, sweet and distant, very faint.

"You hear that?" I whispered to Vicky.

"Mmm?"

"Bells."

Pause.

"Go to sleep."

✳ ✳ ✳ ✳

Things were screwed up at work the next day. For one thing, the phones were broken. I had an important call to make to Syracuse, New York, but I kept getting whistling and crackling noises instead. The operator wouldn't answer. I finally told Rose to report it to the office manager, and spent the rest of the morning talking to my dictation machine. When I got back from lunch, Rose had the transcription on my chair. I put my feet on the desk with a contented sigh, uncapped a red pen, turned back the cover sheet, and read:

Sleepers Awake, the voice is calling,
On the battlements the watchman cry:
Wake, city of Jerusalem! . . .

The telephone rang. I groped for it.

"Bill Johnson, please," said a faraway, staticky voice.

"You have the wrong number."

"This isn't Johnson's Formal Wear in Des Moines, Iowa?"

I said no, hung up, buzzed Rose, and handed her the memo as the phone rang again.

"Bill Johnson, please," said a faraway, staticky voice.

I hung up. Rose was staring at the memo blankly. "That's funny. Something must be wrong with the word processing system. I'll try to . . ."

The phone rang. I answered it, watching her out of the office suspiciously.

"Bill Johnson? Of Des Moines Iowa?"

"No, Bob Wilson, of Washington, DC, the same guy you've gotten the last half dozen times."

"Sorry about that, Mr. Wilson. Tom Gibbs from New York City. I'm in formal wear. How are the phones down your way?"

"Screwed up."

"Same here. I've been trying to get through to Des Moines all morning. Seems like the trunk lines are out of whack. I can get Washington, Boston, Chicago, and LA OK, but the farm lands don't answer. Funny."

The phone rang once more that afternoon. I picked it up, expecting Tom Gibbs, but it wasn't Tom Gibbs; it was a wide, distant hum, a faint gabble of ten thousand crossed lines overlaid with the electronic buzz of some vast malfunction, like a telephone call from Entropy itself. I hung up with a shiver and a quick prayer that It didn't intend to come visit in person.

I was in a bad mood when I got home.

"Where's the newspaper?" I complained, after searching the living room for it. "You didn't throw it away again, did you?"

"It didn't come," Vicky called from upstairs. "I left you some green beans on the stove."

"Green beans?" I went and looked at them mournfully.

"I've got rehearsal, honey." She came downstairs, beautiful in a blue skirt and pink, floppy sweater, eyes vivid with makeup, and gave me a barely touching kiss that wouldn't smear her lipstick. "And when I get back we have to go over to Mrs. Roemer's. She swears she has ghosts. I promised we'd come and make sure there aren't any. I think she's gone crazy, poor old lady."

"Ghosts? Honey, I don't want to go over there tonight. I'm tired. You wouldn't believe – "

In the backyard, crickets trilled in subtly shifting patterns, the air still and just a little damp. Moonlight cast a dark deck shadow on the grass. I was leaning on the railing before going back inside to my spy book, when I heard the faint, sweet sound of bells.

I held my breath. The lights of Vicky's car had just disappeared down the hill. The sound seemed to be coming from around the side of the house.

I tiptoed down the wooden steps and through crackling leaves, poked my head past the gutter downspout at the corner.

High in a young maple in Arland Johnston's side yard, unseasonable firefly lights floated.

I snuck forward, the soft earth of iris beds silencing my steps. For a second it crossed my mind that Arland had hung out his Christmas lights two months early: I thought I saw tiny haloed saints and angels with trumpets.

Then they all winked out at once.

I stood looking up into the tree, now lit only by the pale moon. As I watched, a single leaf let go and fluttered down.

I heard the bells again, faint and faraway.

The firefly lights were floating around a tree in old Mr. Jakeway's back yard, down at the bottom of the street.

I crept across silent asphalt moon-tinted the same deep, dusty blue as the sky, along the sidewalk in tree-shadows, and pushed through a hole in Mr. Jakeway's hedge, getting scratched and poked.

I picked my way through his quarter acre back yard, trying to tell clumps of weeds from junk auto parts that could break your leg in the dark. Gnarled tree branches hung almost to the ground.

A cobra blur coiled around my leg and yanked me into the air.

I tried to scream, but only a faint gurgling came out. I hung upside down, breath knocked out of me, spinning slowly, arms and free leg struggling wildly in the air.

The rope around my ankle jerked. There were grunts from above, and I started going up again, slowly. Hands took hold of me and pulled me onto a thick tree branch four stories off the ground.

An old man squatted on the branch. For a second I thought he was Mr. Jakeway, but then I saw that he was even older, with a sour, wrinkled face, and no hair. He wore a long, dingy robe that the moon lit gray, with big buttons down the front. He peered at me through wire-rimmed spectacles. Around him crouched half a dozen kids in their early teens, watching me solemnly. Three of them held me onto the branch.

The old man croaked: "I am the Angel of Death."

I stared at him. Then I did something I never would have expected: I started to cry. I could see our house down the street, yard awash in pale leaves, my old Nissan parked in front, a bag of newspapers on the walk waiting for the recycling truck. I had never seen the neighborhood from up here; already it looked far away and out of reach, like a picture of someplace you used to live but will never see again.

"Please stop crying," said the old man irritably. "I'm not going to take you yet. At least, not if you promise to stop poking around where you have no business. We're having enough trouble right now without you."

I wiped my shirtsleeve across my nose hopefully.

"Do you promise to stop snooping? To leave those little lights alone? And not to tell anyone about us?"

I nodded eagerly. One of the teenage kids looped the end of the rope they had pulled off my ankle around my chest.

"See that you don't," the old man croaked as they lowered me rotating toward the earth. "If you do – "

When I reached the ground, I struggled out of the rope and ran blindly until I was inside my house, locked the door, drew all the curtains, and dialed 911.

It took them a long time to answer. After I had given my name and address, I said: "There's a weirdo in a tree at the end of my block who claims he's the Angel of Death. He's got some kids with him. They've got a rope snare rigged up that almost broke my back. This guy is dangerous, officer – if you could see his face – "

"Angel of death – up in a tree – rope snare – " a heavy voice on the other end repeated slowly, writing. "And what address would this be at, Mr. Wilson?"

"It's the first house on your right as you turn onto Thayer Place. I don't know the exact address. You're sending somebody right over?"

"It'll probably be half an hour, Mr. Wilson, before we can get to it. We've – "

"Half an *hour*? Officer, there's a dangerous maniac – "

"If you'll let me finish, Mr. Wilson, we've got about thirty other emergency calls, and we just don't have the cars to cover them. I suggest you stay inside and keep your doors locked until we can get out there, but I wouldn't panic. The other wild calls we've had tonight have turned out to be hoaxes."

"This isn't a hoax!"

"I didn't say it was, sir. But look, we've got a report of a giant lizard prowling around Sligo Creek – ate somebody's dog, says here. We've got a report of a *mushroom cloud* over on Colesville Road. We've got ghosts all over town. We figure it's one of these kids' Dungeons & Dragons clubs, or some people very confused about when Halloween is, so I wouldn't get too concerned. Just stay inside until the officer gets there."

As soon as I put down the phone, a scream sounded faintly from next door.

I spent a minute that felt like an hour chewing the end off my thumb. I figured the Angel of Death guy and his kids were murdering Mrs. Roemer. I wondered what I should do about that.

Another scream.

I banged out along leaf-covered sidewalks. All of Mrs. Roemer's windows were lit and her front door was ajar. Mrs. Roemer herself was standing in the middle of her small, well-furnished living room, wrinkled hands on her hips, looking around with solemn belligerence.

"He's back," she announced in her hoarse voice as I stopped in the doorway, gasping. "Him and his alcoholic mother and his sponging sister."

"Who?" I yelled, trying to keep my teeth from chattering.

"Terrell."

"I – I thought he was dead."

"It was such a relief to me. I learned to love him afterward; he left me this house and a lot of money, God bless him. But he's back. Him and his alcoholic, sponging family."

"Mrs. Roemer, I've got a terrible emergency – "

"You look in the basement," she told me. "I'll go upstairs. If we can't find them, we'll have to look in the attic."

And she started up the stairs, yelling quaveringly: "Terrell! Terrell! You come out right now!"

It took me awhile to get her calmed down. She wouldn't let me leave until I had crawled around in her attic, poking a flashlight into dusty, cobwebbed corners. Maybe I didn't hurry as much as I could have; with the Angel of Death guy prowling the neighborhood, Mrs. Roemer's attic felt comfortably remote and full of dark hiding places. Thankfully, I didn't find her dead in-laws crouching in any of them. When I peeked out her front door twenty minutes later, I was relieved to see the red and blue lights of a police car rotating silently at the end of the street.

I jogged down to where a policeman and old Mr. Jakeway stood by a purring squad car, the mist of their breath rising into blue depths where the moon shone mistily. Another policeman was crashing around in the brush behind Mr. Jakeway's house, shining a flashlight up into the trees.

"Hey there, Bobby," said Mr. Jakeway. "Officer here tells me you saw some kids up in my trees."

"An old man and some kids. But that was an hour ago."

"Well, they're gone now," said the policeman.

"Officer, I know it sounds strange, but they were there. They pulled me – "

"You're not the only report we have on them," said the policeman, looking at a clipboard with his flashlight. "At least the old man. We got a call over on Pershing Drive, an old man fitting that description trampling through people's flowerbeds. Went off in a big foreign car, says here."

"You think they're foreigners? Terrorists?" Asked Mr. Jakeway, thrusting his old, grizzled head forward.

"I don't know what they are. We've gotten a lot of strange calls tonight, is all I know."

"Psychological warfare, maybe," said Mr. Jakeway, nodding and looking into our eyes one at a time. "It could be. You never know what they're inventing in those laboratories. Some kind of gas, maybe, makes you see people up in trees when there aren't any."

The other policeman crashed out of the bushes, looking scratched and out of breath.

"You ought to come cut down some of those weeds back there," he told Mr. Jakeway.

✳ ✳ ✳ ✳

I had left the front door of our house open; it spilled a rectangle of light onto the walk in the still, cricket-trilled air, and I could hear the phone ringing half a block away as I walked back up from Mr. Jakeway's.

I rushed in and answered it.

It was Vicky. "Bob? Hi."

She never calls me "Bob" unless somebody is listening. In the background I could hear music and voices.

"I'm going to be a little late tonight. Something wonderful has happened."

"Where are you? Are you all right?"

"Of course I'm alright. I'm at rehearsal. Honey, you'll never guess what happened."

"Are you coming home? There's some weird things – "

"I'm going to be a little late. Honey, there was a producer at rehearsal tonight. None of us knew it. Stewart introduced us afterward. His name is Ken, and he's doing a show at the Kennedy Center in March. *And he signed me up for a part. With Tim Curry.*"

"That's great, honey, great! But I wish you'd come home, because – "

"Bob? The lines getting staticky. We're going out to celebrate and sign the contract. Can you hear me?"

"I can hear you fine – "

"Hello? Bob? Oh, he's gone," she said disappointedly to someone at her end, and hung up.

Aside from a few distant crackles, the phone was dead.

I got my keys, locked the front door behind me. The gas station at Dale and Piney Branch glared with white neon, self-serve customers dawdling over their hoses. Overfed diners tottered out the door of the Chesapeake Crab House. I pointed the Nissan toward town. Half an hour later I was banging on the locked door of the Souris Studio storefront on 14th Street, cupping my hands on the glass to peer into a dim entrance with a coat rack, a few shabby chairs, and a display for theater programs, but no people. I stood in the smoky, rundown darkness trying to imagine where one would go to celebrate a contract. Then I walked back to the parking garage where I had left the car.

It was on the third sublevel. I went down urine-smelling concrete steps, crossed the oil-stained, neon-lit ramp. I had the door unlocked when a voice behind me said: "Can you give me a ride?"

The ramp had been deserted a second before. "No," I said, and yanked the door open.

"Please. Someone is following me. Please."

She was small and slim, with fashionably tousled blonde hair, breathtaking dark eyes. She wore black tights, a black leather jacket, pink patent leather shoes with buckles. Her face was wild, lips trembling. She came closer between the cars.

"*Please*," she said.

The heavy throb of an engine echoed down the ramp, and her pupils dilated crazily. Her breath came in tearing gasps.

I moved away from the car door with a quick gesture. She scrambled to the floor of the passenger seat and crouched there, head down.

I got in, backed out, and headed up the ramp. At the first turn I had to edge past a black Mercedes limo coming down. I edged close enough to see through the tinted glass of the back seat.

An old man with a bald, wrinkled face sat there. He wore a gray robe with big buttons, wire-rimmed spectacles. He didn't see me; his eyes were straining through the windshield as if looking for something.

I didn't yell, but my heart pounded. I paid the garage attendant in his cubicle of light with a shaking hand.

We were rattling over potholes on 14th Street before the woman said: "You know him." She was staring up at me.

"I'm going to call the police."

She laughed shortly. "The police," she sneered. She threw herself into the passenger seat. "Take a right here. You can use my phone."

As we drove it began to rain. I suddenly had the feeling that I was leaving behind everything familiar to me, my whole life.

She directed me down 22nd Street. A few blocks down, I pulled over by a brick building with wide front steps between stone lions, brass and glass entrance doors glittering with chandelier light. The building elevator was elderly but highly polished. The third floor hall was silent, lit discreetly by brass leaves with bulbs behind them, carpeted in a red floral pattern. The woman unlocked a door near the end, then locked and bolted it behind us.

"Phone's over there," she said, her hand a pale blur in the dark. She hurried into another room.

Rain pattered on the sills of open windows, and the glare of streetlight showed black and white outlines of magazines, clothes, and dishes scattered over deep chairs and a sofa, low glass and metal tables. Shelves held expensive stereo components and a turntable, books, and vases. Shadowy art prints hung on the walls.

The woman was opening and closing drawers in the other

room. She hadn't turned on any lights. I dialed 911 on a telephone shaped like a banana. It was busy.

"You have a phone book?" I called.

"Somewhere." She sounded preoccupied.

A phonebook-sized binder lay on a table at the end of the sofa; but when I opened it I found myself looking at an eight by ten glossy photograph of her wearing only a gold necklace, her delicate, beautiful body stretched out on a bed. I closed the book with a snap.

The woman's voice said behind me: "Look, I need a ride somewhere. It's a matter of life and death. Can you help me?"

From where I stood I could see out the window. "No," I said. "Not yet."

She came around the sofa. She was wearing a white plastic raincoat over a white dress and white stockings, carrying an overnight bag. I held her so she wouldn't get too near the window. Streetlight glow lit her face silver gray.

A black Mercedes limousine was parked across the street.

"Oh my God," she whispered. She started to shake.

I got her by both wrists, whispering: "Shhh." I was imagining the Angel of Death and his chauffer listening in the hall outside.

"No!" She screamed in a sudden frenzy. "No!" She tried to wrench her wrists away from me.

I wrapped my left hand around her face, pinioned her arms with my right, and dragged her struggling into the next room. One of her blue rubber boots kicked off and hit the wall. I crushed her down on a big unmade bed, held a pillow over her head to muffle her screams. After awhile lack of air made her quiet.

I took the pillow away enough to say in her ear: "Maybe they don't know we're here."

She lay still.

I helped her sit up. Her face was red, swollen, wet, her breath gasping with sobs. I put my fingers to my lips and crept back into the living room, listened at the front door. The elevator opened once, but voices and footsteps went away in another direction. There was no other sound. I tried the telephone. There were only buzzing and crackling noises on it now. I sat down against the wall behind the front door, my ears straining against the patter of rain and the distant sound of traffic.

After a long time I peered out the window again. Streetlights glittered on wet pavement. The black limousine was gone.

The woman was asleep in her coat, one boot on, her face calm and intent like a child's. She woke with a start when I touched her.

"They're gone," I told her. My voice seemed to come from far off somewhere. I had started to shake.

She looked up into my face for a minute. Then she began fumbling with the buttons on her dress, breath quickening.

$$* \quad * \quad * \quad *$$

I woke up next to her after midnight, exhausted. Her pale skin seemed to glow faintly in the dark, as if there was a light inside her.

I lay and watched her. Gradually she woke up too.

When she was awake, I said: "I don't understand what's happening."

She propped herself up, sitting against the head of the bed, got a cigarette from the night table. Tendrils of smoke curled around her pale hair, pale shoulders.

"You're dead," she said.

I didn't say anything to that.

"Everybody's dead. Everybody at once," she went on. "Altogether. Whoosh. Wholesale global disaster, Sunday evening about 5:30. You might have seen a flash or felt a sharp pain. I won't tell you what it was, since it's no longer your business, but almost a billion people died in the first half hour, and more are coming all the time.

"Almost nobody noticed. But now you're starting to notice. Now your old consensual reality is starting to break down, to be rebuilt by more powerful forces: desires, obsessions, fears."

I got out of bed. I felt dizzy.

"I have to go," I said. "Home."

"You don't have a home anymore. Just a blackened spot on a

tiny piece of dust buzzing around a spark of light in a far corner of the universe. And a dream image that could vanish any second. You might as well stay here." She smiled, letting a wisp of smoke curl out through her lips.

"I can't," I said thickly, hunting for my underwear in the pile of clothes by the bed. "My wife –"

By the time I turned the Nissan onto Thayer Place, it had stopped raining. Untidy maple branches looming over the front walk in the dark dripped on the waterlogged bag of newspapers. I was heading shakily for the front door when there were steps behind me on the sidewalk.

A bent figure was jogging painfully up the hill. I stumbled backward, the adrenaline of fear tearing through me, but it was only Mr. Jakeway, unshaven jowls wagging, sunken eye sockets filled with shadow.

"Bobby," he rasped. His thin, trembling hands took hold of my shoulders and he leaned on me, breathing hard. "Have they got you too? Or are you awake?" His breath smelled faintly alcoholic.

Before I could answer he went on: "They're lying, Bobby. Nothing's happened. *Nobody's dead.* Don't believe 'em, boy." He leaned on me harder, put his arms around my shoulder. "They want us to move aside. Just move aside and give up. They're using some kind of gas. Black gas. Thank goodness I found you, Bobby," he said hoarsely. "Everybody else is walking around in a dream."

I stared at the glitter of his eyes in the dark. I felt strange.

"Who?" I finally blurted out. "Who?"

"I don't know *who*," he whispered hoarsely. "But they're not from here. Aliens, maybe. I seen them walking through the streets, spraying black gas. We got to do something, Bobby, before they – "

"Somebody told me it was a worldwide disaster – " I stammered miserably.

"That's their lie! It's a lie, Bobby. They want us to – "

"So what do we – what do we do?"

The question seemed to agitate him. "We have to wake up the

others! We have to wake everyone up! Quick! Where's your wife? I'll go after Arland. Come on!"

His panic infected me. I ran up the walk to our front door.

The living room – tidy and familiar, yellowish light from the floor lamp by the couch throwing familiar shadows – turned my panic into cold, jittery sweat.

"Vicky?" I called.

No answer.

Out the window, Mrs. Roemer's bright new kitchen caught my eye. Something was going on in there.

A man and a woman sat at a table by the kitchen window, talking tensely. I couldn't hear what they were saying. The woman looked vaguely like Mrs. Roemer, but young, with an obsolete hairdo. The man was unshaven, jowly, tired-looking.

There was a muffled scream, and the woman dived across the table and buried a paring knife in the tired-looking man's forehead. They tumbled down out of sight, the woman screaming wildly.

My heart pounded. A darkness came over my eyes. I sat down heavily on the couch.

When I started to think again, I was exhausted, drained, too tired even to see clearly: the wall, floor lamp, and coffee table next to me looked translucent, unreal.

I became aware that voices, laughter, and footsteps were approaching along the front walk. The front door flew open and a dozen people came in. As they did, the living room changed. The walls turned from blue to peach and fled outward in a long, curving line; the hardwood floor became plush blonde carpet and sagged to shape a huge sunken living room with grand piano, Chinese screens, round, furry chairs and sofas, dark lacquered cabinets, soft lighting, tropical plants. My body felt peculiarly stiff. I looked down with difficulty. All I could see of myself was a large Chinese vase displayed on a carved stand.

The people who piled through the arched, open front door looked too grown up to be carrying on the way they were. The men wore tuxedos with flowers in the lapels, the women glittery outfits that seemed to be half evening gown, half bikini. They were all young and beautiful. They crowded, laughing, chattering, and squealing, up a wide, curved staircase.

I was still too tired to move, so I sat numbly for another few minutes, until two people came back down the stairs. Music and merrymaking sounds came faintly from above.

The two people, a man and a woman, leaned on the grand piano not more than a stone's throw from me. The man was broad-shouldered and tall, with the kind of face Michelangelo used to carve, hair curling carelessly over his collar. He gazed at the woman is if there was nothing else to see in the world.

She was my wife. A little bigger in some places, a little smaller in others than I remembered her, dark ringlets thicker, the West Virginia jaw trimmed down slightly, but unmistakably Victoria Kathryn Wilson. She was wearing a tight, slithery dress of gold sequins that showed off most of one leg, and that I had to admit looked great, even though it was embarrassing the hell out of me.

I tried to stand up and make a fuss. I couldn't move or talk.

"You haven't given me your answer, darling," murmured the man, gazing down at her. She was gazing at him too, in a way I didn't like. "You can't leave me hanging like this. *Please.*"

"How can I answer? How can I even *think* right now, Billy? Everything is so wonderful! I feel as if I'm in heaven!" She put her drink on the piano and kicked off her high heels. "Do you think it's a dream? An Oscar nomination, highest-grossing first week in history – "

"And all because of you," he said. "You made that film what it is. Without you it would be nothing."

"Oh, Billy – "

He drew her close in his strong arms, crushing her to him, and as their lips touched a shudder went through him.

"Hey!" I managed to yell in outrage.

I thought Vicky glanced at me, but the man didn't seem to hear.

"It's funny," he said when they were done slobbering on each other. He seemed ready to cry. "Here I am, the most powerful man in Hollywood – I really thought I had it made. Any woman in the world would do anything to get in my next picture. But the one I really want – the one I *must* have – won't have me."

He knelt down in front of her, looking up with imploring eyes. "Please," he whispered. *"Please . . ."*

"Oh, brother," I groaned.

"Will you shut *up*?" Vicky screamed at me, stamping her foot. "What are you doing here, anyway? I didn't come snooping around your corny private eye scene with that slut, did I? Get out of here! Leave me alone!"

Her rage hit me like a wave. Everything turned translucent again, Vicky and the Hollywood producer like ghosts with lights glowing inside them. The producer didn't seem to notice Vicky yelling – he stood up and took her in his arms again. And as they kissed, something funny happened: the light inside Vicky seemed to flicker and go dim, while the light inside the producer got stronger, as if he had drawn some of her light into himself.

And there was something else – someone I hadn't noticed before, sitting on a distant loveseat, half hidden by a dwarf palm, hands clasped patiently over his long gray robe, wire rim glasses patiently watching the oblivious lovers.

I struggled, trying to shout a warning, but I couldn't move or make a sound.

Ghostly music played. Vicky and the producer started to dance, close and slow, gradually swaying over near where I sat stiff and dumb. Soon the producer's tuxedoed bottom swayed languidly in front of my face. I lunged forward with all my strength, and bit it desperately hard. He screamed and jumped out of Vicky's arms, whirling in astonishment and rubbing himself.

Vicky's face was ugly with rage as she kicked me off my stand to shatter against the wall.

I stood in the trough of a mountain in heavy night rain, showing my thumb to interstate traffic that made a pale ribbon through murky darkness up the mountain's shoulder. Every few minutes lightning struck the summit, lighting wooded hills, and sending out a crackle and boom. I wore an old army surplus poncho, I was 17, the rain was warm, and the crowded, lonely highway made me feel somehow alive, vital, like a sailor on an uncharted ocean. When a little white car pulled out of traffic up the shoulder, I ran, lugging my knapsack, and climbed into the front seat next to a girl.

She was slender and young, wearing jeans and a floppy sweater, tousled blonde hair falling to her shoulders, dark eyes that flashed at me, then watched the mirror for an opening in traffic. Her pale hair and skin seemed to glow in the dark.

"Where you going?" she asked.

It seemed strange that I couldn't remember. To hide my confusion, I pulled my poncho off over my head, getting water on the front seat. I felt the car accelerate.

"Okay," she said softly. "Come and say goodbye."

We climbed the mountain along with the other traffic. Ahead of us, the storm sent out a flash and a boom.

High up, the highway was bordered by jutting boulders and pines, the mountaintop bulking black in the gloom. At a sign that said "Authorized Vehicles Only," the girl suddenly jerked the steering wheel to the right.

"Whoa!" I said, steadying myself.

We were climbing a rutted track among the boulders, the lights of the highway abruptly left behind. Pine trees swayed and moaned in the rain and wind, dead leaves whirled and scattered before our lights.

"Where are we going?" I asked the girl. Not that I objected. When you're 17, and a beautiful girl wants to drive you somewhere strange –

There was a blinding flash that seemed to obliterate everything, and a splitting *bang!* that shook the mountain.

When my eyes recovered from the lightning, I saw that the track had turned steeply up, and the little car's engine strained, its wheels spinning on a slope it couldn't climb. The girl killed the engine and lights and we got out into wet, rushing air that smelled of ozone and scorched rock. My skin prickled with electricity. Not far above black clouds roiled, muttering heavily.

The girl was a pale blur scrambling through high grass that bent hissing in the wind. I scrambled up the slope after her.

Something loomed above me: a huge rock cropping out of the very top of the mountain. She was climbing it.

"Hey!" I yelled, laughing. "This is crazy! We've got a get out of here!" The storm scattered my words. I started after her, fingers straining on narrow holds, shoes slipping on wet rock, wind and rain tearing at me blindingly. When I reached the top, I was gasping.

The girl was naked, standing on the topmost pinnacle of rock, arching her body upward, straining her hands toward the clouds. The rocks steamed, and the smell of burning electricity was strong. The glow of her skin reminded me of something. Dizzy chasms of wind rushed below me.

"Hey, this is crazy!" I yelled over the wind. "We have to get out of here!"

I reached for the girl's straining body.

A blue spark jumped between us, lighting for a second her white skin, her crazy eyes, the hair standing up from her head like a silver mane. Then she was clawing at me, pulling me desperately to her, and suddenly I wasn't afraid anymore. I pulled off my clothes, throwing them out into the darkness. The rock was hot and charred under my feet. Then I took hold of her again. She was wild with lust, and we grappled, coupled, until the mountain seemed to rock thundering on the roots of the world.

There was an enormous flash that cut the flesh from us in an instant, and I was illuminated from within: I saw our bodies flaming in the rushing air, and all the cracks and straining strength of rock under us, pushed up to the air from the liquid searing center of the Earth, saw the live green things that crept and grew over the mountain toward the light, pushing upward by millimeters even in that second, saw birds huddled in their nests in swaying branches, saw animals crouching in their holes, a little river frothing at the foot of the mountain, and all rivers running to the oceans, the whales gliding silent and deep through the cold blue oceans, birds singing over the nests of their young in the evening, saw a young man leaning on a bridge in the evening, staring down into quiet water.

And as the vision faded and I plunged through darkness like a dying spark from a firework rocket, I saw, seated in the midst of everything, an old, old man in a gray robe, hands folded patiently on his stomach.

* * * *

. . . a fresh October day with pale blue sky, yellow leaves fluttering down. I was sitting on my back deck, so tired that it was an effort to breathe, to hold my head up, so tired that the long yellow sunlight seemed aged and brittle, the breeze cold. Vicky sat in the chair next to mine head bowed, hands lying useless in her lap like an old woman's.

Slow footsteps came along the flagstones at the side of the house, along with a heavy, rhythmic *clunk*, as if whoever walked there leaned on a staff. The footsteps climbed the wooden steps, and an old man came into view. He was tall and stooped in his gray robe, bald, wrinkled face grave and thoughtful.

He look down at us for a few minutes. Then he intoned in a strong, old voice:

"The first seed of life is desire. Life is the unwinding of desire, like the unwinding of a spring. When desire is burned away, the next world comes.

"I sent you images, reflections of your own desires, to help you to the next world."

Then a profound blue light shone from him, dimming the sun, and it was as if his body had turned inside out, had become hollow – had become an opening or doorway in the air of our backyard through which blue light shone from some other place, where I thought I could see stars. Flanking the door were two tall, shining figures.

Then they and the door and the old man were gone.

A haze had a come over the afternoon sun, making the sky pale. Mist was creeping through the bushes at the bottom of the garden. Birds sang and fluttered on the old grape arbor in Mrs.

Roemer's backyard. I was too tired to move, or even think, almost too tired to watch the mist roll in silently, softening the outlines of trees down on Thayer Avenue. After awhile the yellow leaves of our oak dripped with moisture, and the sky had turned twilight gray through what was now a thick fog. The few sleepy songs of birds were muffled in its stillness.

It thickened, so now I could only see halfway down the hill. Mrs. Roemer's grape arbor began to slip out of sight. My hand had somehow gotten locked with Vicky's, but I couldn't turn to look at her. A surf, invisible in the fog, seemed to roll under us now, as if the ocean washed around the foundations of the house. Soon I could see only the horizontal bar of the deck railing in the mist, and the oak tree's shadow leaning over us as soft gray silence closed around.

My eyes were heavy and my chin drooped to my chest, but somewhere, maybe deep inside, someone seem to be shaking me and saying "wake up, wake up."

Then I fell asleep.

Dream Walking

The Amana had been a Medical Building 30 years ago, but its downtown neighborhood had long since gone to seed, and it had become a resting place for struggling travel agencies, hopeless dentists, and dilapidated solo practitioners, their names listed on the faded building directory as on a cheap mausoleum. The single working elevator was painted industrial beige, and lacked mirrors. That was no loss to Dexter Grant, who would simply have studied himself with distaste anyway: a large, gym-muscled, middle-aged man in an expensive suit, handsome but gray, like an aging bachelor lawyer who realizes there is no place to go from where he is but down, the realization sapping all the color out of him.

The Life Revision Institute was on the Amana's fifth floor, off a narrow hall smelling faintly of sanitizing cleansers and old, musty wood. The plastic laminate sign on the door said:

Life Revision Institute
"Asleep and Awake – A Greater Life"
Dr. P. Thotmoses II, PhD

That stopped Grant briefly. Thotmoses II – like the Egyptian Pharaoh? No name had ever appeared on the Institute's online lucid dreaming lessons; nor, until the previous week, had a street address. In the year since he had found the Institute's classified ad in an obscure part of Craigslist, this was the first lesson that had required an office visit.

He went in.

The waiting room was elegant in a threadbare way, with dark, antique furniture, paintings, and tarnished brass lamps giving quiet, clubby light under the ceiling fluorescents. It was empty except for a receptionist behind a small desk. A beautiful receptionist, he saw as she looked up, black eyes wide, as if the last thing she had expected was a customer. She was perhaps in her mid-20s, and exotic, her eyes perfect almonds, skin pale and fine. Her black hair was held in a bun by two lacquered chopsticks, and her back and shoulders in a shiny Chinese style sheath were very straight.

He wondered whether the sad, teasing quirk in her smile was a sign of bittersweet life experience or just a twist nature had given to her lips.

"Dexter Grant for a three o'clock appointment."

She carefully turned over the pages of an appointment book with long fingers. "If you'll have a seat, I'll let Dr. Thotmoses know you're here."

Her voice was light and melodious, like a bell. He sat and watched with an ache as she spoke briefly into her phone, then began reading something on her desk, averting his eyes whenever she glanced up, a youthful beauty he was too old to possess, though perhaps something like her was the only earthly thing that could cure what had come over him --

"Mr. Grant?" A deep, hoarse voice said, startling him. The man was very big, almost freakishly so, and very stooped, perhaps so that he could look into people's faces. He was old, with white hair and loose, pink jowls on the long, soft face, like a kind headmaster that the students made fun of behind his back. His ill-fitting gray suit was rumpled.

He smiled with a touch of melancholy humor, a touch of guile, as if he knew what Grant had been thinking watching the receptionist. "I am Dr. Thotmoses. Will you come in?" He raised a hand the size of a frying pan toward an inner door.

The inner office was small and windowless, crowded with a large oak desk, a chair, and two bookshelves. Grant took the chair while Thotmoses squeezed himself behind the desk, put on reading glasses, and squinted down at an open folder, his head wavering a little as with a geriatric tremor.

He read slowly in his deep, hoarse voice: "Dexter Grant, 47, occupation attorney, never married, only child, all relatives dead."

Grant, irritated by this recitation of his private information – though he himself had provided it – nodded.

Thotmoses tilted up another sheet of paper. "A man who has everything," he boasted. "Good job, good health, good social life. And a great deal of money."

"What is your interest in my money?" Grant snapped.

"Oh, dear, no!" said Thotmoses, his rheumy, oyster-sized eyes pained. "What I mean is: why would a man who has everything wish to practice Life Revision? What does this life lack for him?"

It had started one Thursday morning, warmed with the feeling of the approaching weekend, when it had occurred to Grant suddenly, for no particular reason, to wonder how many more weekends before they were finished, before he ended up in a hospital somewhere, and then a small obituary in the newspaper, then nothing. Somehow he had been hypnotized all these years by this unending round of five days, then two days, then five, always looking forward to something, some satisfaction or illumination that never seemed to arrive.

"Remember that Life Revision is effectively irreversible, since it takes place at a physical level, in the brain."

Grant nodded.

Thotmoses' big hands shuffled clumsily through the folder, and he squinted at another paper. "Your test answers show all the experiences of an advanced lucid dreamer. You have learned to maintain the waking level activation of your primary association cortex even in deep REM sleep. Though of course you don't need to know the underlying mechanism any more than an athlete knows the biochemistry of muscle tissue." He gave a sincere squint and a brief, practiced smile, as if to say: don't worry that you're a layman, I can simplify it for you. "It used to be assumed that waking and sleep are incompatible, but that was disproved at Stanford in the '70s and '80s. In lucid dreams one's afferent centers, speech centers, sensory centers, everything, act just as they do in waking, as if you are actually walking around, talking, doing the things you are doing in your dream. The only difference being that the connection between these brain centers and the body is interrupted in the brainstem, causing paralysis, sleep atonia. You dream lucidly nearly every night now, correct?"

Grant nodded. He felt a sudden jolt of anticipation or apprehension.

"Good. So now for the next step. No more mental exercises before bed for you. You need something more powerful, to stabilize your dream experiences."

Thotmoses stood up until it looked like he would go through the ceiling, but instead he opened a door Grant had thought was a closet, and switched on a light. In the center of a tiny, windowless room a dentist-type chair stood among electronic device boxes stacked on wheeled shelves. The chair had arm- and leg- straps with metal buckles, and bundles of wires ran to a helmet-like thing on a boom. Grant stood too, with some alarm.

"Don't worry," said Thotmoses, with another skin-deep professional smile. "This is mostly imaging hardware. The process is very gentle. Your brain gets more of a workout at your average real estate seminar." He leaned down and press switches on two open laptops. Their screens flickered, and lights on a tall stack of black boxes flickered on in response.

"How many people have – done this?" Grant's palms were wet.

"Not many," Thotmoses. "Not many people are interested in Life Revision, and even fewer get as far as you have with the exercises. It takes a certain – hunger."

"But -- what are your qualifications to do this?" Grant stuttered. "What are you a doctor of, I'd like to know?"

"It's completely painless," Thotmoses said, watching the laptop screens. "I put you into a deep hypnotic sleep before you begin." He straightened stiffly and regarded Grant innocently. "Of course, your fee for this lesson is fully refundable," he said mildly, "if you decide not to continue."

That night Grant woke in a dank basement apartment crowded with secondhand furniture, and it was morning.

He lay in a rumpled sofa bed. He held still for a minute, studying a crack in the ceiling. Then he wondered if he was dreaming, a question he had taught himself to ask 100 times a day, and especially whenever he first woke up. He sat up, got his watch from a wobbly bed table, and looked at the writing on its face, just below the 12. "Timber," it said in tiny letters. He looked up at the crack in the ceiling then back at the watch. "Arctic," the tiny letters said now. He *was* dreaming, then. Text and numbers were notoriously unstable in dreams; they changed 75% of the time on two readings, 95% of the time on three, making a simple test. If you didn't check, you would often just go on along illucidly, rationalizing the most outrageous oddities. It was only when you could say to yourself "I am dreaming" that you became really lucid.

Grant studied the apartment. It was his old place on North Campus, where he had returned to go back to school. It had stayed empty all those years waiting for him, like the tomb of a college student pharaoh, mail accumulating in a great pile under the front door slot. He got up and walked across the cold floor tiles to poke through the pile; there was an ancient letter from his mother with faded, curling photographs; a defunct class bulletin; a postcard from a forgotten girlfriend. The atmosphere they exhaled of other days brought to his mind an old scene: the long hill where the giant residence halls and classroom buildings stood deserted on their enormous lawns on blank, late August afternoons after the end of summer classes, the shuttle buses from main campus groaning up the hill nearly empty on their hourly off-term schedule.

The heat of the afternoon entered him, and then he seemed to be standing on an empty sidewalk infinite and blank as the hot sky, sweaty and full of restless, frustrated melancholy, the melancholy of a solitary student who worked between semesters cleaning the giant university kitchens and dining halls. In dreams there was nothing solid to keep you from getting lost in your thoughts, and because your thoughts were the places you were in, you easily drifted from scene to scene. Thotmoses had told him that the new treatment would correct this, Grant remembered now, help stabilize the lucid dreams so that eventually they became as real as life. A new life.

With an effort, he imagined the dank, mildewed smell and cold floor tiles of the apartment, and found himself back there. After all, he had to clean the place up; he had a date tonight.

His heart jumped as he remembered that it was with the black-eyed receptionist from the Life Revision Institute.

The colors of the apartment began to fade; he could vaguely feel his body lying in bed, asleep. His excitement had begun to wake him from the dream.

Grant spun around in the middle of the room, arms out, like a child making himself dizzy. Spinning was one of the best ways to keep from losing a lucid dream; the whirling sensation seemed to pull the attention back to the dream body, blocking the authentic sensory input from the physical body. Though sometimes when you returned to the dream, the scene had changed.

He walked on a dark uphill street, chilly gusts shaking drops of the rain that had fallen earlier in the night from the branches of old trees, bushes hissing and swaying over fences like sentient things in greenish streetlamp light. Near the top of the street a gate opened onto a garden in whose darkness untrimmed rosebushes waved and nodded. A patter of drops fell from the overhanging branches of a huge oak as he followed the walk toward the tall Victorian house. There was only dim, yellow light behind the lace curtains in the windows, and he wondered for a moment if she was home; but a few seconds after he knocked she opened the door, taut and nervous and beautiful in a yellow jacket and black jeans.

Grant had had a splitting headache when he came out of the hypnotic sleep in Dr. Thotmoses II's treatment chair, and it lasted most of the week despite two bottles of aspirin. He took Monday and Tuesday off work, and telephoned Thotmoses several times in a fury, threatening him with lawsuits and criminal prosecution.

Thotmoses had assured him that the headache was normal and would go away, and it did, slowly, until, on Friday when he approached the door of the Life Revision Institute for his follow-up appointment, he was well again and didn't feel like suing anyone. In fact, his thoughts were running in a different channel altogether, and he was woefully nervous. All that week he had seen the Institute receptionist every night in his dreams: naked, riding on the shoulders of a huge ape; baking bread in a stone kitchen in the citadel of an ancient city; on a dark city sidewalk, her eyes reflecting the smoky night.

As before the waiting-room was empty, and the girl looked up with her wide black eyes.

But this time when she saw him, a flush crept up her neck and cheeks, and she stared back down at her desk.

Grant's heart was hammering, his palms wet, voice cracked. "I'm here for my appointment. Dexter Grant."

She nodded and opened the large appointment book with a rustle that was loud in the silence. It was nearly empty, he saw, his name penciled into the middle of a blank day. Her shoulders were bowed as if from shock. She was wearing a black dress shirt today, its two top buttons undone over a milky throat, the third tight from the pressure of her breasts. Black tresses fell about her shoulders like sable water.

"What's your name?" he asked, stomach quavering.

Her eyes were shocked and wondering. "Anna."

"Grant."

She nodded miserably.

"Anna," he said, trying to keep his voice steady. "Have you by any chance – will you – would you go out with me?"

She looked up at him, and with a sinking heart he knew she would refuse, he had made himself ridiculous, blown it by stumbling straight into a clumsy invitation instead of coolly –

"Yes," she said, barely audibly.

Out of the corner of his eye he caught sight of Thotmoses, who had appeared silently again, and was watching them with his foolish, knowing smile.

✳ ✳ ✳ ✳

"No kidding," said Grant, lying in his king size bed, relaxed and happy the way a man can only be when he has laid claim to the woman of his dreams by making love to her.

Anna leaned an elbow on her pillow, hair tucked behind her ear, her almost unbelievably lithe and beautiful body seeming to glow faintly in the dark. It was Friday night, or maybe Saturday morning. After his checkup with Thotmoses Grant had steeled himself and asked her to dinner. Things had gone faster than he had dared expect, and afterward she told him shyly that she had dreamed about him every night that week.

"It's weird," he said enthusiastically after telling her that he had dreamed about her, too. "And you're taking his life expansion lessons?"

"Yes." Her voice was soft but still rich, bell-like. "I can't afford to pay, so Dr. Thotmoses is letting me earn my way. Actually, I had my neuro session last week, right after you."

Grant got his watch off the night table. 2:02 a.m. Out of habit he checked the tiny letters just below the 12. They said "Thought." He looked away, and then back. "Moses," they said now.

"Oh, shit," he said, sitting up.

"What is it?" She asked, alarmed.

"I'm dreaming. Shit." His heart sank like a stone. "I should have known better than to think you would actually sleep with me."

"What? That's not true," she said. "Let me look."

He showed her the watch. She looked away for a second and then back.

"Well, that doesn't mean --"

"Yeah," he said ashenly. "Okay." He lay back on the pillow and closed his eyes, ignoring her protest.

The Life Revision lessons had included half a dozen ways to wake yourself up, but falling asleep in your dream worked best for Grant, like a return through the mirror to real life. Sure enough, a few minutes after he had closed his eyes, blocking out the dream faux-sensory input, he felt himself lying in a different position. As his sleep atonia paralysis wore off he stirred an arm, then a leg. Then he opened his eyes.

To his immense excitement, a beautiful girl with tousled black hair was opening her own sleepy eyes and smiling at him in gray early morning light.

"You see?" She murmured. "I told you." She stretched and he took hold of her, feeling the delicious slender flex of her muscles and bones.

But then anxiety filled him again. How did she know what he had dreamed she had said? The falling asleep in your dream trick usually worked, but false awakenings were common too. He picked up his watch. On his first read the tiny letters spelled: "Careful"; on his second: "Thought."

He tried to smile at her, his chest full of pain again. "False awakening," he said. He turned away to put the watch back on the night table so she wouldn't see his dejection. But what does it matter, he thought. She's just a dream. Gone in the morning.

He lay back down and closed his eyes grimly.

The doorbell rang.

His eyes opened involuntarily. He shut them again, tried to ignore it, but it rang again after a minute.

"I'll get it," he said, climbing out of bed. It was too uncomfortable not to answer your doorbell, asleep or awake.

Anna got up to. She took his breath away; long and smoothly curved, her messy hair and the triangle between her legs very black against her pale skin. He handed her his robe, searched in a drawer for sweat-pants and pulled them on. The doorbell rang a third time as he stiffly descended the stairs. Anna, in the oversized robe, stood at the rail of the open hallway overlooking the two-story foyer.

Grant opened the door. Dr. P. Thotmoses II stood there in a shabby scarf and a wrinkled raincoat several sizes too small for him.

"Ah, Mr. Grant," said Thotmoses. "I apologize for coming so early, but I'm going away, and I wanted to be sure I caught you before I left." It was dawn, Grant's big lawn and the quiet street beyond hazed with grey mist.

"Well – come in," said Grant, startled.

"Just for a moment." Thotmoses took a single step onto the slate floor of the foyer. He had on huge black galoshes. "Ah, Anna, my dear," he said, catching sight of her. He didn't seem surprised. "Everything is going well, then. Both of you may be thinking that something odd is happening." He looked at each of them in turn. "I just came by to give you a few words of encouragement."

"This is a dream," Grant announced to him, as if it would make any difference to a dream character.

"My dear Mr. Grant." Thotmoses raised a huge hand. "It is now time for you to give up that mode of thought. Look around. Look, for instance, at Anna. So beautiful. She walks, talks – you do talk, Anna my dear, don't you?"

"Yes," said Anna shyly, her hands on the railing.

"She walks, talks, breathes, is charming, does everything a 'real person' does. In 'real life' how do you know Anna is real? The answer is that she walks, talks, breathes, etc. You have no more reason to believe she isn't real here than in 'real life,' do you? As far as you are concerned, this is just as real as 'real life,' isn't it?"

Grant and Anna protested at once. "Why are you talking to him? This is my dream," Anna said. "I know what's real and what's not," Grant said. "I did a triple-read test on my watch."

"Ah," said Thotmoses, untidy eyebrows rising over his large, corrugated brow. "So you can identify absolute reality based on some tiny letters on your watch. Hm. And Anna, my dear," he looked up at her, "are you certain two people can't have the same dream?"

She just stared down at him.

"This is why I had to wait so long to let you have the neurological treatment," he said to her, waving a hand at Grant and the house. "I had to wait until Mr. Grant was ready. It would be inhumane to set anyone on the road of Life Revision alone, and I never do that. Reality is consensual, after all. I am delighted to find you two together, though I must confess what you may already have guessed." He smiled kindly. "I administered posthypnotic suggestions causing a powerful mutual attraction. Did you dream about each other? Yes. But even when that wears off, I suggest – strongly suggests – that you stay together. Not that two such wonderful young people would have any reason to part. Anna is so beautiful, and Mr. Grant has enough money to carry you forward until you can function normally in your new, richer world. Thus my interest in your savings, Mr. Grant," he finished with a little bow.

Thotmoses stepped backward out the door and waved fondly. Grant noticed that he had begun to turn translucent. As they watched, he became nearly invisible, a figure made of mist.

Grant and Anna spoke again at the same time. "But what about --" "You told me --"

"Goodbye," said Thotmoses merrily, both his form and his voice beginning to curl like smoke. "Remember to discuss any strange experiences carefully. Congratulations! Stay together! Awake and Asleep – A Greater Life!"

With that he smudged completely. Grant stepped out into the damp, cool air and put his had through what was left, making it swirl gently merging into the dawn mist. Then he came back in and shut the door. Anna watched him climb the stairs.

"That was weird," she said, a trembling edge to her voice.

"Yeah," he said. "I want to wake up."

She grabbed his arms. "Grant."

He looked into her urgent young face.

"Are you sure we should? Wake up? Even if it's just a dream, it's so –"

It began to fade even as she spoke, as if in response to his intention, colors fading, the heaviness of his prone body intruding upon the feeling that he was standing up, the feeling of Anna's hands –

He opened his eyes looking at the ceiling of his bedroom in gray early light.

". . . reassuring being here," said a light, soft voice. He turned his head. Anna lay next to him, fast asleep, a little spittle on the pillow by her mouth. But her hands were fumbling shakily toward him, and she was talking. "I mean, if we do wake up alone, it'll be so – lonely."

"Shit," said Grant, and grabbed his watch. His heart started to beat fearfully. He wanted to wake up. He looked at the tiny letters. They said: Kenneth "Kenneth Cole" and below that: "New York."

He studied the ceiling for a few seconds, then looked quickly back: "Kenneth Cole -- New York." He tried again, and then a fourth time to be sure, and the relief that flooded him made him so buoyant that for a second he thought he had lifted off the bed into the air. But you could only do that in dreams.

"I mean," said Anna, still asleep, her hands now lying long and beautiful on the sheet, "Dr. Thotmoses says we should stick together."

"You were talking," Grant said as he poured tea. His breakfast nook was all bay windows looking out over lawn and trees soft in the midst. "In your sleep." He was still disturbed by the dream he had had -- they had both had, bizarrely -- but the sight of her at the table in his bathrobe made him so dizzy with happiness that he had to concentrate to think about it.

"So?" Anna asked, her mouth full of toast. "People talk in their sleep." She seemed as happy as he was, so happy that it made her animated, waving her toast she talked. He had covertly checked his watch several times, but the result was always: "Kenneth Cole – New York." Too, all the appliances in his kitchen were working perfectly, and he had been able to turn on the lights on his first try. Machines -- and especially lights -- usually didn't work right in dreams.

"Not in REM sleep. Remember sleep atonia? Keeps you from moving around, like those cats when they damage their brain stems, and they run around in their sleep, acting out their dreams."

"*You* thought you would wake up and I wouldn't be there," she mocked him. "You thought I was a dream."

"You don't think it's weird that we dreamed the same thing? Exactly?"

Her face got thoughtful. "And we dreamed about each other all last week."

"That was from Thotmoses hypnotizing us – no, wait a minute; that was part of the dream." He pondered, trying to keep it all straight. "Well, what about this: did you have a headache after your treatment in that chair? Low down, like almost in your neck?"

"Yes," she cried, eyes wondering. Her hand went to the back of her neck. "Yes. You did too?"

A thought had come to him. "Let me look."

She turned her head, and he lifted her heavy, shiny hair. At her hairline, right where the spine met the skull, was a small red spot, like a healed puncture wound.

"What is it? Is there something there?"

"Look at mine. Do I have a little red spot? Like a needle pricked me?"

She put her thumb on the back of his neck, and he thought her voice shook a little.

"Yes, it's there. What is it? What did Dr. Thotmoses do to us?"

※ ※ ※ ※

After breakfast they tried to watch TV, ordered pizza in the afternoon. Grant called the Life Revision Institute several times, but no one answered. They drove to Anna's tiny downtown apartment and picked up some clothes so she could stay with him a few days. It was exciting, like getting ready for a big snowstorm, though the only intimation that something was supposed to happen had come from their dream of Thotmoses. They were restless all day, and at night Grant had a hard time sleeping, but he must have finally dozed off, because the next thing he knew he and Anna were waking up talking to each other.

"You're his secretary," Grant said in the dark after they had gotten over the spookiness of that. "He's never said anything to you about this talking and moving while you're in REM?"

"No," she said slowly. "I may have typed something about it. I have a feeling I did, once."

"Do you remember what it said?"

"No. When you type your brain's not involved, you know?"

"I bet you remember at some level, though. I bet we – you could incubate a dream about it. I mean, maybe we can learn something before we confront him Monday. Bastard. If he's damaged us, I'll sue him into ground beef. Come on, program the dream, okay? 'I'll have a dream where I remember when I typed for Dr. Thotmoses about moving in REM sleep.' Okay?"

She murmured it over and over and finally was quiet. He drifted off too after a while, holding himself conscious inside by watching the colored geometric designs your visual cortex makes while you're falling asleep. After the designs had faded, he opened his eyes. He was in bed, Anna next to him. He double read his watch. It said "Watch" the first time and "Thotmoses" the second. Anna, feeling him move, set up, blinking.

"Oh, we're here," she said. "We want to go to the Institute, right?"

"Not necessarily; just remember what you typed."

She shook her head. "I visualized sitting at my computer at the Institute and reading it off the screen."

"Maybe I can spin us there . . . " Grant said, and then realized that didn't make sense. It was Anna who had to "go to" the Institute and dream about what she had typed. "We'd probably both better spin," he concluded. "We might be talking to each other in our sleep again --" A sudden chill went through him, and he sat bolt upright. "You know what? I bet that's why Thotmoses killed our atonia, if that's what he did; so that we'll move and babble to each other in REM, give each other cues so that we dream the same things. Maybe that's part of stabilizing dreams. What did he say about consensuality? But that was in a dream too." It was getting more and more confusing. "Come on, let's see if we can go to your Institute."

They both stood up and spun, focusing on the Institute, but every time they stopped they were still in Grant's bedroom.

"We should drive," Anna said finally.

She was right. Do the action your unconscious associated with approaching the place you wanted to go. Often even starting such action would change the dream scene to the desired place.

But not this time. Still in his robe and slippers, Grant guided his car through nearly deserted 3 a.m. downtown avenues. The air, smelling of sidewalk dust and garbage, was cool and damp on his bare legs as they got out of the car under a street light in front of the Amana building. Anna had chosen to get dressed before they came, and he wished he had too, now; but he reminded himself that he was home in bed, so it didn't make any difference. Anna unlocked the street door.

The fifth floor hall was barely lit, and the dead air had the sour, musty smell of old wood. Anna's key in the Institute lock sounded loud. The waiting room was pitch dark until she switched on a lamp, yellowish light silhouetting her slim shape.

"This seems so real," she said in a hushed voice.

"Dream stabilization," Grant muttered.

She turned on the computer at the reception desk. It's hard disk chattered, and the screen faded up to a lurid white glow. Grant shuffled over to stand behind her.

The face of a man appeared on the screen, making them both jump.

It was Dr. Thotmoses. He smiled, and said tinnily from the built-in speaker: "Anna, dear, look over by my office."

They looked, and Grant heard Anna's short scream over the pounding of his own heart.

Thotmoses stood there. Half in shadow he looked bigger than ever – and then Grant's heart went so fast that he nearly fainted, because growing out of Thotmoses' head were curling horns, like a ram's horn.

"Is this what you are looking for?" Thotmoses asked, and held something out to them.

They were frozen, Anna sideways in her chair, poised to flee, eyes wide. There was a piece of paper in Thotmoses' outstretched hand.

Dreams can't hurt you, Grant reminded himself. Frightening things had to be faced, integrated; often they were important suppressed material.

Nauseated with fear, he forced his numb legs to move.

"Yes," he croaked. "Thank you."

He got just close enough to stretch his arm out and pull the paper from Thotmoses' hand.

Anna screamed in terror.

Thotmoses had changed. Instead of a human head, he had the head of a ram, and his one visible foot was a cloven roof.

Terror blared in Grant. He ran in awful slow-motion, dragging Anna by her arm, their footfalls like heartbeats in the hall, their gasps echoing in a stairwell; they swam wildly through the lobby doors and Grant's car yanked them away from the curb. It was only when they were safe out of the confining streets and speeding along the vast, empty commuter highways that Anna began to cry, in shaking, hysterical sobs.

They pulled into Grant's driveway as the eastern sky was beginning to pale, and without a word went back up to bed. Grant badly wanted to wake up, though he was exhausted. Anna was wan and yawning, still shaking As he lay holding her, the warmth of her body soothing his own, he realized that the dream had gone on for hours now, much longer than any REM cycle he had ever heard of. And the way they had had to travel all the way downtown and all the way back, and the fatigue – the hair prickled on the back of his neck. *Could they have been awake?* Or sleepwalking, actually driving downtown in a dream? He itched to turn over and check his watch, but he didn't want to wake Anna.

"Are we still dreaming?" she asked, sounding wide-awake.

He turned over and fumbled for his watch, did a triple-read. "We're awake."

"But when did we wake up?"

"I don't know."

They lay there for hours, thinking, occasionally speaking. It was strange but restful, as if their brains no longer needed rest, but their bodies did. It was late morning before Anna stirred and said: "I need to take a shower."

She got up with youthful quickness and went into the bathroom. The sound of the shower soon gave way to vigorous toweling, and when she came back into the bedroom in Grant's bathrobe, hair wrapped turban-like in the towel, her cheeks were pink and her black eyes sparkling, as if she had had a full night's sleep.

She sat on the side of the bed, thrusting her hands into the pockets of the robe. Something rustled, and she drew out a crumpled paper. She smoothed it.

Her whispered "Oh!" made Grant sit up and look over her
shoulder. It was a letter:

Dear Anna and Mr. Grant:

Forgive me for addressing you through this letter but,
experience has taught me to make myself scarce when my
students are first awakened; their initial incomprehension
of the Life Revision intervention can cause unpleasantness.
The closest thing in the medical literature to what you are
experiencing now is called "REM sleep behavior disorder"
or RBD, a rare condition in which the normal muscle atonia
and sensory gating that keep the body still and insensible
in REM sleep are disrupted, resulting in the person "acting
out" his dreams. RBD is caused by damage to the brain's
tegmento-reticular tract, which normally carries the
neurological messages causing paralysis and insensibility to
the spine. The Life Revision intervention involves insertion
of a needle into the blood vessels serving the tegmento-
reticular tract, and the introduction of precise amounts of
a toxin specific to certain cells.

Of course, there is a crucial difference between RBD
and your condition. Before the intervention, each of
you completed an intensive course in lucid dreaming.
Consequently, unlike victims of RBD, who act out their
dreams in complete unconsciousness, both of you are
capable of remaining completely awake even in deep REM
-- and with the tegmento-reticular track disrupted awake
not only subjectively but objectively as well, walking about
and interacting with the world while also in deep dreams.
Indeed you have learned to be Awake and Asleep.

It is painful for me to know that you may believe that
you are the victims of an unscrupulous act of unconsented
surgery. But remember that both of you asked for it, having
concluded, each in your own way, that the life you knew
was not worth living. And you were right. The picture
of reality that has grown so strong in modern times has

convinced people that meaning is something we impose on the world, something we make inside our brains – and this has driven the direct perceptions of inherent meaning into the unconscious, so that our dreams seem as overloaded with meaning as our lives are devoid –

It ended there, as if the writer had been interrupted.
Anna turned to Grant, lips pale. "What – ?"
"The paper Thotmoses gave us last night," he said, throat dry. "I must have put it in my pocket when we ran."

Downtown the wind was chill and fresh under scudding clouds, as if it blew from a nearby seacoast of whose existence Grant had not known before, where fishing boats and huge ocean-going ships moored in the surging cold blue water that fell to infinite depths a mile out, as though the town verged on the edge of infinity itself. He wondered if the seacoast had been there all the time, if his memory that it had not was just a mental artifact, like the opposite of déjà vu. The earth seemed to rock slightly in the rush of wind, sunlight, and cloud, bringing to his mind the cries of seabirds, the tourists in summer, the lazy hush of the waves, or their roaring on days of chill wind like this one.

A gust around a street corner brought a chill of tiny raindrops. He and Anna hurried forward. The gray front of the Amana building was like a blank, aging face staring at the lowering sky. But as Grant watched there was a flicker around its top.

"You see that?" he muttered to Anna, who held her coat shut at the throat with a slim gloved hand.

She didn't answer, but he knew by the direction of her eyes that she did see it, greenish light flickering around the fifth floor of the building now resembling insubstantial figures flying upward into the gray, now resembling flickering horns.

After the wind outside, the Amana's small, shabby lobby seemed very still. The fifth floor was silent except for a dirty radiator across from the elevator ticking out heat, and the sour floorboards creaked fretfully as they went along the worn runner.

The plaque had been unscrewed from the Life Revision Institute's door, leaving it looking bare and flimsy. Anna unlocked it.

"He's gone," she said.

Emptied of furniture the waiting room seemed big and shabby, like a vacant welfare office. Grant and Anna walked through the inner rooms. There were signs of hurried moving – electric outlets with their covers removed, the inner office door taken off its hinges, a few cardboard boxes and some packing tape lying around, the dusty floor disturbed by footprints. When Anna wasn't looking Grant surveyed the prints for hoof marks. It was ridiculous, of course; the ram's-head and hooves had been some kind of REM overlay on reality created by their dreaming brains, like a hallucination. Hadn't it? Or had they perhaps seen a sign of the man's inner character -- a sign that someone in ordinary waking consciousness would miss?

The innermost room was small and irregular with a single, dirty window, beginning to streak now with rain. Grant leaned his head against the window idly. Below him the narrow street was gray, long streaks of rain pattering in puddles, and beyond gray roofs the city fell away, mist hanging over the buildings, the dark green of a small park, a flashing red light on a transmission tower, the neon of stores a dozen blocks away – and a sudden sense of the vastness of the world broke in on Grant like light from a door opening on a prison cell. He sensed somehow the vast turning of it, the falling of the rain on streets and roofs, roads and fields, trees and hills, small animals breathing in their holes, birds quiet in their nests in trees, car headlights through the rain on dark country roads, yellow lights of houses, cliffs at the edge of the ocean with the sound of waves, the vast, vertiginous ocean itself heaving in great swells a mile deep, and then the stars singing silently in their unthinkably far vacuums, turning in their titanic, slow-motion pinwheels, flying out in their infinitely slow, infinitely rapid explosion from a center that was the center of *him*, his own bursting heart, and he stood and watched it all from this room. Anna stood quietly behind him, an Angel with great pale wings of light folded around her.

A Greater Life.
Could it really be?
If it was, maybe he could get used to it.

My Informant Zardon

My informant Zardon, a private investigator in interpenetration universe L-2 with whom I exchange letters, sent me this report of a case he had:

"I was in the Fladian Peninsula, a geologic curiosity much like your Florida: a narrow spit of percolating rock through which the ocean flows with scarcely any hindrance, heavily forested above, with popular resorts on the coasts. I remember, my first or second day there, standing at the top of a wide, foot-scarred beach, the cries of children and washing of surf coming clearly through the still air. A looming haze on the horizon reached toward the land with tentacles of cloud and a faint electricity. The water was like warm, choppy glass, the more delicious because soon the storm would make the beach deserted, darkness would fall, there would be lightning, and the swimmers, sitting or lying now in rocking, gurgling water, would be cozy in their beach cottages. Up the bluff behind me, amid the cool humidity of trees, the stillness was heavy and penetrating, as if silent, invisible raindrops had already begun to fall.

Days later, or earlier – in an unconnected time, it seemed – I drove on a winding road over thickly forested hills, the ocean showing now and then between vine-hung branches. A long way from anywhere, I came upon a house with a yard grown so wild you couldn't tell where it ended and the woods began; ivy grew shabbily in place of a lawn, mingling at its edges with the forest leaves and overhanging the mossy retaining wall along the road.

The house itself was dark weathered brick, set so close around with huge oaks that it looked almost like a natural outcropping of rock. Brick steps led to the front door. On the middle step, in the damp, quiet evening the forest made of afternoon still shimmering on the ocean, I first saw the woman; eyes in evening light glistening, skin glowing faintly against the forest's slow brown and green decay, motionless, as if time had frozen, she caught on the steps like a fly in amber.

I was to know her better. In another time, seemingly disconnected, we stood on an observation walkway built over jutting rocks on an ocean mountain. Beyond the concrete parapet, leaves of a forest like a still green ocean fell away in rills and cliffs.

"I love you," I confessed in the high, airy silence.

She laughed softly.

A saying goes: "Memory is difficult, and distance truly separates." From your descriptions, it seems that distance doesn't separate at all in your world! Here is an example: Because the woman seemed to be an important link in my investigations on the Peninsula, I tried to remember where I had seen her before. I seemed to remember her in Ionia, a region of gently rolling plains corresponding somewhat to your Central Midwest. The distance between the Fladian Peninsula and Ionia is uncertain, but vast. Looking at maps in our world is dizzying, like looking down from a great height; not only because the red and blue lines representing roads and railways seem to shift and meander as you study them, but because a vague racial memory warns you that each foot of distance between two places is filled with strange events, and that people don't always end up where they aim to go. There is a vertigo in maps.

Arriving in a little Ionian town, stricken with travelbend, I had wandered into a garden party at a local philanthropic institution. I was received kindly: people in my world have much sympathy for travelers. My bags were taken up a cool, echoing staircase, I was given a glass of pale wine and sent out to join the other guests, scattered in chattering and laughing groups about the large grounds, sitting in garden chairs under trees or lounging on blankets on yellow summer grass. The sun, high and diamond-

bright, had made me sweat carrying my bags through the quiet
streets from the train station, but here a breeze stirred. I felt my
body relaxing, the spinning disorientation of travelbend slowing.
I found myself sitting against the trunk of a tree, a little way from
a girl.

She had honey-colored hair, eyes like green crystal, a thin,
shapely body in a pale green sun dress, a pale, friendly face. She
asked me: "Dew thick on the train?"

Then, with the sudden reinterpretation of sound you get when
you realize you've misheard something, I knew she had actually
said: "Duluth ink on the brain?"

But that wasn't it either; my travel-addled brain gave me a
dozen reinterpretive echoes: "To use thin kilts a strain?" "Do you
think kitsch will reign?" "To Youth Inc. a twill rein?"

"Um –," I said, putting a hand to my head to stop it from
spinning.

She looked at me closely then.

"Oh, I'm so sorry!" she gasped, and put cool, apologetic hand
against my cheek.

Later, gradually, with a rising hiss and a movement of wet air,
it began to rain.

I could not have predicted it, but now I realized that light and
shade had slowly merged, the sky had piled up with mountainous
clouds, a cool gust had blown, and now a big drop splashed into my
wine, followed by a thunder crash.

The green-eyed girl was staring straight up, blinking her eyes
and laughing. I studied her. Was she the woman from the Fladian
Peninsula?

And suddenly the air was full of rain, thick and sweet, filling
me with its intoxicating smell. A cry went up from all the people,
and I realized that, of course, this was *Io*, the July thunderstorm
that ends the summer drought, and of course the thunderstorm
was the occasion of the party.

The green-eyed girl stood up. The rain – rushing between us
like rippling bead-curtains, washing color and light so that shifting
curtains of silver seemed drawn all around, and beyond them a
roar like an approaching tidal wave; gleaming with celestial light

from above the clouds – the rain had wetted her sun dress to near transparency, showing the smooth, ivory shape beneath.

She took my hands and we were dancing, laughing hard in the torrent, separated from the world, whirling around, splashing in mud, seeing no one, stumbling and falling, laughing harder, out of breath, her rain-cold wet skin friendly as my best friend's.

Dancing in the muddy street outside the gates as the rain gets less.

Pulling me by the hand through small-town streets as darkness falls, our wet clothes clammy in the chilly air, the smell of growing fields from a few blocks away where the town ends.

Creeping through the back garden of a big house in the dark, smell of tomato plants in soft earth. Pulling me through the black doorway of a half basement, where she means for us to sleep.

But someone, or some*thing*, is already there: a huge, man-shaped shadow moves in the blackness, moaning like a ghost disturbed. We run away wildly, but I have the feeling she knows who he is, knew he would be there.

Was she the same woman I had seen in the Fladian forest? The Fladian woman's hair was curly and dark, her figure fuller, her eyes blue – but people and things are different in different times and places. Connections between events are difficult in our world, even as the events themselves stay the same.

As my investigation proceeded, I needed to find out more about her. My client had given me instructions for contacting a paid informant on the Peninsula, to be used only in urgent circumstances: I ran a classified advertisement for three days in obscure back issues of the local newspaper:

> Love you
> In the world's tallest building
> Valentine

On the evening of the third day, I set out for Shadeview.

Shadeview is a village in the central Peninsula, away from the beaches, where rich people go when they don't want to bother with anyone who isn't rich. I came there in late evening. In the center of town was a small, deserted park. The air was dark blue, heavy, still, like the air that hangs in jungles, black at the edges where the forest stood, pricked by stars and windows. I walked silently across trimmed grass. In the center of the park was a square holly hedge, taller than a man. I went through an opening in it. Surrounded by the hedge was a square concrete pool, lit orange by underwater lights, filled with foot-long carnivorous fish.

I waited, and after awhile someone came through another opening in the hedge. It was the woman, wearing a black leather bodysuit, orange light making shadows of her eyes. She stood just inside the opening.

"What do you want to know?" she asked softly.

I tried to hide my astonishment. After a minute, I blurted: "Who you are. And what your involvement is with my client."

She smiled. "Come with me."

Beyond the park a dark garden sloped up under cedars holding their clumps of leaves like nocturnal clouds. The whirring of crickets closed around us. A big house loomed. We went through a side door in an ivy-covered wall, climbed stairs to a high-ceilinged room with sharp-edged blue-green chairs set around a huge glass dining table. A chandelier above the table was made of blue-green bulbs with trapezoids of glass hanging on wires. Sharp metal flower stood in vases.

The woman's boots click on the blue enamel floor. Her figure was slender and hypnotic in the tight leather. I followed her into the next room.

It was dim, carpeted in fluffy white, with deep, silk-upholstered couches. Lacquered cabinets stood against flower-papered walls. A big window was open on the garden, letting in tendrils of plants, the whir of crickets, the smell of crimson night flowers. The woman was walking quickly; I had to hurry to keep up with her. The next room had walls and ceiling of black slate, a floor of white gravel, squat brass charcoal braziers giving off acrid, intoxicating smoke

--

Suddenly I realized that she had tricked me.

In our world, meaning – the most highly ordered form of information – has a certain limiting parameter of accretion, which has been precisely defined by the scientists. If a subject moves through dissimilar events faster than this limiting rate, meaning "bends" (undergoes a continuous topological deformation), or, in extreme cases may "collapse" (undergo a discontinuous nonlinear transformation). In the former case, "travelbend," meaning reassumes a comprehensible shape once the event motion slows or ceases, though reconfigured in ways often bewildering to the poor traveler. In "event collapse," however, the relationship between pre- and post-collapse circumstances may be completely undiscoverable.

By rushing me through these wildly different rooms, the woman was trying to overload my already travel-stretched capacity for new events, and so to escape. "Wait!" I yelled, and ran toward where her alluring backside was disappearing through the next doorway – too late. I barely had time to see a room of carved arches fading into a dimness of bookcases when the crushing intoxication of travelbend hit me, and my brain would no longer organize.

At one point I got a letter from my client. I had been sitting under a beach umbrella all morning. Perfect immobility and surroundings that change little are best for thinking, and I needed to think. The case was getting away from me, the threads of it unraveling; soon it would dissolve completely, the event window would close, and I would return north with my client's problem unsolved. Hazy sunlight sparkled on blue water and a breeze blew from far ocean regions. Children squealed, and seabirds cried in their more airy voices. Around noon, a mailman in crimson uniform and fez strode along the beach yelling out the names of those who had received Express Mail, his sandal bells jingling. Of course we have no hyper-rapid forms of communication like your telephone and radio – messages moving at such speeds would become incomprehensible. Letters are carried at a cautious pace inside featureless metal containers to minimize travelbend; even so, they must be interpreted with care when received. Express Mail, carried a little faster, is only used when urgency justifies obfuscation. I was irritated to hear the mailman calling my name: more events at this stage of the case were unneeded. I waved him over and paid him; he handed me the familiar sequined envelope and strode away calling other names. The letter was addressed to "F.C. Zhardun, Southern East Coast, Fladian Peninsula." Mail is addressed vaguely here: undue exactness only causes trouble if the address bends or collapses in transit.

I tore open the envelope ready to confront confusion; still, I was astonished. It held only a dozen-year-old clipping from a northern newspaper. The headline read: "Deserter Rapes, Kills Woman," and under it separate photos showed my client and the Fladian women. The story began: "A Special Forces deserter brutally raped and stabbed a local woman during an express elevator ride from the top of the city's tallest building, police said today.

"The soldier, who reportedly jumped a troop train several days ago, pushed through a crowd of horrified witnesses in the lobby of the World Industry Center, leaving behind the blood-soaked body of 21-year-old – "

But my eyes kept wandering up to the two photographs: my client, a huge, square-jawed man, enormously strong, enormously determined, in this picture younger, his black hair unflecked with gray; the woman dark-eyed and beautiful even in the rather fuzzy print.

In another time, seemingly disconnected, I first met her. I drove back to the house in the woods where I had seen her. The night air was close and still under vine-hung trees; a single cricket creaked languidly. A lit window glowed on gnarled tree roots like lizards writhing in the thick ivy. I had to knock several times before she came to the door, though she was only sitting in the next room. It was long and narrow, lit by a dim floor-lamp. She sat on the couch near gauze curtains that stirred faintly in windows facing the ocean, motioned me to a chair.

Her face was half in shadow. "How may I help you, Mr. – ," she consulted my card, " – Zardon?"

"I'll be very frank, Miss – "

She didn't supply the missing noun.

"I'm a private detective," I went on. "My client is a successful

253

businessman in a northern city. Lately he has had a string of bad luck in both his business and personal lives. For certain reasons, he believes this bad luck is emanating from the Fladian Peninsula. I am here to locate and eliminate the source of it."

"And has this something to do with me?"

A breath through the window brought the cool, haunting smell of jasmine, filling me suddenly with the memory of making love to her, lying in dry grass outside a little Ionian town, she gasping, her slender, strong body thrusting against mine, the vertigo of travelbend singing in my head, until I felt myself shooting toward the stars as if in an express elevator in the world's tallest building.

I had never remembered that before.

"Are you all right, Mr. Zardon? May I bring you a glass of water?"

The water was full and rich, as if it had soaked the roots of flowers before coming to the cracked ceramic glass she gave me. The crack, as I saw it while drinking, assumed the shape of a flower stem, graceful and lithe as her body.

I handed back the glass, wiped my mouth.

"However I pursue you, you deflect me," I muttered.

"Why, Mr. Zardon, what extraordinary things you say," she said, sitting on the couch again, her hands cradling the cracked glass interestedly. "I don't remember ever seeing you before. Of course, that doesn't mean I *haven't* ever." She laughed softly, with a hint of taunting.

The moon was rising outside the window.

"Do you like to swim?" she asked suddenly. "Would you go swimming with me?"

A path ran under dark trees, through brush and coarse grass to the beach. The water was lukewarm, with restless, gentle swells, gray in the moonlight, with the faintest tint of unlit green.

"So your investigations have led you to me?" she asked as the water rocked us a hundred yards from shore.

Only then did I notice the shadow that circled around and under her in the water, huge and dark and man-shaped.

I swam desperately back to shore, dreading every second to feel its hands dragging me down. I stood trembling on the beach.

She was a moon-ripple, slowly coming nearer, rising from the water, wet silver and ebony.

"Don't you understand?" She hissed, barely audible over the surf. "He killed me 13 years ago, and now I have his soul." She reached a hand back toward the water, where a black ripple moved unquietly. "Tell him I will *not* let him go. I've only started to pay him back."

"But – you're alive."

"Yes, isn't that funny? The elevator in the World Industry Center moves so fast, and I had just traveled into town that morning – at the same moment his knife cut into me, I had acute event-collapse, and was somewhere else.

"But I can still see feel his hands on me, can feel my life spurting from the cuts, and even as I stand here, I'm a rotten skeleton lying in the ground, darkness pressing all around me, lonely . . ."

In one part of the sky it is raining, in another part it is morning, in another part deep night. The woman leans over me, breasts taut against black leather, shafts of yellow sunlight, raindrops, and blackness falling around her into my car. I am in the driver's seat, and she is programming the dashboard for a long trip.

Her voice is soft, flutelike: "I'm sending you far away. But the time you get unbent, I'll be long gone. Nothing personal: I loved you once. Maybe that's why he hired you." Her voice trembles. Crimson flower petals tremble in a breath of moonlight, stir in a dawn breeze, shake in rain.

She closes the door: the car starts away. The last thing I remember is a sign saying "Shadeview City Limit."

Saluting you affectionately my friend (and waiting eagerly for more tales of your own strange world), I am

Sincerely yours,
Zardon"